PRAISE FOR

THE CURE FOR
# DREAMING

"[a] gripping, atmospheric story of mind control and
self-determination."
—*Kirkus Reviews*

"A strong female protagonist, realistic dialogue, and
well-written prose allow readers to become immersed
in Olivia's rather unique
(and sometimes frightening) world."
—*School Library Journal*

"Fluid boundaries between what's tangible and what's
intuited, lucidity and unconsciousness, sanity and
madness are particularly apt for this story
about hypnotism and emotional manipulation."
—*Horn Book*

"Winters continues to be a refreshing, incisive talent
with a unique perspective."
—*Booklist*

Also by
Cat Winters

*In the Shadow of Blackbirds*

*The Steep & Thorny Way*

# THE CURE FOR
# DREAMING

## CAT WINTERS

### Amulet Books
#### NEW YORK

PUBLISHER'S NOTE: This is a work of fiction. Names, characters, places, and incidents are either the product of the author's imagination or are used fictitiously, and any resemblance to actual persons, living or dead, business establishments, events, or locales is entirely coincidental.

The Library of Congress has catalogued the hardcover edition of this book as follows:

Winters, Cat.
The cure for dreaming / by Cat Winters.
pages cm
Summary: In Portland, Oregon, in 1900, seventeen-year-old Olivia Mead, a suffragist, is hypnotized by the intriguing young Henri Reverie, who is paid by her father to make her more docile and womanly but who, instead, gives her the ability to see people's true natures, while she secretly continues fighting for women's rights. Includes timeline and historical photographs.
Includes bibliographical references.
ISBN 978-1-4197-1216-6 (hardback)
[1. Supernatural—Fiction. 2. Suffragists—Fiction. 3. Hypnotism—Fiction. 4. Fathers and daughters—Fiction. 5. Portland (Or.)—History—20th century—Fiction.] I. Title.
PZ7.W76673Cur 2014
[Fic]—dc23
2014012019

ISBN for this edition: 978-1-4197-1941-7

Text copyright © 2014 Catherine Karp
Book design by Maria T. Middleton

Image credits: Bettmann/CORBIS: pages vi–vii; Library of Congress, Prints & Photographs Division: pages 40, 78–79, 111, 123, 164, 224, 283, 330, 344–45; Courtesy U.S. National Library of Medicine: pages 55, 90, 204.

The quotation from Mark Twain on page 55 appears by permission of the Mark Twain Foundation.

Printed and bound in U.S.A.
10 9 8 7 6 5 4 3 2 1

Amulet Books are available at special discounts when purchased in quantity for premiums and promotions as well as fundraising or educational use. Special editions can also be created to specification. For details, contact specialsales@abramsbooks.com or the address below.

ABRAMS
THE ART OF BOOKS SINCE 1949

115 West 18th Street
New York, NY 10011
www.abramsbooks.com

For Carrie,

MY SISTER AND LIFELONG BEST FRIEND.

KEEP SHINING.

"She was looking thin and pale and weak;
but her eyes were pure."

—BRAM STOKER, *Dracula*, 1897

# CHAPTER ONE

# A CHARMED INDIVIDUAL

PORTLAND, OREGON—OCTOBER 31, 1900

The Metropolitan Theater simmered with the heat of more than a thousand bodies packed together in red velvet chairs. My nose itched from the lingering scent of cigarette smoke wafting off the gentlemen's coats—a burning odor that added to the sensation that we were all seated inside a beautiful oven, waiting to be broiled. Even the cloud of warring perfumes hanging over the audience smelled overcooked, like toast gone crisp and black.

Up in a box seat to my left sat Judge Acklen's son, Percy, in an ebony suit and a three-inch collar that made him look far older than his seventeen years. The electric lamplight shining down on his head coaxed a rich redness to the surface of his auburn hair, which made me think of Father's favorite saying about my mother's strawberry curls: *Red hair is a symptom of dangerous, fiery passions.*

Percy shifted toward the orchestra seats, and I could have sworn, even from that distance high above me, he glanced at me and smiled.

A sharp elbow jabbed me in the arm.

"Stop gawking at him, Livie," said Frannie—my dearest friend, despite the jabbing. "That boy is a vampire."

"A vampire?" I snickered and rubbed my walloped bicep. "Here I thought *I* was the one who'd read *Dracula* too many times."

"Percy Acklen would do nothing but make you feel small and meaningless."

"You never even talk to him."

She patted my hand. "Neither do you, my friend."

I shut my mouth, for she was right. Percy and I had never exchanged as much as a simple *Good morning* or an *Excuse me for stepping on your toe.*

"Forget him," said Frannie, "and enjoy your birthday treat. You're worth a thousand Percys."

Our friend Kate, a dimpled blonde whose married older

sister was supposed to be our chaperone for the evening, plopped down beside Frannie after chatting with other girls at the back of the theater.

"Why is Livie blushing?" she asked, leaning forward.

"I'm not blushing." I fanned myself with my program. "I'm just flushed from the heat."

Frannie frowned up at Percy and twisted the end of her waist-length braid, but she was a good-enough friend not to betray my silly infatuation.

I folded the upper-right corner of the program's front page until the tip of the cream-colored paper met the bold-faced words at the center:

### Tonight's Performer
# THE MESMERIZING HENRI REVERIE
## Young Marvel of the New Century

"Maybe as a birthday present to yourself, Livie," said Kate, flapping open her own program, "you should volunteer to join this Mr. Reverie on the stage. Maybe he'll teach you how to hypnotize your father into being less of a grouch."

"Maybe." I gave a small sniff of a laugh, but I greatly doubted anything could fix Dr. Walter W. Mead.

The lights dimmed, submerging us all in the dark, save for five small candles that flickered inside a row of jack-o'-lanterns in front of the closed red curtain. A hush fell over the audience. Electric footlights rose to life in a fog of white and orange.

A full-whiskered man in a green checkered suit plodded across the apron of the stage, which set off a hearty round of applause from a thousand pairs of gloved hands. The gentleman waved his arms to quiet us down and offered a grin that turned his eyes into tiny crescents.

"Good evening, ladies and gentlemen," he said in a booming voice that rumbled up from the barrel of his round belly. "And a Happy Halloween to all of you. I am William Gillingham, your stage manager, and I'm ecstatic to announce that we have a bewitching show for you tonight. Young Monsieur Henri Reverie, barely eighteen years old, has traveled all the way from Montreal, Canada, to exhibit his enthralling hypnotism skills."

Additional exuberant applause echoed across the theater, and again Mr. Gillingham settled us down with a wave of his hands.

"Thank you, thank you—I'm overjoyed by your enthusiastic response. Some of you sitting out there in the audience will be invited onto the stage to fall under Monsieur Reverie's spell. The rest of you will bear witness to his remarkable powers over the human mind. I assure you, this talented young man will cause your jaws to drop and your eyes to open wide in astonishment. For musical accompaniment, he's brought along his sister, the highly talented Mademoiselle Genevieve. So . . . without further ado, I present to you"—

Mr. Gillingham turned with an upward sweep of his right hand—"the Reveries."

The curtain ascended and revealed two mahogany chairs, facing each other at the center of the stage, and a canvas backdrop painted to look like a star-kissed nighttime sky. On the left, a young woman with long golden ringlets sat in front of a monstrous pipe organ made of dark wood and gleaming copper. The stage lights brightened to their full brilliance, and the girl's peacock-blue evening gown gave off an otherworldly glow that made her appear more spirit than mortal.

She reached toward the instrument's keys and pressed a single D note twelve times in a row—the sound of a church bell chiming midnight. Chills shuddered down my spine. The pumpkins' toothy leers seemed to burn brighter.

Silence swallowed up the theater again, but before we could all lean back into the comfort of the calm, Genevieve Reverie lunged toward the keys and played a series of eerie notes that swelled into a passionate rendition of Camille Saint-Saëns's "Danse Macabre." She hunched her shoulders and plowed her feet into the instrument's pedals, as if she were racing through the streets of the underworld on a tandem bicycle, on which we were all unwitting passengers. I clutched the armrests. My head seemed to spin around and around and around, but I smiled and straightened my posture, for I adored a good Halloween fright.

A cloud of white smoke crept across the floorboards from

both sides of the stage. Genevieve's playing intensified, and the mist grew and billowed into a wall of burning orange that blurred the girl from view. The air tasted like my parlor whenever Father lit the fire in the hearth but forgot to open the flue. Those in the first few rows coughed into their gloves. The rising music warned that something was about to happen—something horrifying. The stage was about to erupt in flames. *We'd all burn up on Halloween night!*

"Are you all right?" whispered Frannie.

"Yes." I nodded with a laugh. "It's just better than I imagined."

The song reached its climax, racing, rising, climbing, higher and higher.

Smoke stung my nose.

I braced myself for fire.

But, no—instead, a young man stepped out of the clouds onto the apron, and the audience drew a collective gasp. A woman in the front row actually screamed. I gripped the armrests with all my might, for the boy looked like the devil—I swear, he resembled Lucifer himself with his black suit and crimson vest and his face shining red in the pumpkins' lights.

"Good evening, *mesdames et messieurs*," said the boy in an accent that sounded French and dangerous and deliciously sophisticated. "I am Monsieur Reverie." He gave a deep bow with his hand pressed flat against his stomach.

Silence greeted him. Our brains took several moments

to absorb the fact that this was our entertainer for the night—Henri Reverie—not the ruler of hell. Weak applause trickled across the theater, but it gained speed and volume as everyone roused from their stupors. Relieved laughter boomed through the crowd. I settled back in my seat, eased my viselike grip upon the armrests, and clapped along with everyone else.

"*Merci.* Thank you." The young man turned toward the reemerging pipe organ and stretched his arm toward the girl at the bench. "Isn't my sister astounding? Please, won't you give a warm round of applause for Mademoiselle Genevieve Reverie."

We all applauded Genevieve's performance, which far surpassed the uninspiring efforts of an amateur organist like myself. Genevieve panted as if she might collapse, and her golden ringlets uncoiled and wilted across her shoulders like limp strands of seaweed. Oh, how I envied her passion.

The applause dissipated, as well as the smoke, and the theater collectively exhaled a calming breath. The stage settled back to normal. Henri Reverie's skin faded to a less-diabolical shade without the orange smoke rising around him, and his short hair, a bit mussed on top and parted on the right, revealed itself as dark blond, a tad lighter than the hue of fresh honey. He was attractive, I suppose, with red lips and a rosy blush of health in his cheeks.

He stepped closer to us and spoke again. "*Merci.* Thank you for coming here today. My name is Henri"—he pronounced his name *On-ree*—"Reverie, and I have been studying the arts of mesmerism and hypnotism with my uncle ever since I was twelve. I use a combination of techniques from the great masters, including animal magnetism, deep relaxation, and the remarkable power of suggestion."

Genevieve played a hushed rendition of "Beautiful Dreamer."

"In a moment"—Henri strolled across the stage, his hard soles clicking against floorboards—"I am going to invite my first volunteer to come onto the stage with me." He placed his hands behind his back, which pulled his coat farther open, allowing the crimson silk of his vest to wink at us in the footlights. "There is no need to be afraid of what you will encounter with me. I am going to temporarily take you away from your worries. You will submerge yourself in a depth of relaxation such as you have never experienced before, and you will awake feeling better than you have felt in your entire life. All your troubles will dissolve into nothingness the moment you let me guide you into the beautiful world of hypnosis."

Despite my previous fear that Henri Reverie was the devil, his words melted in my ears like spun sugar. I needed a temporary escape from life. Yet I wasn't brave enough to say so.

"Is there a young lady in the audience who would like to be my first volunteer?"

A dozen hands flew into the air. And then at least two dozen more. Silhouettes squirmed and arms flailed throughout the darkened audience.

"Let me see—how should I choose?" Henri grinned and scratched his smooth chin. "Tell me, is anyone here tonight for a special occasion? A birthday, perhaps?"

Next to Frannie, Kate shot her hand into the air and shouted, "My good friend over here is celebrating a birthday."

Henri Reverie pivoted our way. Fear stabbed at my heart.

Kate stood and urged me to my feet by tugging on my hand. "She's turning seventeen today."

Murmurs of disappointment over not being chosen rumbled through the crowd. Frannie took my other hand and said, "Do it, Olivia. Don't be afraid. It might be fun."

Henri strutted closer to us. "You have a Halloween birthday, *mademoiselle*?" he called down to me.

I cleared my throat and answered in an ugly, croaking voice, "Yes."

The hypnotist smiled with those red lips of his. "Then legend says you are a charmed individual. You can read dreams and possess lifelong protection against the spirits. Come up here with me, and let us see how you fare with hypnosis."

"Go on, Livie. Don't be shy." Kate steered me toward the aisle as if she were herding a lost sheep into a pen. She then clapped her hands together, which triggered yet another thundering round of applause.

I tripped my way down the center aisle in the dark. Classmates from school called out my name in encouragement, and someone patted my arm as I struggled to figure out how to get onto the stage with the disorienting clapping ringing in my ears.

"Over here, *mademoiselle*." Henri waved me over to the left side, where I found a short flight of wooden steps. He reached out his gloved hand for me to take.

I hesitated a moment, wondering what my father would think of me climbing onto a stage with a young man who had reminded me of the devil only minutes before. Yet I reminded myself of Henri's promise of escape: *You will submerge yourself in a depth of relaxation such as you have never experienced before.*

The hypnotist wrapped his fingers around mine and helped me climb to the floorboards above. Our respective pairs of gloves separated our hands, but I felt the warmth of his skin beneath the smooth fabric. Hot white lights smoked by my feet and glared down at us from the ceiling like an army of small suns. I shielded my eyes while Henri led me to the center of the stage, continuing to hold my hand.

"What is your name?" he asked in a voice for all to hear.

"Olivia Mead," I answered in a decibel only he would be able to detect.

"Do you live here in Portland?"

"Yes. I attend Portland High School."

"Ladies and gentlemen," he said to the audience, "I present to you Mademoiselle Olivia Mead of Portland, Oregon, my first subject of the evening. Do any of you know Miss Mead?"

"Ask her about her father," called a husky male voice from the audience. "Mead the Mad."

I lowered my head and stiffened my shoulders, but Henri gave my hand a squeeze and pretended not to have heard the horrifying remark.

"Is this raven-haired beauty known for her brute strength?" he asked, at which several people laughed, possibly because I was never typically referred to as a beauty. "Would you like to see this delicate young feather of a girl become as strong and rigid as a wooden plank?"

The audience clapped and cheered, and Kate yelled out, "Go on, Livie. Have a bit of fun."

Henri turned to me and said in a quieter tone, "Come with me, Miss Mead. You have nothing to fear."

I drew a shaky breath and allowed him to lead me to the chairs in the middle of the stage. The echo of our footsteps ricocheted across the entire theater and sounded far too loud to my ears. Genevieve transitioned into Brahms's "Lullaby."

"Please, sit down." Henri held the back of the chair on the left.

I seated myself on a springy burgundy cushion, my posture tense and rigid, my back a solid board of oak. I never laced my corset to a point where I couldn't breathe, yet the steel stays dug against my ribs and kept oxygen from settling into my lungs. Every part of me ached and itched.

Henri, still standing behind me, removed his white gloves. "Ladies, Miss Mead will need to remove her gloves and hold my hands directly. I am going to transfer my energy into her, which will enable her to fall into the desired state of relaxation and open her mind to me. I apologize if I offend anyone, but this has been the tradition ever since Franz Anton Mesmer popularized this astounding technique." He stepped around me to the other chair and took a seat. "Miss Mead, please take off your gloves and hold my hands."

I swallowed and hesitated. Prickly beads of sweat bubbled across my forehead. Genevieve's lullaby strengthened in volume, perhaps to assuage my fears.

*Don't be rude and delay the show,* I scolded myself the way Father would complain whenever I dawdled before leaving the house for an event. *What are you waiting for? Chop-chop!*

I slipped off my gloves with my eyes directed toward my nut-brown skirt. Henri's bare right hand reached my way, and, with trembling fingers, I took it. Our other hands joined as well. His skin, smooth and hot, smoldered against mine.

"Look into my eyes," he told me.

I gave his face a brief glance, noting how blue his irises were, but the idea of staring into the face of a stranger felt unnatural. I tittered and focused instead on the starry backdrop.

"Miss Mead," he said in the gentlest male voice I'd ever heard, "are there any worries you would like to escape?"

My smile faded. My mind skipped back to a scene from earlier that day. I saw a small group of women with yellow ribbons pinned to their left shoulders. They shouted for equality on the steps of the courthouse. My own voice, along with Frannie's and Kate's, rang through the air in support. A barrage of rotten eggs smacked my arms and chest and oozed milky gray yolk down the lace of my blouse with a stink that made me gag. Fierce-eyed men—men who might have known my father—barked at us to go back to our homes where we belonged, and I ran off to scrub away the filth and my guilt until my fingers turned red and raw.

"Miss Mead?" asked Henri Reverie. "Would you like me to take you away from the world for a while?"

I glanced back at him, and his eyes held mine. Such arresting blue eyes—bright river blue, without any flecks of green or gold to distract from the principal color. They pulled me toward them and beckoned me to stay. They wouldn't let me go. Nor did I want to leave them.

"You are going to feel a great deal of warmth pass from my fingers into yours." He squeezed my hands—not enough to hurt, but enough to show me he was there. The balls of his thumbs pressed against mine. "It is going to feel like gentle flames, starting in your palms and fingertips . . ."

Heat tingled down my thumbs and spread across my hands.

"And then it will move into your wrists and slowly, slowly up your arms."

The warmth glided through my blood, past my elbows, and up to my shoulders in a strange, pacifying wave. Henri's blue eyes continued to hold my full attention.

"You may feel your arms grow numb, and that is perfectly

fine," he said, and my arms indeed felt strange and heavy. "The heat and numbness will make you tired. Very tired." He inhaled a deep breath that inspired me to do the same. My lungs expanded with air that soothed me down to my bones.

"As the warmth pours down through your torso like heated milk," he continued, "and travels slowly, gently across your hips and to your legs, you are going to find yourself so relaxed, you cannot keep your eyes open."

My eyelids fluttered.

"Close your eyes."

They fell shut.

"Keep them closed. Fall into a deep, deep sleep."

My hands, weighing several tons, dropped away from his fingers, and my chin slumped to my chest. I sank deep inside the darkness in a languid, dreamlike fall. Nothing hurt or troubled me any longer.

I felt divine.

"As I pass my hands over you," said Henri, "you will travel farther into this wonderful stage of sleep and be unable to open your eyes. Keep going downward, downward, and hear only my voice. Turn off all your other senses. You will only hear, taste, feel, smell, and see if I tell you to do so. For now, just focus on my voice and the magnetic force of my hands passing over your body. Sleep. *Sleep*. Keep going farther into sleep."

Downward I kept sinking. Downward, downward, downward. Gentle nips of heat sizzled across my skin, all the way to my toes, and my body melded into the chair until I became a part of the batting and the nails and the wood.

I continued to hear Henri's voice, directed to the audience. The word *test* came up, and *cymbals*, and *Remarkable, isn't it?* But nothing else mattered until he told me, "Stand up, Miss Mead."

I did as he asked. My eyes remained closed, and my body may as well have been made of stone, but somehow I was able to get to my feet.

"I am going to press my hand against you, and my touch will cause every muscle inside your body to go rigid."

His fingers cupped the back of my head, and a hardening sensation spilled down to my feet, as if he had unscrewed the top of my skull and poured a fast-drying plaster inside me.

"Rigid!" he called near my ear. "You are an iron bar that cannot bend. Every part of you is stiff. Nothing can cause you to falter. You are as solid as a board."

He spoke again to the audience, calling up "strong male volunteers." Firm hands lifted me into the air, beneath my shoulders and legs. I rose up high, my arms glued to my sides, and settled across two bars, one behind my neck and the other below my ankles.

Henri's voice whispered inside my mind. "Lift yourself out of your body, Miss Mead. Float up to the top of the stage, and I will return you safely after you have had some time to enjoy yourself. You can hear Genevieve's organ music again . . ."

The organ filled my ears with a rich and dreamlike melody.

"Open your eyes."

I did.

"See the shine of the lights. Let their radiance beckon you to them. Allow Genevieve's music to carry you away. Do not fight it, lovely girl. Just go."

I rose out of my petrified bones.

"Yes . . . go."

I drifted upward—a weightless feather immune to the burden of gravity, lured by the pull of the vast ceiling above with its rows of metal catwalks and blinding lights that breathed wispy plumes of smoke. Genevieve's music carried me up to the bulbs and allowed me to lie in a foggy bath of golden rays without a worry or a pain. Henri disappeared. Memories of gaseous eggs on my chest disappeared. Fears of what Father would say about the courthouse rally slipped away. I was nothing but a feather.

I floated for hours . . . or so it seemed.

I could have drifted much longer if Henri's voice didn't call up to me. "Miss Mead," he said. "Are you ready to come back now?"

I tried to hold myself up there in that luxurious land of electricity.

"I need to bring you back so someone else may have a turn. You have done beautifully, but it is time to wake up."

"No," I said, but I felt myself deflating. A withering hot-air balloon with the gas turned low.

"I am going to sweep my hands upward, starting at your feet, and count from one to ten."

"No."

"Yes, Miss Mead . . . and by the time I reach ten, you will feel wide awake and rested." His presence burned at my feet. "One, two—you feel the magnetic force between us fading—"

I sank back to the ground, closer to the stage.

"Do not fight it. Three, four—you are slowly stirring back to life. Five—your senses are returning to your body. You can feel the heat from the stage lights again . . ."

My hair warmed, and my mind was able to recognize the music playing: "Evening Prayer" from the opera *Hansel and Gretel*. The sheet music was part of my collection back home.

"Six, seven—do not fight it, Miss Mead, please do not fight it. Eight—very good, you are almost there—nine . . ." He placed his hot hand against my forehead. "Ten. Awake."

I opened my eyes, and the hum and the glare of the lights made me jump. I found myself standing upright at the center of the stage again.

"Let us give a warm round of applause for the lovely and cooperative Mademoiselle Mead." Henri lifted my hand in the air, and applause assaulted my ears like the blasts of gunshots at a sharpshooter show. My legs wobbled as if made of sand, and I had to grab hold of Henri's coarse sleeve to keep my knees from sinking to the ground.

Henri put his arm around my back and guided me to

the stairs. I resisted the urge to lean against his shoulder to support my drooping head.

The clapping died down.

Genevieve finished her music.

The hypnotist let me go.

He didn't say another word to me as I clutched the handrail and descended from the stage with my gloves somehow back in my hand—not a whisper in my ear or a simple *Thank you for joining me.* At the bottom step, I peeked over my shoulder and caught him watching me, as a doctor would monitor a patient he was releasing from the hospital after a surgery. But then he smiled. A warm smile that heated my blood and made me forget Percy Acklen sitting high in his box seat above the darkened theater.

The hypnotist then turned back to his show.

I returned to my seat.

Our relationship seemed to be over.

# CHAPTER TWO

# WOMANHOOD PERFECTED

When I sat back down, Kate covered her mouth as if she were stifling a laugh and Frannie whispered, "Oh dear, Livie. That went much differently than expected."

"How do you mean?" I asked, but the woman behind us shushed us, and Frannie murmured that she'd explain later.

The next volunteers ventured onto the stage in a group of ten, and they were a motley collection of males and females of varying sizes, shapes, and ages. Under Henri's spell they waltzed to "The Blue Danube," forgot their names, and performed other embarrassing but relatively harmless feats.

During all the demonstrations, I was nothing more than a heap of melted butter that oozed against my red velvet chair in the audience. I felt as if I had awoken from a hundred-year nap, every part of me rested and content, aside from an odd, smarting sensation in one wrist. I almost possessed the confidence to go home and tell Father I had participated in a women's suffrage rally in the center of the city.

Almost.


"SO, TELL ME, LIVIE," KATE SAID WITH BARELY CONCEALED excitement after the theater lights stirred us back into reality and we rose to our feet, "what did it feel like when lovely Monsieur Reverie was on top of you?"

"I beg your pardon?" I halted in mid-stretch. "What did you just say, Kate?"

"You heard what I said." She smiled with a glint in her hazel eyes. "He instructed you to stiffen, and then he laid you out between those two chairs and stood on your stomach to show how rigid you became."

"What?" I pressed down for signs of bruises below the protective barrier of my corset. "He stood on top of me?"

Frannie nodded and bit her bottom lip. "He did, Livie. That's what I meant by 'Oh dear.'"

"Didn't you feel him?" asked Kate.

"No."

She laughed. "You didn't feel a man at least thirty pounds heavier than you standing on your body?"

"No."

"You were honestly that hypnotized?" Frannie put her hands on her hips. "You didn't hear the cymbals he crashed next to your ears or feel the pins he poked into your wrist to see if you were alert?"

I rubbed my left wrist. "Is that why my skin tingled after I got back to my seat?"

"Oh, Livie." Kate shook her head, her fair curls wobbling across her forehead. "You're always missing the excitement, even when you're smack-dab in the middle of it." She swiveled toward the aisle and held up the hem of her skirt. "Come along, ladies. Let's try to pull Agnes away from her suffragist troops and their election-day plotting and remind her she's our chaperone."

Frannie and I grabbed hands to keep from losing each other in the crowd, and I followed her swaying braid up the aisle, while she followed Kate's bright green-and-black plaid. Strangers stepped on my feet at least three times, and I couldn't help but think everyone was staring at me, the girl who had let a young man balance atop her stomach.

Out in the lobby we had to wait ten minutes to fetch our coats, and then we found ourselves swept along in a warm wave of bodies that pressed toward the theater's exit. On all sides of me people buzzed about Henri Reverie's skills.

"Quite a talented young man."

"Such persuasion. Such power."

"I would have liked to see him try that hogwash on me. My mind is far too sharp and alert for that sort of humbug—I can promise you that."

I glanced over my shoulder, for I thought I heard my name amid the commotion.

"Olivia." An arm waved, flashing a jeweled cuff link. Auburn hair and a handsome face with fine cheekbones came into view ten feet behind me. "Wait," called Percy Acklen.

I squeezed Frannie's hand in the crowd's swift-moving current. "I think Percy is calling to me."

She laughed. "What?"

"Percy Acklen is calling and waving to me."

She turned as well, and although a parade of elbows and shoulders smacked against us, we stood there, frozen.

Percy made his way to where we waited and stopped two feet from me. I could smell his divine, musky cologne.

"May I drive you home, Olivia?" he asked.

"Drive me home?" I looked to Frannie to ensure I'd heard him correctly.

She gaped, her jaw dangling open enough for me to see the little gap between her bottom front teeth.

A rotund gentleman with a heavy black beard fell against Percy, and the force of the blow knocked Percy's chest against mine. He grabbed my arms to steady himself but carried on with his conversation as though we hadn't just crashed together with our cheeks pressed close. "My father bought me my own buggy." He let go of me and stepped back to a more respectable distance. "I'd love to give you a ride."

I cleared my throat to find my voice. "Didn't you come to the theater with your parents?"

"They brought their own carriage. I drove separately."

"Frannie? Livie?" called Kate from the exit, bobbing up and down like a buoy. "Where in heaven's name are you?"

"We're coming, Kate," said Frannie. She glanced my way with concern in her eyes. "You're coming, too, Livie, right?"

My heart pounded. I felt I'd stumbled across a crucial fork in a road after a long journey, and choosing the wrong path might alter my entire life. Going home with my friends as planned would mean safety and comfort and normalcy. Yet driving away with Percy, unchaperoned—Percy who was gazing at me as if I were something rare and enchanting he'd just unearthed—well, that was an entirely new adventure.

I buttoned up my gray wool coat. "I'll go with Percy."

PERCY'S BUGGY WAS AN ELEGANT BLACK CONTRAPTION with fresh paint, a curved roof, and a seat, meant for two, upholstered in padded green leather. He stepped in beside me and rocked the vehicle until he got himself situated.

I tucked my gloved hands inside my coat pockets, for the night air was chilled and damp with the type of mist that stung my cheeks and nose. *Fairy kisses,* my mother had called that type of weather when I was small enough to believe in mystical creatures.

Percy fitted his silk top hat over his head. "Where do you live?"

"Twelfth Street, near Main."

"That shouldn't take long." He gathered up the reins. "Are you ready?"

I nodded. "I am."

"Let's be off, then." He made a clicking sound out of the side of his mouth, and his white ghost of a horse pranced away from the theater with the steady clip-clop of hooves. The carriage bumped and jostled over potholes in the dark, so I grabbed the crisscrossing bars running up to the roof to keep from bouncing out to the muddy street.

"You have a beautiful horse," I said when we were two blocks west of the theater.

"Thank you. His name is Mandolin."

"Oh, that's pretty."

"Thank you."

I leaned back against the seat and wondered what I was doing with exquisite Percy Acklen and his gorgeous black buggy.

Silence ruled our drive across the city, even though I longed to ask him what books he liked to read outside of school and what he thought of hypnotism . . . and Halloween . . . and bicycling . . . and a dozen other subjects. Words failed me, however—as they were apt to do around attractive boys. All my imagined questions struck me as either dull or nosy.

I focused on the glow of the arc lamps dangling from overhead wires and the darkened stores, including my absolute favorite, McCorkan's Bicycle Shop, which featured two pairs of ladies' riding bloomers in the front window. We traveled past rows of houses—oversized gingerbread homes with rounded towers and sprawling porches topped with jack-o'-lanterns that reminded me of Henri Reverie leaping out of smoke. The carriage wheels squelched through soupy puddles and clattered across stony patches of road so poorly paved, the surface might as well have been dirt. The air carried the scent of Halloween bonfires and magic.

We turned left, and Percy urged Mandolin into a fast trot, perhaps to impress me. My backside bounced against the seat hard enough to rattle my teeth.

I clutched the buggy. "Is it safe to go this fast in the dark?"

"Are you scared?"

"A little."

"It's Halloween. You're supposed to be frightened."

"Frightened of the dead arising . . . not of imminent death."

"Ha! I'll slow down, then." He adjusted the reins, and the horse eased back into a walk. The buggy swayed in a gentle rhythm, and I relaxed my stranglehold on the bars. "There, boy," cooed Percy. "There's a good horse."

Our narrow, two-story house came into view to the south, its ugly red clapboards too dim to be seen with the clouds blocking the moon.

"My house is the third one on the right," I said with a nod toward the place. "The skinny one with the big maple in front."

"All right."

We drove close enough for me to see a light flickering behind the lace curtains of one of the side windows in the back. Father's study.

Percy called out another "Whoa," and the buggy rocked to a stop in front of our curb. Mandolin whinnied. Rain pattered against the vehicle's roof, which made me think of poor Frannie and Kate trudging through drizzle and hopping aboard streetcars to get home, and there I was, sitting in the height of luxury on padded green leather.

"Well," I said, "I should probably—"

"You looked beautiful on that stage tonight, Olivia." Percy turned toward me, briefly illuminated by a delicate strand of moonlight that stole through the clouds.

I sat up straighter. "I did?"

"Yes." His eyes—black in the night, a beguiling greenish-brown in the daylight—stayed upon me. "I don't know if you remember it, but that hypnotist laid you out between two chairs. You were as stiff as a board, with only your neck and your ankles supported, and you were as lovely as Sleeping Beauty."

I snickered. "I was?"

He scooted closer to me on the seat with the soft whisper of leather. "My father leaned over to me and said, 'Now, that's womanhood perfected, Percy my boy. That's the type of girl you want. Silent. Alluring. Submissive.'"

My stomach lurched. I tried to appear unfazed by his

father's words, but my mouth twisted into an expression that must have looked as if I were swallowing down those milky gray eggs from the courthouse attack.

Percy laughed. "I said those were my father's words. Not mine."

"Oh." I sighed. "I'm glad. You don't think women ought to be silent and submissive, then?"

"You *are* silent, Olivia. I've never heard you speak one word in any of the classes we've had together."

"That doesn't mean I like to be silent."

Unfortunately, my argument ended there, and I indeed fell silent again. As did Percy.

Down the street, a dog howled. A pitiful wail.

"'Listen to them—the children of the night,'" I said before I could think to regret quoting *Dracula* in the middle of an already awkward moment.

Percy straightened his neck. "What did you just say?"

"I beg your pardon?"

"What about nighttime children?"

"Oh . . ." I wrapped my arms around my middle. "I just . . . I have a strange attraction to horror novels."

"Which ones?"

"I'm reading *Dracula* . . . for the fourth time."

"The fourth time?" He whistled and shifted his knees in my direction. "Doesn't the library mind you checking it out so often? I've heard it's all the rage."

"I saved enough money to buy my own copy as soon as

it showed up in Harrison's Books last year. Have you read it yet?"

"No." He tugged at his stiff collar. "My father only allows classic literature in the Acklen household. Friends have to sneak me copies of anything new and exciting."

"I could lend you my copy if you'd like."

"Really?" He scooted another inch my way. "You'd help corrupt me?"

I sputtered a laugh. "*Dracula* may frighten you, but I doubt it will corrupt you. At least . . . I don't think it will. There are some . . . scenes . . . I suppose some people would find . . ."

"What?" He tilted his head. The right corner of his mouth arched in a wry smile that Frannie would have hated. "What types of scenes are there?"

My face flushed. "I'm not going to say. You'll just have to read them."

"You'll definitely have to lend me your copy, then. Show me what I'm missing." He pressed the side of his arm against mine, clearly meaning for me to feel him.

I froze. My heart rate doubled, and I was certain he could detect my pulse jumping about beneath my sleeve, even with all that fabric separating us.

"Well . . . ," he said.

I lifted my eyes. "Yes?"

"I suppose I should help you down before the vampires

crawl out of their graves and drink your sweet, invigorating blood. What do you think?"

I nodded. "I suppose you should. There aren't any Van Helsings in the neighborhood."

"Who?"

"You'll see."

He shifted his weight and climbed out his side of the buggy, another smile half hidden on his face in the moonlight. His leather soles squished toward me through the shallow mud; then he stopped below me on the damp sidewalk and hooked his fingers around the crisscrossing metal next to my arm. "Thank you for letting me drive you home."

I folded my hands in my lap to keep them from trembling. "May I ask you something about that?"

"Yes."

"Um . . . well . . ." I drew a breath that made my tongue go dry. "You didn't ask to drive me here merely because you liked how I looked when I was in that trance, did you?"

"Well . . ." Percy beamed at me in a way no one ever had before, his head tipped to the left, his dark eyes glassy and wistful. "You really were a beaut up there, Olivia. You should have seen the way the lights shone down on your black hair and your sleeping face."

"But have you ever felt—" My skin warmed over. Words wilted at my lips, but I forced myself to finish my thought. "You've never seemed to notice me before this evening. Am I only attractive to you because I was lying unconscious across two chairs on a stage?"

"No . . . that's not . . . I just . . ." He rubbed the back of his neck. "I'd never thought of you that way before. You've always simply been . . . Dr. Mead's daughter."

"Oh." I nodded. "I see. You're afraid of my father like everyone else."

"No, I'm not afraid. It's just . . . well . . . your father has never worked on my teeth, but he certainly took care of my mother's and father's mouths—I can tell you that much. He fitted them with the finest dentures money can buy."

"And is that so terrible?"

"Your father smiled the entire time he was yanking out my father's molars. As if he enjoyed it."

I swallowed and squirmed. "He's not smiling when he's pulling out teeth. A natural reaction to luring a person into opening his mouth is to make a funny little grimace. I used to play dentistry with my dolls, and my grandmother observed me making the same face."

"I've heard he also enjoys the use of leeches."

"Only to relieve inflamed gums. It's standard dentistry practice. They do the job beautifully."

"They suck blood out of patients' gums beautifully? Is that what you're saying?" His eyes shimmered with amusement. "My goodness, Olivia. You do like horror stories, don't you?"

"You see? This is why I don't talk much in school. You're laughing at me."

"I'm just entertained that sweet little Olivia Mead is defending the use of leeches inside people's mouths." He inched his hand down the metal bar, closer to my skirt. "You have to admit, it is a little shocking."

I picked at my coat's cloth-covered buttons.

"Please, Olivia"—he nudged my leg with the back of his hand—"don't be angry."

"I'm not angry. It's just not easy being the daughter of . . . my father."

"I understand. I've got an infamous father, too. He's been known to make grown men cry in court."

"Oh." I met his eyes again, noting the softening of his expression. "I didn't think of that. I suppose you might truly understand, then."

"I do. I really do." Percy offered me his hand. "It's starting to rain harder out here. We should get you inside before it pours."

"Will you come up to the door with me to meet my father?"

He helped me down from the carriage with a backward glance at the house.

"My father doesn't extract teeth and leech gums just for fun, Percy," I said with a smile. "His home office is solely for emergency treatments, not for torturing his daughter's drivers."

Percy blanched. "He keeps dental tools in the house?"

"I promise, you'll leave here tonight with all the contents of your head intact."

"Oh. Well . . . good." He tucked my hand inside the crook of his elbow. A wind kicked up around us, forcing him to press his top hat against his head with his free hand. "Come on. We're going to get soaked."

We ran up the brick front path just as the rain gained force and pelted the ground with a clatter that sounded like the applause Henri had received when I was standing on the stage with him. Up on the porch, we ducked under the cover of the roof and shook water off our sleeves.

"Come inside for a moment to get dry." I turned the doorknob with an embarrassing squeak and poked my head inside. "Hello? Father?"

Silence met my ears. The only movements within the house were the twitching flames of the entry hall's sconces, which threw shadow and light across the rusty-brown wallpaper. The air smelled of gas from the lamps' hissing jets, and there were lingering whiffs of the pot roast supper Father and I had shared earlier that evening.

"Father?" I called into the silence, stepping inside the entryway with a moan from the unvarnished floorboards. Our home had never seemed so much like the sinister abode of a mad, leech-loving dentist until that moment. "Are you still awake?"

"I need to talk to you, Olivia." Father clomped out from his office at the back of the long hall, dabbing his forehead with his handkerchief the way he usually did when he was anxious. When he saw I wasn't alone, he stopped and blinked, as though trying to clear his head of a brandy-induced hallucination.

"Olivia?" He tucked his handkerchief into his coat pocket and patted down his graying black hair—a longer and scragglier mess than most professional gentlemen's. "You didn't tell me you were bringing a guest home."

"Father, this is, um, P-P-Percy Acklen, Judge Acklen's son. He kindly drove me home from the hypnotism show."

"He did?" Father bounded our way with a jolly smile that rivaled Santa's in my illustrated copy of *A Visit from St. Nicholas*. The leftover stink of one of his cigars muffled Percy's musky cologne. "What a pleasure to meet you, Mr. Acklen." He shook Percy's hand with rapid pumps that jerked the boy's shoulder. "I'm Dr. Mead, a great admirer of your father's newspaper opinion pieces. He's a just and wise man."

"Thank you, sir." Percy slid his hand out of Father's and stretched his fingers with a crack. "He'll have another piece printed soon. A group of women gathered on the courthouse steps this afternoon and protested their lack of a vote in next Tuesday's election."

My heart stopped.

Father's eyes flitted toward me for the briefest of seconds. "Oh?"

"The protest turned somewhat volatile." Percy removed his top hat. "My father yelled out the window for them to all go home before he set the police on them."

"I don't blame him. That must have been appalling."

Father darted another quick glance my way, which turned my stomach into a flip-flopping jumble of nerves.

*He knows I was there.*

"Well"—Father cleared his throat—"that sort of behavior is inexcusable for a woman. If my own daughter ever dared to throw a tantrum like that on the courthouse steps, I'd pull her out of school and send her straight to a convent." Father snorted. "And I'm not even Catholic."

Percy laughed as if he had just heard the wittiest joke ever uttered, perhaps to humor Father, but he straightened his posture and sobered when he caught my unsmiling reaction. "Oh, I doubt Olivia has ever done anything wrong in her entire life, sir. There's no need to worry about her. In fact, the entire city just witnessed her strict obedience this evening."

Father stiffened. "What do you mean?"

"She was hypnotized. That hypnotist fellow we went to see—Henri Revelry—"

*"Reverie,"* I corrected Percy.

"He called her up to the stage and put her under his spell. She did everything he asked of her."

Father spun toward me. "You were hypnotized tonight, Olivia?"

I nodded. "Yes."

"And you did everything asked of you?"

"Apparently so."

"Well, g-g-good. Good girl." He slipped his handkerchief out of his pocket and dabbed his forehead again. "That's my Olivia. An exemplary model of fine manners and strict obedience."

"And she was positively breathtaking," added Percy. "If I may be so bold, sir, I'd say tonight on that stage your daughter was the loveliest thing I've ever witnessed."

"Really?" Father cocked his head, sounding a little too skeptical that I could have been that lovely.

Percy fussed with the brim of his hat. "May I ask you a question, sir?"

"Of course," said Father.

"I was wondering if I might take Olivia with me to an event Friday night. Sadie Eiderling invited me to her birthday supper."

"Sadie Eiderling?" Father's eyes expanded at the mention of the local beer baron's daughter, and I swear I could see the glow of rich golden ale sloshing about in his dazed irises. "You want to take Olivia to a party at the Eiderling mansion?"

"I realize you don't necessarily know me well enough for me to escort your daughter to such an event, but I'm a respectful young man with a reputation for impeccable behavior."

Father rubbed his lips and seemed to weigh his decision with great care.

"If you need to think about the proposal before answering," said Percy, "I'd understand . . ."

"Yes, let me get back to you before I extend such a privilege to Olivia. I'll send a note over to your house tomorrow evening."

"Thank you, sir. I appreciate your considering the offer." Percy planted his hat back on his head, and I could feel the enchantment of the evening dissolving into the ether. "Well, I hate to scuttle off so quickly, but I need to go home so Mother doesn't worry. Thank you for letting me drive you home, Olivia. Good night, Dr. Mead."

"Good night, Percy," I said.

"Good night, son." Father closed the door and allowed Percy to dart back into the rain and the darkness.

I lunged for the staircase behind me.

"Wait."

I turned and braced myself against the banister. "Yes?"

"After you left for the theater this evening"—Father shoved his handkerchief into his breast pocket—"I received a telephone call from one of my most prestigious patients, Mr. Underhill."

"Mr. Underhill?"

"He owns one of Portland's largest shipping firms."

I shrugged. "I've never heard of him."

"He was at the courthouse this afternoon."

I gulped and turned my attention to the toes of the rain-freckled shoes peeking out from beneath my skirt.

"Olivia," said my father, "look me in the eye."

I did as he asked, raising my chin to bolster my confidence.

He lifted his chin as well. "Why did you humiliate yourself by standing in that crowd of hysterical women? Mr. Underhill said men pelted you with rotten eggs."

"That is correct, sir."

"Why were you there?"

"A friend's sister is a member of the Oregon State Equal Suffrage Association, and I decided to see what all the fuss was about."

"Mr. Underhill said you were chanting *with* the women."

"That is correct."

"Why?"

"Because I would like to vote for president when I'm older."

Father pinched his lips into a scowl that turned his face lobster red, and his entire body quaked, as if blasts of lava were about to spew from the top of his skull. "Olivia Gertrude Mead, my hope for you since the day your mother left was that you would grow up to be a rational, respectable, dignified young woman who understands her place in the world."

"But—"

"You're lucky Percy Acklen's father didn't see you standing out there on his courthouse steps, or that distinguished young man never would have taken an interest in you."

"I—"

"Was he hypnotized into falling in love with you?"

"No!"

"Well, then, if you spoil this unexpected bit of luck you've been handed this evening, I will keep to my word about ending your education and sending you away."

"But—"

"No. You are done talking for the day." He shoved a finger

in my face. "I lost Mr. Underhill as a patient because of you. He was supposed to be leeched tomorrow afternoon, but he demanded to know how he could trust me with his mouth when I can't even control my own daughter. He called me an embarrassment to the men of Portland, and he uninvited me from the election-night ball of the Oregon Association Opposed to the Extension of Suffrage to Women."

"What? That's ridicu—"

"You will go to your room, change into your nightclothes, and turn down your lamps without reading or writing a single word. You will go to sleep while contemplating your poor decision and figure out how you can compensate for your ills tomorrow. You need to prove you won't embarrass me if I let you go to that party with Judge Acklen's son." He lowered his finger and steadied his breath. A bulging blue vein pulsated in his forehead, and for a moment I feared it would burst and kill him right there in front of me.

"Go!" he shouted.

I scrambled up the stairs with thumps and bangs and skids, failing to sound like a "rational, respectable, dignified young woman." I sealed myself inside my bedroom—my cherry-blossom-pink Elysium of lace and literature and freshly dusted china dolls in long satin dresses. Father had already lit my frosted gas lamps, so there was no need for me to fumble in the dark for a match.

I grabbed the little steel hook from the top of my chest of drawers and undid the dozen black buttons running down my ankle boots. "Unfair," I muttered under my breath as I worked to free my cramped feet. "So unfair. I'd like to see *him* silenced for a change and sent off to a monastery. How would he like that?"

My stocking-covered feet broke loose from their leather prisons, and I stretched out my toes across the cold floorboards.

From my bedside table, the Count's dark blue castle on the brown cloth cover of *Dracula* beckoned: *Read me, read me. Only thirty more pages to go before Mina will be saved from Dracula's bloodthirsty curse.*

I slid my arms out of my coat and caught the reflection of my movements in the standing oval mirror by my window. A tired girl with a plain face and a distinct lack of fire in her pale brown eyes peered back at me from the glass. Stray strands of hair the color of wet river sludge had fallen out of my topknot and stuck to my cheeks after my ride through the city and the scramble through the rain with Percy. I brushed the hairs aside with the back of my hand and heaved a sigh that made my shoulders rise and sink.

The only other evidence of mischief on my body, the only sign my seventeenth birthday wasn't quite as proper as it should have been, was a dusty pair of footprints on my dress, right above my stomach and thighs.

"He could see plainly that she was not herself.
That is, he could not see that she was becoming
herself and daily casting aside that fictitious self
which we assume like a garment."

—KATE CHOPIN, *The Awakening*, 1899

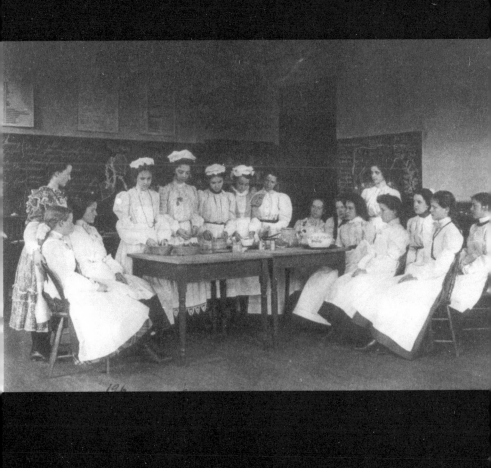

# CHAPTER THREE

# UNLADYLIKE DREAMS

B y the time I had dressed for school and was heading downstairs the next morning, the house smelled like poached eggs, black coffee, and a touch of rosemary from the Macassar oil Father used for slicking down his hair. He was already seated at the breakfast table, below his favorite photograph: an appetite-souring image of a pair of bone dentures, with six of the bottom teeth missing.

"You're in the newspaper, Olivia," he said from behind a sheet of newsprint.

My stomach tightened. "I am? Why?"

Before he could answer, Gerda, the Swedish girl we hired to help with the cooking and cleaning, blew through our swinging kitchen door with the silver coffeepot. She smiled when she saw me, her butter-blond hair and crisp white apron cheery contrasts to our moth-brown walls and dim lighting. "Oh, good morning, Miss Mead," she said in her lovely Swedish lilt.

"Gerda"—Father rustled the newspaper down to the table—"return to the kitchen, please."

Gerda and I exchanged a look.

"Gerda," said Father in a warning tone, "a private family matter needs to be discussed."

"Yes, sir." Gerda nodded and disappeared through the door, which flapped shut behind her as if it were swatting her away on her posterior.

I clenched my fists and prepared for the worst.

Father slid the paper across the table. "*This* is why you're in the newspaper."

My lips parted at the startling image on the front page of the *Oregonian*: an illustrated picture of me, lying supine in my hypnotized state. As Kate, Frannie, and Percy had all told me, I was propped between two chairs, supported beneath my neck and ankles, and my body looked as rigid as the Steel Bridge crossing the Willamette River. A sketched version of Henri Reverie stood on top of me with his arms stretched out to his sides, as if he were balancing on a tightrope instead of a girl.

Below the picture was a caption:

*Young hypnotist Henri Reverie stands atop mesmerized*
*Olivia Mead, daughter of Portland dentist Walter W. Mead.*

"I'm so sorry." I scooted the newspaper back across the table and sank into my chair. "Kate volunteered me to go on the stage with that hypnotist, but I didn't even want to do it. I had no idea Mr. Reverie was standing on top of me after he put me in my trance."

Father picked up the paper again, but instead of bristling and grumbling, he sat there with the flames of fascination flaring in his pupils. "Young Mr. Reverie's persuasion over you was clearly quite powerful."

"Yes," I said, a nervous quaver in my voice.

"I'm curious about hypnotherapy myself. I've read several articles about dentists who use trances to subdue their thrashing patients." Father scratched his beard with an audible rustle of hairs. "The article states that between performances, Mr. Reverie is offering his hypnotism skills to help individuals overcome their addictions and fears. He's staying in Portland until next week."

"Oh." I unfolded my napkin. "I'm sure he'll be helpful to men addicted to drink."

"Are you also becoming a temperance crusader, Olivia?"

I looked up, caught off guard by the question as well as the squeak of fear in his voice. "I beg your pardon?"

"I keep reading about that lunatic of a woman, Carrie Nation—the old hag who's smashing up saloons in Kansas with stones and bricks and billiard balls." He stared me down with probing brown eyes that themselves resembled billiard balls. "Do you ever harbor urges to commit violent acts against men?"

"No! Of course not. Just because I want to vote doesn't mean I'm going to turn savage."

"Women who want the vote seem hell-bent on outlawing liquor, too. They're ready to attack."

"Father, I just—"

"I'm considering telephoning this Henri Reverie and hiring him to help you."

I half slipped off my chair. "Help me with what?"

"I want him to put an end to your growing signs of rebelliousness."

"I am not rebellious." I gripped the edge of the table. "I may have gone to a suffragist rally and upset one snobby patient, but no one else has ever complained about my behavior. Not at school—not anywhere. You're just punishing me because of Mother."

"I'm ensuring you won't become like your mother." Father folded the newspaper into two crisp halves. "If Percy Acklen drove you home last night because he has marriage on his mind, what do you think he'll do if he catches word you were at that protest?"

"He probably won't—"

"I'm not done talking, Olivia. If Percy feels he won't be able to command his own domestic ship, if he worries you'll turn wild on him, he'll run as far as he can in the opposite direction. You'll never again have a young man with means and money take an interest in you. You'll have no options for your life."

"I'm only seventeen. I don't care about marriage right now. My schoolwork is good enough that I could go to college and study to be a teacher. Or a writer."

"You are not going to be a teacher or a writer."

"Why not? Plenty of young women are taking jobs these days."

"Only desperate and unfeminine ones. The only reason I even allow you to go to that school is because I hate to think what would happen if you were on your own while I'm at work."

"What?" I gasped. "School is my key to the future, not my nursemaid."

"Your future is to become a respectable housewife and mother. Women belong in the home, and inside some man's home you'll stay."

I squeezed the table's edge until my fingers and my voice both shook. "You're angry because you couldn't keep my mother inside this home—that's what this is all about. But it's not my fault you drove her away."

Father's mouth fell open, and his eyes refused to blink, as if I'd stabbed his heart with the barbed tips of my words.

"I—I—I'm sorry," I said. "Please, Father—please don't hire that hypnotist to remove thoughts from my brain. My mind isn't like a rotten tooth. You can't just take it away."

He stabbed at his egg with his fork, and that angry blue vein from the night before throbbed again in his forehead.

"Father, please—"

"Don't you understand?" He slammed his fist to the table and made the dishes jump. "I'll be making your life easier for you by freeing you of these unladylike dreams. It's for your own good, so don't make me out to be the villain here. The world will seem far less difficult when passions that can never be fulfilled are gone from your stubborn head."

"I don't want them to be gone. I'd rather be able to dream and fail than to never feel the pull of another way of life."

"That's a silly, frustrating way to live."

"But—"

"The subject is closed. If I decide it best to hire the hypnotist, I will."


ON MY WAY TO SCHOOL, I PASSED POSTERS FOR HENRI Reverie's performances, taped to utility posts and shop windows. The corners of the papers curled and fluttered in the cool November breeze, and each notice resembled the other: a black background, tall yellow letters, and a pair of large blue eyes staring out from above the phrase Young Marvel of the New Century!

I plodded onward, but every other block, Monsieur Reverie watched me travel through the city.

Up ahead of me, the high school's spire clock tower pierced the gray sky high above the corner of Fourteenth and Morrison, a sight that always reminded me of a postcard my mother sent me from Notre Dame Cathedral on her thirtieth birthday. Our school was actually quite colossal and impressive on the inside, too, with dark wood fixtures, electric lighting, fifteen classrooms, a library, a laboratory, a museum, two recitation rooms, an art room, and an assembly hall. The curriculum was modern. The classrooms were integrated and coeducational.

He sent me to a progressive school. And yet my lunatic father was still considering hiring a stranger to obliterate my thoughts.

Algebra was challenging enough without worrying about a cure for female rebellion, but with that new fear bearing down on me, I failed to complete five equations on the weekly examination. In domestic science I somehow lost my little white baking cap and caused a small grease fire that singed the cuff of my right sleeve. History was a blur of dates and long-dead generals (although, to be fair, that tended to be the case every day in history). And in physical education, down in the musty high school basement, I twisted my ankle when

Mrs. Brueden squawked at us to jog faster in our whooshing black exercise bloomers.

English fared somewhat better.

Percy was in that class with me.

My eyes drifted to the back of his combed auburn hair one row over and three seats up, and with nearly soundless squeaks, I swiveled back and forth in my stiff oak chair, my elbows resting against the steep slope of my desk.

Percy scratched his shoulder with his chin, his eyes turned downward, and I held my breath, wondering if he had caught me staring at him. His eyelashes rose. His gaze met mine. The right side of his mouth curved into one of his sly grins, and I smiled, too, while the back of my neck prickled.

"Mr. Acklen, what do you believe Longfellow meant in this last stanza?" asked Mr. Dircksen, our white-haired teacher with furry sideburns that reminded me of rabbits sticking to his cheeks. His broad shadow loomed across Percy's desk and somehow chilled my own arms with gooseflesh.

Percy returned his attention to his reader and straightened his posture. "Um . . . I think it means, sir, we're all trying to see more in life than what there actually is to see. The moon makes everything look more . . . spiritual. I think."

"Are you positive about that?"

"Yes. That's my interpretation, at least."

"Mr. McAllister, would you care to go one step further?"

Quick-witted Theo McAllister launched into a detailed interpretation of the poem, and Percy's shoulders relaxed.

He peeked backward again to see if my eyes were still upon him—which, of course, they were.

I mouthed three words to him: "I brought *Dracula*."

"What?" he mouthed in return.

*"Dracula."* I pointed to my toffee-colored book bag hanging on a hook on the wall next to all the other bags.

"Ah." He nodded, and with an eyebrow cocked, he added, "Corrupt me."

My cheeks burned. Percy snickered.

"Mr. Acklen!" Mr. Dircksen whacked Percy across the head with the palm of his hand, hard enough to knock him out of his chair. "The first rule in this classroom is respect."

Everyone in the room collectively stiffened. My stomach turned with guilt as Percy—red-faced, shoulders hunched—crawled back into his chair and rubbed his ear.

Mr. Dircksen stood up tall above Percy's desk with his hairy neck stretched high. "Turn around in that chair one more time, and you'll be facing the paddle in the principal's office. Do I make myself clear?"

Percy combed his hand through his hair. "Yes, sir."

Mr. Dircksen then pointed a bony finger at me. "You, in the back there. I forgot your name."

I choked on my own saliva.

"What is your name?" he asked in a voice that slapped me on the back and made me cough out the words.

"Olivia Mead."

"Miss Mead"—Mr. Dircksen tapped his reader against his

opened hand—"do *you* require a firm reminder of the first rule of this classroom?"

"N-n-no, sir." I shook my head until the classroom went fuzzy.

"Good. Now, where were we before this interruption?"

I clutched my desk, doubled over, and spent the rest of the class trying to remember how to breathe.

AT PROMPTLY ONE O'CLOCK, MR. DIRCKSEN EXCUSED US. I grabbed my book bag and hustled out to the hallway ahead of my classmates, hoping for a whiff of fresh air, but all I inhaled was the smell of pencil shavings and other students. Even worse, Henri Reverie's eyes haunted me from another black poster that someone had pinned with thumbtacks to the burlap-covered bulletin board across the hall, next to a notice for the school's banjo club. The dramatic yellow letters—all capitals, all screaming to be seen—peeked at me from between the passing hair bows and the male heads with severe parts combed down the middle.

## THE MESMERIZING HENRI REVERIE

"I'm glad he didn't wallop your head, too," said Percy from behind me.

I spun around, my book bag sliding to my elbow.

Percy walked toward me, his satchel slung over one shoulder, his hair falling into his eyes. He rubbed his ear again. "I'd use a word to describe teachers like him, but that would guarantee I'd get the paddle."

"I'm so sorry about that. Here"—I dug into my bag and tugged out *Dracula*—"keep it. It's yours now."

"Keep it?" he asked. "But you love it."

"It's the least I can do."

He flipped the novel over and studied the cover illustration of Dracula's angular castle perched atop a lumpy hill. "I like the way the little bats are soaring around the towers. It looks like a corker of a book." His eyes returned to mine. "But I don't know. I think you owe me more than just a ghost story. Don't you?"

I shrank back. "I—I—I don't—"

He cracked a smile and nudged my arm with his elbow. "Don't look so terrified, Olivia. I just meant I think you need to work even harder to persuade your father to let me take you to that party." He reached out and stroked a piece of my hair and, with it, my cheek. "Will you do that for me, Sleeping Beauty?"

"Yes, of course." I peeled my eyes away from his red ear. "I'd be happy to."

"Good." He dropped his hand to his side. "Tell him I won't bite, unlike"—he patted the novel—"your friend Dracula here."

He tucked the book into his satchel and wandered away.

Frannie's face came into view from around the corner to the stairwell, and as she approached she peeked over her shoulder at Percy disappearing down the steps. Without slowing her stride, she grabbed me by the elbow and steered me toward the music room at the opposite end of the second floor.

"So," she said, "was he kind to you when he drove you home last night?"

"Very kind. But something awful happened to him just now."

"What?"

We passed a boy named Stuart from English who was pantomiming Mr. Dircksen's attack on Percy to a group of his friends in front of the library.

I lowered my voice. "Mr. Dircksen smacked Percy in the head in front of the class . . . and he threatened to send him down to the principal for a paddling. Percy and I had just been exchanging whispers about *Dracula*."

"A paddling on the backside?" Frannie lifted her chin, her eyebrows raised. "Well, now. That's highly appropriate."

I stopped and shook her arm off mine. "Why on earth do you hate Percy?"

"It's nothing," she said, but her face went red and splotchy.

I took her by the arm and pulled her aside, one door down from Stuart and his friends.

"It doesn't seem like nothing, Frannie."

"I just . . ." She shifted her weight between her feet. "I just think he's a snob, that's all. And snobs are only fun in Austen novels."

"Are you sure you don't have a particular reason for hating him?"

"Just watch yourself with him—that's all I'm going to say." She hooked her arm again through mine and pulled me toward the opened chorus room doors. "I've heard he flits from girl to girl and doesn't care about their reputations. Watch out for his hands."

"His hands?" I asked.

"On your bottom, you ninny. I've heard he's a grabber."

She tugged me into the music room, and we sealed the subject of Percy closed.

I OPENED MY MOUTH AS FAR AS MY JAW COULD STRETCH and joined my girls' chorus sisters in rehearsing "Silent Night" for the Christmas concert.

In the middle of the second verse, just as my vibrato was gaining strength and feeling good in my chest, my friend Kate entered the room with a folded piece of paper tucked between her fingers. Her new black shoes with buttons on the sides clip-clopped across the floor to the beat of the metronome sitting on Mr. Bennington's piano.

Mr. Bennington stopped conducting and scratched his waxy mustache. "Let us take a short break, ladies."

Kate handed the teacher the note. Mr. Bennington pulled his wire reading glasses out of his striped coat pocket and squinted through the lenses, as if he couldn't quite decipher the words.

"It's for Olivia," said Kate.

My insides liquefied. I wondered why the devil someone was sending *me* a message in the middle of the school day.

"Olivia." Mr. Bennington peeked up at me. "Come read this note and then return to your position."

"Yes, sir." I climbed down from the risers, out of the depths of the deepest altos stuck in the back, and took the piece of paper. Kate patted my back as if I were receiving a summons to the gallows and clip-clopped out of the room.

I unfolded the note.

"Let us take it from the beginning," said Mr. Bennington.

My classmates cleared their throats and stood up tall, while I read two sentences scribbled in Father's squiggly cursive:

*My daughter, Olivia Mead, must come to my dental office directly after school. She should NOT go home.*
*Respectfully,*
*Dr. Walter Mead*

My blood froze. I reread those phrases at least three more times apiece. Our rather somber rendition of "Silent Night" seized the room with a harmony that pricked the little hairs on the back of my neck, and Father's ominous second sentence stared me in the eye.

*She should NOT go home.*

> "He had the calm, possessed, surgical look of a man who could endure pain in another person."
>
> — MARK TWAIN, "Happy Memories of the Dental Chair," 1884

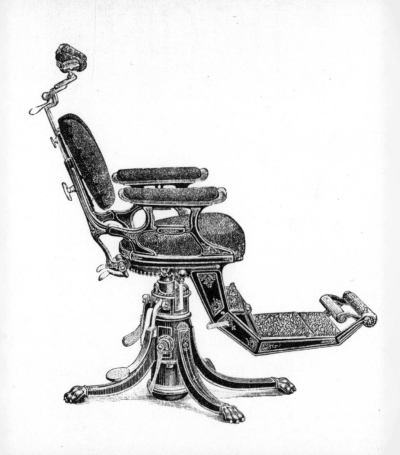

CHAPTER FOUR

# THE CURE

I n Father's downtown office, tucked in the heart of Portland's business district, a door with a frosted glass pane
separated his mahogany-lined lobby from the windowless
operatory in which he tended to his patients' teeth and
gums. I could see him moving beyond the glass—a distorted figure in a trim white coat, bending over the silhouette
of a man tipped back in the padded dental chair. Laughter erupted from the patient, first in snickers, then in loud
brays and hiccups that told me the man had inhaled a bag
of nitrous oxide, otherwise known as good old laughing gas.

I seated myself in a rigid chair in the lobby and stared up at Father's four-foot-wide oil painting of a pair of silver dental forceps shining against a green background. I recalled Percy's utter dread of my father's profession (even though Father worried *I* would scare Percy away), and I slunk down a little farther in my spindle-back seat, wishing Father were a bookstore owner like Frannie's pa, or even a chimney sweep or a sailor. Someone who didn't hang pictures of torture devices on his workplace walls or cause men to suffer from fits of laughter while they shouted out, "No! I'm not ready!"—as was happening beyond the frosted glass beside me.

I eyed the main door to the street and debated bolting home. *I can claim I never received the note,* I realized. *I could say that I—*

The front door opened.

Henri Reverie stepped into the lobby.

I drew a sharp breath and averted my eyes. My shoulders inched toward my ears. *He's come to take away my free will. I knew it!*

Henri removed a dark square-crown hat from his head, closed the door, and lowered himself into a chair across from me, below the painting of the forceps. He was dressed in a three-piece suit and tie, all as black as midnight—a shadow with cobalt-blue eyes and blond hair. His complexion was poorer than I remembered, probably due to all the lard-based greasepaint theater people had to wear on their faces, according to my mother. His slumped posture gave him the shifty look of a peddler trying to pass off bottles of booze as magical cure-alls.

"No!" cried the patient in the operatory.

I gave a start—as did Henri.

"Noooo! I'm not ready! Nooooooo!"

Shrieks and loud smacks and another fit of hysterical laughter came from beyond the glass. Henri grabbed hold of his armrests with whitening fingers, and his knees swerved to his right, toward the door, as if he were about to flee.

A smile twitched at the corners of my lips. I relaxed my shoulders and folded my hands in my lap, for I realized something absolutely delightful: Henri Reverie's fear of my father's dental practice gave me the upper hand in our current situation.

*Interesting.*

"Are you here for an appointment, Mr. Reverie?" I asked.

"Stay still, Mr. Dibbs!" yelled Father from beyond the door. "If you don't stop flailing about, I'll need to clamp your wrists to the chair in addition to your head."

Henri grimaced as if his own head were being clamped to a chair, while Mr. Dibbs cackled and whooped and let loose the screams of a man suffering the tortures of the Spanish Inquisition.

"I said, are you here for an appointment, Mr. Reverie?"

"I—" Henri's blue eyes shifted toward me for a swift moment, but they veered straight back to the bobbing and ducking figures beyond the frosted pane. "Yes, an appoint-ment."

"A bad tooth?" I asked, sitting up straighter, stifling another smile. "Swollen gums? Do you need your tissues leeched of blood?"

A howl of pain echoed through the office walls. "No!" cried Mr. Dibbs in a decibel that made my ears ring. "No! I wasn't ready."

"It's all done," said Father. "The extraction was a success. Hold this ice over the wound and rest a few minutes. You're fine."

The patient sobbed and moaned and then cackled with laughter. "You had a blasted smile on your face, Dr. Mead. You looked like you enjoyed ripping my tooth from its socket."

"Nobody enjoys the sight of a decayed bicuspid rotting away in an inflamed mass of bleeding gums, Mr. Dibbs. Take better care of your oral health, sir."

Father's distorted image came closer to the frosted glass; his beard and white coat grew sharp and clear behind the pane until I could almost see the browns of his eyes. He opened the operatory door and poked out his head. "Ah, good. You're both here. I'll lay Mr. Dibbs on the cot and bring you in."

I jumped to my feet. "I am not going in there like one of your patients."

"Now, don't be difficult, Olivia." Father let go of the doorknob. "Mr. Reverie has kindly agreed to help you accept the world the way it is."

"You actually hired this person"—I pointed toward the still-seated hypnotist—"to extract my thoughts in your operatory, as if my brain were a decayed thing, like Mr. Dibbs's disgusting bicuspid? Do you know how cruel and horrifying this is?"

"Olivia . . ." Father put out a cautious hand and trod toward me as though I were a rabid dog. "I told you, I only want the best for you. Don't have a conniption."

I lunged for the front door, but my father pounced and took hold of both my arms before I could escape.

"Olivia, please." He spun me toward him. "Please behave for me. Your mother—she abandoned the both of us, not just me. She left you behind, too."

"I know that." My eyes smarted with tears, and I saw a blurry version of Henri Reverie turning his face away from us, pretending not to hear, which made me want to cry all the more.

"She said she wanted the vote, too," said Father. "I hear her voice in yours. You can't do that to some poor husband and child one day. I won't let you break people's hearts."

"I'm not going to be like her."

"You've got to change."

"No."

"Think of your future sons and daughters. Think how much better your childhood would have been if your mother had accepted her place in the world and ignored her selfish dreams."

"She did it all wrong." I wriggled my shoulders and struggled to break free of his grip. "I won't be like her, I swear. Please don't pay him to take away my thoughts."

"Please do not be afraid, Miss Mead."

I turned and looked straight into Henri Reverie's eyes—a mistake.

"Do not be afraid," said the hypnotist again in a voice that soothed me as much as when I had succumbed to his anesthetizing words on the stage. Those eyes of his—those potent blue irises that tugged me toward him—swallowed me whole and assured me there was nothing to fear inside that dental office. There was nothing to fear in the entire world. My muscles slackened. My worries evaporated into the sweet nitrous oxide in the air.

Father let go of my arms.

"It is a pleasure to see you again, Mademoiselle Mead," said Henri, rising to his feet. "I can tell you are nervous about my presence here, but I promise, your session in this building will be as relaxing as your trance yesterday. *Ne vous inquiétez pas.* Do not worry."

I exhaled a sound between a laugh and a gasp and tore my eyes from his, an action that hurt as much as pulling a thorn from my finger. "How can I possibly feel relaxed," I said, "when I don't know what's about to happen to me?"

Henri walked toward me with footsteps that scarcely made a sound on the lobby's dusty floorboards. "I swear to you, Miss Mead, you will not be harmed in any way. You will feel the same sense of well-being and euphoria you experienced when you reemerged from my trance on the stage. Do you remember that beautiful sensation?"

He stood in front of me and trapped me again with those unshakable eyes. The flaws in his skin and light stubble on his chin faded to insignificant blurs compared to those two orbs of brilliant blue. My breath grew shallow and fluttery. My veins seemed to flow with hazy waves of Father's laughing gas instead of blood.

Henri took my hand, and a rush of warmth passed between us. I remembered that warmth all too well.

That sensation was my undoing.

He jerked me toward him by my arm and called out, "Sleep!"

My face crashed against the buttons of his coat.

"Melt down, melt down." He cupped his hand over the back of my head, and my body slackened against his chest. "Let yourself go, downward, downward, downward."

He dragged my rag-doll body across the floor and plopped me into one of the lobby chairs, still holding the back of my head. "Keep going down, Miss Mead. Keep easing deeper into sleep. Melt down. Let go, let go."

A lock clicked into place. Curtains clattered closed.

"Teach her to accept the world the way it truly is," begged Father in a voice that trembled and cracked. "Make her clearly understand the roles of men and women."

"I'll try my best, *monsieur*—"

"And tell her to say 'All is well' instead of arguing whenever she's angry. Please. Her rebelliousness has got to be removed if she's going to survive."

I was too submerged in a warm and comfy eiderdown blanket of peace and darkness to care anymore what that silly man was blathering on about. Henri took hold of my left hand, and a numbing shot of heat flowed up my arms and fanned throughout my body to my farthest extremities. I gasped. My chin melted to my chest. The entire world slipped away, except for the soft lull of Henri Reverie's voice.

"You are doing beautifully, Miss Mead. But now I need to take you into an even deeper level of hypnosis. I am going to stand behind you and use my hands to guide your head in a complete circle. Each revolution will send you further and further into the desired state of relaxation."

His warm hands clasped my temples and revolved my head in a gentle, circular motion that slowed my breathing and dropped me down into a tingling world of blackness. My shoulders slumped forward.

"Yes, very good . . . you are melting even deeper now." He rotated my head again, tilting back my chin until my neck was stretched and exposed. "You are doing so well. Keep going . . . all the way down. All the way down . . ."

Two delightful revolutions later, my chest collapsed against my legs.

"Excellent. Wonderful. I am so impressed." He seemed to

shift his position and kneel in front of me. His hand cradled the back of my skull. "You are now submerged in one of the deepest levels of hypnosis. Say *yes* if you understand me."

"Yesss," I mumbled with heavy lips into the wool of my skirt.

"*Magnifique.* Now, Miss Mead, I want you to listen to me, for the next part of my instruction is extremely important." His lips bent close to my ear, and his voice traveled directly inside my head, as if he were taking up residence in the middle of my brain. "When you awaken, you will see the world the way it truly is. The roles of men and women will be clearer than they have ever been before. You will know whom to avoid. Say *yes* if you understand me."

"Yesss."

"Good." He exhaled a feathery sigh against my cheek. "Now, some of the things you see with your new vision might make you angry. However, you will be incapable of uttering angry words. Whenever you are upset, all you will be able to say is 'All is well.' Say it right now."

"All is well."

"Good. All is well. You will see the world the way it truly is. The roles of men and women will be clearer than they have ever been before. Instead of getting angry, you will say 'All is well.' Say it once again."

"All is well."

"Wonderful. I am so glad you understand. I am going to bring you back up again. Let us just take our time and do this slowly. I will count to ten, and you will feel my hands rising up from your feet. One . . . two . . . You feel the force between us cooling, weakening . . ."

The blanket lifted off me, and I rose like a swelling loaf of bread.

"Three . . . four . . . five . . . let it go, you are doing splendidly, Miss Mead . . . let it go . . . six . . . seven . . . eight . . . you are almost back . . . nine . . ." He pressed his hand against my forehead. "Ten. Awake."

I opened my eyes.

"Oh—my Lord!" I sank back against my chair and grabbed the armrests. "Oh, God!"

Henri Reverie kneeled on the floor in front of me, and he had turned into the most delightful creature upon which my eyes had ever feasted. Flawless skin. A perfectly structured nose. Sumptuous red lips that looked ripe and full and ready to be touched. Pure blue eyes with bottomless pools of dark pupils that reflected his sincerity and concern. Concern for me.

"Do you feel all right, Miss Mead?" he asked in a voice like a distant echo, as if spoken from the opposite end of a tunnel. He leaned forward on his knees, and I couldn't help but reach out and sift my hand through his hair, which slid through my fingers like golden threads of sun-bright silk. The rest of the world darkened into shadow around him. All I could do was look at him—really look at him.

"Olivia!" snapped Father, also in a faraway voice. "Why are you touching him?"

I lifted my face toward Father to try to describe Henri's confounding beauty, but my tongue froze when I caught sight of a fiend in a white coat standing in the lobby where my father should have been. The brute's red eyes gleamed bright and dangerous, and his skin went deathly pale and thin enough to reveal the jutting curves of the facial skeleton beneath his flesh. His graying beard resembled the flea-infested fur of a rat.

"What is it?" asked the fiend, his canine teeth as sharp as the fangs of a wolf or the deadly tip of a scythe. "Are you cured or not?"

I clutched the armrests until my fingers ached, and my knees knocked against each other with the thumping of bones and a wild rustle of skirts. I opened my mouth to shout, *You look like a monster! What's wrong with you? Get away from me. I hate you!*

Yet only three limp words emerged from my lips.

"All is well."

CHAPTER FIVE

# THE WORLD THE WAY IT TRULY IS

I bolted.

I didn't even wait to see what Mr. Dibbs and his bloody tooth socket looked like back in the recesses of the operatory. The monstrous version of Father shouted something about catching me, but I darted out the front door and down the street before anyone could chase me down.

Outside, the world felt as if it had tipped sideways and knocked everything askew. The air had grown too thin to breathe. Shop windows reflected blinding sunlight that throbbed behind my eyes. The city had turned as bright and vivid as a theater stage at the height of a performance, yet the noises of my surroundings—carriage wheels, trotting hooves, peddlers hawking wares from carts—sounded muffled and tinny. Even my sense of smell dulled as my eyes viewed the world with startling clarity. I saw two women across the street with blood on their necks. A man in a business suit and derby hat came my way, and his face was as gaunt and pale and fanged as Father's.

I panted and slid my hand across the cold sandstone walls for support and somehow managed to run across the street and down the next block—before I stopped in front of an establishment that was caging up women.

Yes, *caging women.*

On a corner lot where a regular storefront should have stood, a giant copper cage held five ladies prisoner. Their shoulders and hats squished together in a crowd of feathers and fine wool dresses, and they buried their noses inside some sort of pamphlet that distracted their attention from the freak-show absurdity of their situation.

Out in front of the entrapment, a female carnival barker—I didn't even know women could be barkers!—in a red-striped jacket and a straw boater hat yelled, "Welcome! Welcome! Come see the only proper place for women and girls."

A young blond woman in a tailored blue suit took a pamphlet from the barker and climbed inside the cage with the other ladies. The barker promptly shut the cage door and locked it tight.

"Miss Mead!"

Footsteps ran toward me, and before I knew what was coming, Henri Reverie grabbed me by my arm. "Are you all right?"

The hypnotist had returned to his shady young showman appearance, and he smelled as dusty and smoky as the letters Mother wrote from backstage dressing rooms. Sounds regained their full volume. Henri's hair lost its brilliance.

"Th-th-they're caging up women," I said. "They're locking them up right here . . ."

I turned and pointed, but instead of the copper cage, I saw a brick building with a wide white banner hanging above the glass door.

## HEADQUARTERS
### THE OREGON ASSOCIATION OPPOSED TO THE EXTENSION OF SUFFRAGE TO WOMEN

A slender middle-aged brunette with an entire stuffed quail perched upon her hat—not a strange female carnival barker—stood in front of the opened door, and she caught my eye and said, "Would you like to come inside and see what we're all about, dear?" She held out a pamphlet and smiled with a fine pair of false front teeth, undoubtedly fitted by Father. "Read about the hair-pulling, face-scratching women of Idaho who turned into heathens once their state allowed them to vote. We'll teach you about the proper sphere for ladies."

I yanked myself free of Henri and continued down the block.

Henri followed, and our feet clapped across the sidewalk in near unison. He caught me by my elbow before I could cross another street. "What are you seeing?"

"All is well."

"Tell me." He grabbed both my shoulders and turned me around to face him.

"All is well!"

"I need to know if everything went as planned with our session. Tell me what you see."

"All . . ." A frustrated cry burst from my lips. "All is . . ." Itchy tears filled my eyes, but the more I fought to hold back my emotions, the more a fit of crying longed to break free. A stray tear slipped down my cheek. A sob exploded from my mouth.

"No, do not cry, Miss Mead. Please . . ." He rubbed both my arms with a rapid *swish-swish-swish* against my white blouse sleeves. "Shh. Please do not cry. Try to talk in a calmer voice. Try to relax. Those three words will only come out of you if you're angry. Take a deep breath."

"No, I don't want to do anything you ask of me. You got your money; now leave me alone, you—" A vicious insult burned up my throat, but the words hardened into a lump of simmering coal that lodged in the back of my mouth. I coughed out that stupid phrase again: "All is well." I shook Henri's hands off me. "Never come near me again."

A swift kick in his shin with the pointed toe of my shoe sent him doubling over to clutch his leg. I tore down the street again, away from the anti-suffrage headquarters and Father's cruel teeth and Henri Reverie's disorienting blue eyes.

*You will see the world the way it truly is. The roles of men and women will be clearer than they have ever been before. You will know whom to avoid.*

HARRISON'S BOOKS SAT THREE BLOCKS NORTH OF THE courthouse, nestled between a dry-goods store and a small hotel, in a row of storefronts Frannie and I affectionately called *Eat, Read, Sleep, and Be Merry*. I panted in front of the bookshop's leftmost display window. When I had caught my breath, I dared a peek inside.

Just beyond the glass the new and successful novels of the season were propped upon low wooden stands—*The Touchstone*, by an author named Edith Wharton. *The Wonderful Wizard of Oz*, the delightful children's book I had read over the summer. *To Have and to Hold. Richard Carvel. A Man's Woman.* And, of course, *Dracula.* My nose bumped against the cool glass, and my shaky breath left a foggy circle on the pane.

A movement beyond the books caught my eye: Frannie's father, with his curly gray hair and little potbelly, passed through the store with a cloth-bound volume in hand. He wore his usual three-piece suit—tan and lined in pale gray stripes—and he fitted his round spectacles over his bulbous nose that was the shape of my rubber bicycle horn.

I dipped down behind the window's display and watched him flip open the book on the front counter, next to the brass cash register. Unlike Father's, his cheeks were pink and healthy. His teeth weren't overly long and barbaric. Everything about him seemed as regular as could be.

I sprang to my feet and pushed my way inside the shop door.

"Oh, thank heavens, Mr. Harrison!" I clasped Frannie's father in a huge hug and buried my face in his itchy striped coat. "You look so normal."

"Hey, hey, hey." Mr. Harrison held me at arm's length and took a long look at my face. "What's all this about, Olivia? Has someone hurt you?"

I nodded but then shook my head in an adamant no. "Is Frannie home?"

"She's doing homework upstairs."

"May I go see her?"

"Of course."

Mr. Harrison dropped his hands from my arms, and I bounded up the staircase that led to the Harrisons' crowded yet homey apartment above the shop.

The front room bustled with the usual whoops and laughter of Frannie's five younger siblings—Martha, Carl, Annie, Willie, and Pearl. They were like a hill of ants, spilling over furniture and books, piling on top of one another, and bumping into the blue-papered walls. Off in the kitchen, around the right bend, someone rapped a spoon against the rim of a pot. I followed a divine scented trail of boiled beef and carrots and found Mrs. Harrison preparing a stew over her big black cookstove, amid a cloud of steam that drifted past her round face. The copper pot spat wet polka dots across the clean white front of her pinafore apron, and she could have used a few more pins to hold down her brown topknot, which was flecked with a scattering of gray hairs. Otherwise, she was perfect.

"Mrs. Harrison!" I threw my arms around her sturdy shoulders. "It's wonderful to see you looking healthy and happy."

"My goodness." Mrs. Harrison patted my elbow with a hand that dampened my blouse. "What's all this about, Livie?"

Frannie peeked up from her McGuffey's Reader at the round kitchen table. "Yes, what is all this about, Livie?"

I let go of Mrs. Harrison, despite her warmth. "I need to talk to you privately, Frannie. As soon as possible."

"All right." Frannie neatened her pile of homework papers and stood. "We'll be up in my bedroom, Mama."

"That's fine, dear." Mrs. Harrison stirred her pot and pressed her lips into a thin smile, but I could tell from her watchful Mama-bird eyes that she sensed something wasn't quite right.

Frannie and I climbed the second flight of stairs, past piles of books perched on the rickety wooden steps—books that always appeared to have wandered in from the shop of their own accord and made themselves at home wherever they found space. The air up there was rich with the perfumes of paper and ink, along with a fine peppering of dust.

Frannie led me into the room she shared with all three of her sisters, a cramped space with two beds, a chest of drawers, and a tall pine wardrobe. She planted herself on the bed that belonged to her and Martha.

"What's wrong?" she asked. "Did your father say something to you?"

"I . . . um . . ." I balled my hands into fists. "I . . . Oh, criminy. When I tell you what just happened, you're going to think I've gone nutty."

"Just tell me. You're clearly not yourself. Wait—" She sat up straight, her brown eyes enormous. "Oh . . . This doesn't have anything to do with Percy, does it?"

"No. It has to do with Monsieur Henri Reverie, *the marvel of the new century* . . . and all that other hogwash."

She knitted her eyebrows. "The hypnotist?"

"Yes. He hypnotized me again, just now, in Father's office."

"What? Why?"

"Father heard . . ." I braced my back against the wardrobe. "He found out I was at the rally yesterday. He thinks I'm turning into my mother. He decided I needed my unfeminine thoughts removed from my brain."

Frannie's mouth fell open. "What? No! Did he really say such a thing?"

"I've heard horror stories of troublesome daughters and

wives getting sent away to asylums. I've read Nellie Bly's *Ten Days in a Mad-House*. What if this is only the first step?"

"What did that hypnotist do to you?"

"Henri told me"—I rubbed my forehead—"I'd see the world the way it truly is, and the roles of men and women would be clearer than they've ever been before. I don't think my father understood what that meant. I'm not sure I do, either . . . Your father looks like someone we can trust. But my father . . ." I tucked my hands behind my back, between the wardrobe and my lower spine, to quiet the tremors shaking through my fingers.

Frannie leaned forward. "Your father what?"

"He looked like a vampire. I swear upon a stack of Bibles, he had fangs and flesh as pale as a corpse's."

Her eyes scanned my face, as if she were waiting for a twitch of my mouth or a flash of laughter in my eyes to reveal I was joking.

I chewed my lip, but I most certainly did not laugh.

"Livie . . ." She let loose a nervous giggle. "You've read *Dracula* at least four times in the past year."

"Yes, I know that."

"And now you're telling me your father looks like a vampire?"

"Yes."

"Don't you think that's a little . . . peculiar?"

"Yes, it is peculiar, but I was hypnotized, Frannie. You saw the power Henri Reverie had over me last night. He's like a sorcerer who changed the world for my eyes alone, and I can't bear the thought of going out there and seeing my father—or any other man—with fangs and bloodless skin and—"

"All right." She sprang off the bed. "I believe you're truly seeing something troubling, but perhaps Mr. Reverie simply stirred up your imagination."

"He's supposed to be *killing off* my imagination. Father hired him to cure me of my dreams."

She winced. "But if these aren't dreams or imaginings . . . what are they?"

"They seem real. They seem true. How can I go home to Father when he looks like that?"

My nose itched as if it required either a cry or a good sneeze. I scratched the tip with the back of one hand.

Frannie walked over to me and coaxed my hand between her palms. "Have supper with us tonight."

I shook my head. "Father will worry when he sees I'm not home."

"We'll ask Carl to run over to his office and tell him we've invited you to stay. And then Carl and I will take you home after supper so I can see for myself if anything looks different about your father. I'll even give you a little sign if he appears to be normal."

"What type of sign?"

"Well . . ." She scraped her teeth over her bottom lip. "I'll say, 'I still can't believe how many times you've read *Dracula*,

Livie. One too many times, that's for sure.' If you hear that, it means what you're seeing is truly just in your mind, and so it must be the work of that malicious, selfish, conniving hypnotist— Oh, wait." She squeezed my hand and looked me straight in the eye. "You didn't tell me how Henri Reverie appeared after the hypnosis."

I groaned and hunched my shoulders.

"What?" She squeezed my hand again. "Was he even worse than your father?"

I shook my head. "That would have made everything far less confusing."

"What did he look like?"

I sighed. "He looked like . . . I can't even bring myself to say it. It almost hurts to admit what he made me feel."

"What?" Her face paled. "What did he make you feel?"

"He looked . . ." I swallowed. "He looked like someone I should trust utterly."

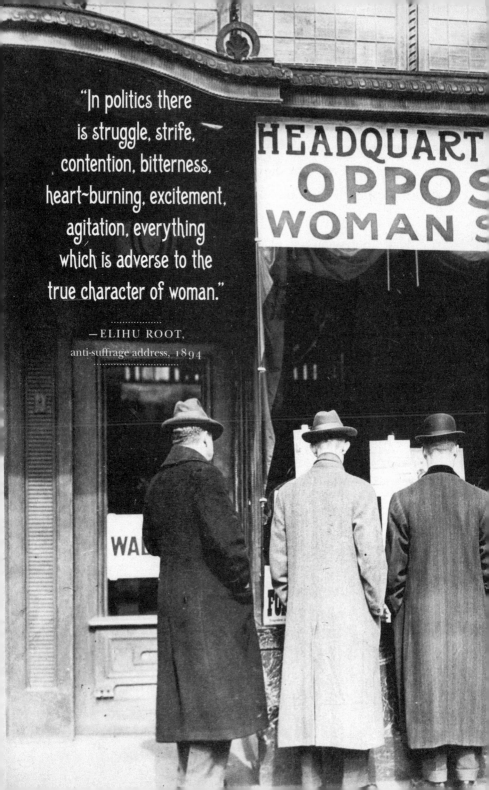

"In politics there is struggle, strife, contention, bitterness, heart~burning, excitement, agitation, everything which is adverse to the true character of woman."

—ELIHU ROOT, anti-suffrage address, 1894

HEADQUART
OPPOS
WOMAN S

# CHAPTER SIX

# THE SILENCER

**A**t supper that evening, the noisy passel of Harrisons chatted and joked about school escapades and camping trips while they stuffed me full of stew and potatoes. Every now and again I caught Mr. and Mrs. Harrison glancing at me with worried expressions, as if they couldn't quite shake the memory of my emotional entrance earlier that afternoon.

After supper, I slid my arms into the thick sleeves of my coat, which, along with my book bag, had been fetched by Frannie's fourteen-year-old brother, Carl, when he went to tell Father I'd be home late. The woolen collar snuggled up to my neck and pervaded my nostrils with the dental office's distinctive odor—a sweet, antiseptic, and metallic potpourri that now flooded me with memories of Henri's hands on my head.

I buttoned up for the outside chill. "How did my father look when you saw him, Carl?"

Carl smiled. "Bloody."

"Bloody?" I asked with a gasp.

"He was leeching some woman, and he had her head locked into a metal contraption to keep her still." Carl tilted his head back to demonstrate, his hands clamped around his temples beneath his curly brown hair. "The leech had wiggled out of the tube wrong and bloodied up the woman's lip, so your father was trying to get the little bugger to travel down to her gums. His hands were smeared in bright red blood."

I lowered my shoulders and steadied my breathing. The fact that the blood was leech related and had nothing to do with fangs and lacerated throats was the best news I'd heard all day.

"I STILL CAN'T BELIEVE HOW MANY TIMES YOU'VE READ *Dracula*," said Frannie from beneath a hissing gas lamp in the dim hallway of my house. "One too many times, that's for sure."

The soles of Father's house slippers whispered their way from his office in the back. I kept my face turned toward the tan rug by the front door as long as I could, but then Frannie gave my back a gentle pat, and I gained the courage to raise my chin.

Father—regular Father, not the cadaverous fiend with the rat-fur beard—frowned at me in the hallway.

"You're not reading that ghastly novel again, are you, Olivia?" he asked. "Haven't you had enough of *Dracula* by now?"

"Yes." I gulped down a nasty taste of bile. "Quite enough."

Carl stuffed his hands into his coat pockets. "You should come to supper again on Sunday, Livie," he said. "Our parents are celebrating—what is it, Frannie?—their hundredth anniversary now?"

"Their twentieth," said Frannie with a roll of her eyes at Carl's exaggeration. "Yes, come. We're planning to sit down at five o'clock. We'd love to have you join us."

"I'd love to be there. Thank you."

Carl opened the door to take his leave, but before following him, Frannie grabbed my hand and leaned in close with a whisper: "Come back to my house if you need anything else. At any time."

I mustered a weak smile. "Thank you."

They closed the door and went on their way.

I stood with my back to Father, facing the exit through which my friends had just vanished while the cool taste of the outside air lingered on my tongue.

"I was so worried about you this afternoon," said Father in a voice cozy and warm with paternal concern.

Despite his tone, I didn't dare turn around.

"Why did you run away like that?" he asked. "You just left me standing there."

"What did you expect me to do? *Thank* you?"

"No—but you made me worry something had gone terribly wrong. Mr. Reverie assured me he found you. He said you had simply been spooked by your new view of the world. But still . . . I was troubled."

I stared at the door.

"Why won't you turn around and look at me, Olivia? Do I look different to you?"

I squeezed my eyes shut and swallowed. "I . . . um . . ."

"What?"

"I . . . I see the world . . . the way it truly is. The roles of men and women are clearer than they have ever been before." I slipped my hands inside my warm coat sleeves and clung to the woolen lining. "I saw a storefront—women, suffrage—a cage."

"What?"

"I saw a cage."

"Suffrage is like a restrictive cage, you mean?"

I pursed my lips. "All is well."

"You understand your place in the world, then?"

I opened my eyes and again peered at the door to the world beyond. "Yes. I understand precisely where I do and don't belong."

Father breathed a sigh. "Thank heavens. It worked."

Another deep sigh, this one accompanied by a small belch. "Well, in light of this new outlook on life, I'll be more than happy to allow you to accompany Percy Acklen to the party tomorrow evening. As long as you promise to be well behaved—and to represent our family with utmost care in front of both Percy and the Eiderlings—I'll have Gerda take a note to the Acklen household tomorrow morning."

"Thank you."

Silence wedged between us again. I assumed he was waiting for me to turn around and face him, perhaps even to fling my arms around his shoulders and tell him, *You were right, Father. My life is so much better now that I hallucinate and can no longer articulate my anger.*

When I showed no signs of moving, he retreated down the hall, his house slippers swishing across the floorboards.

"Time to ready yourself for bed, Olivia," he said as he went. "I'll be finishing my nightcap in my office if you need me."

My stomach clenched into a knot. I steadied myself against the little marble-topped side table we used for collecting mail, and my palm crinkled the copy of the newspaper that featured the illustration of Henri and me. Farther down on the page, a headline I had failed to see that morning jumped out at me in boldfaced letters:

## WHY THE WOMEN OF THIS STATE SHOULD BE SILENCED

The author: Judge Percival R. Acklen.

Percy's father.

I grabbed the paper off the table and tore up the staircase.

Behind my closed door, seated on the edge of my bed, I devoured the entire piece, still buttoned inside my coat and shoes. The letter stated the following:

*As nearly everyone knows, in June of this year, the men of Oregon voted down a referendum that would have given the women of this great state of ours the right to vote. As this upcoming Tuesday's presidential election draws nearer, irate females have taken to the steps of the courthouse in downtown Portland to complain about their lack of a voice in American politics—and to bemoan their jealousies over their voting sisters in neighboring Idaho.*

*What these unbridled women lack is a thorough knowledge of the female brain. Two of my closest friends, Drs. Cornelius Piper and Mortimer Yves, two fine gentlemen educated at East Coast universities, both support the staggering wealth of scientific research that proves women were created for domestic duties alone, not higher thinking. A body built for childbearing and mothering is clearly a body meant to stay in the home. If females muddle their minds with politics and other matters confusing to a woman's head, they will abandon their wifely and motherly duties and inevitably trigger the downfall of American society.*

*Moreover, we would never allow an unqualified, undereducated, ignorant citizen to run our country as president. Why, therefore, would we allow such a person to vote for president?*

*Women of Oregon, you preside over our children and our homes. Rejoice in your noble position upon this earth. Return to your children and husbands, and stop concerning yourselves with masculine matters beyond your understanding. Silence in a woman is feminine, honorable, and, above all else, natural. Save your voices for sweet words of support for your hardworking husbands and gentle lullabies for your babes—not for American politics.*

I ground my teeth together until my jaw ached. This man—this silencer of women—was raising the first boy who had ever looked at me with longing and affection in his eyes.

Poor Percy.

Poor *Mrs.* Acklen.

Poor Oregon.

We were all being lectured by a buffoon.

I thought of Frannie's mother and everything she did to keep their wild household *and* their bookstore running in tip-top order. A fire kindled in my chest, burning, spreading, crackling loudly enough for me to hear it, until I worried my breathing might singe the bedroom walls. My mouth filled with the taste of thick black smoke.

I pulled a sheet of writing paper out of my rolltop desk, dipped the nib of my pen into a pot of velvety dark ink, and wrote a response to his letter with my neatest display of penmanship.

*To Judge Acklen:*

*You state that women were made for domestic duties alone. Have you ever stopped to observe the responsibilities involved with domestic duties?*

*What better person to understand the administration of a country than an individual who spends her days mediating quarrels, balancing household budgets, organizing and executing three complex meals, and ensuring all rooms, appliances, deliveries, clothing, guests, family members, and pets are tended to and functioning the way they ought to be? I do not know of any other job in the world that so closely resembles the presidency itself.*

*Moreover, females are raised to become rational, industrious, fair, and compassionate human beings. Males are taught to sow their wild oats and run free while they're able. Which gender is truly the most prepared to make decisions about the management of a country? Do you want a responsible individual or a rambunctious one choosing the fate of our government?*

*You insinuate that women's minds are easily muddled, yet you entrust us with the rearing of your children, America's future. Mothers are our first teachers. Mothers are the voices of reason who instill the nation's values in our youth. Mothers are the ones who raise the politicians for whom they are not allowed to vote. Why would you let an easily muddled creature* take on such important duties? Why not hire men to bring up your sons and daughters?

I can already hear you arguing that women's bodies were designed for childrearing, but that is not true, sir. Our bodies may have been built for birthing children and nourishing them during their first meals, but it is our minds that are doing the largest share of the work. On a daily basis, we women prove that our brains are sharp and quick, yet you are too blind to see our intelligence.

Furthermore, you have no need to fear that we would forgo our domestic duties if we were to become voting citizens, for we have been trained all our lives to balance a multitude of tasks. We do not let our homes fall into ruin simply because we have been given one more item to accomplish. Worry more about the males who have only one job and no household chores. Their minds are more likely to stray than ours.

Do you call your own mother "undereducated" and "ignorant," Judge Acklen? Was her mind in too much of a muddle to keep your childhood household intact? Was she so easily confused that she was unable to raise a boy who would one day become a judge? I think not. Your mother was undoubtedly a quick-witted, accountable individual who would probably make a far better president than the pampered male you gentlemen vote into office this Tuesday.

I dipped my pen into the inkwell, caught my breath, and read my incendiary words, debating whether the phrasing was too obvious. I tried to imagine what would happen if the writer were identified and made public. Father would likely shove our entire life savings into Henri Reverie's pockets to ensure my mind was altered beyond recognition. There might indeed be a trip to an asylum. I'd even heard rumors of surgeons removing wombs from the bodies of rebellious wives and daughters.

*Unthinkable.*

But maybe . . . if I was careful . . . just maybe the right anonymous signature would disguise me.

I tested out various examples in my head.

– *An Angry Woman*

– *An Irate Female*

– *Your Long-Suffering Mothers, Wives, and Daughters*

– *A Highly Educated Woman*

– *A Girl Who Refuses to Be Silent*

No. Too emotional for the tastes of stubborn men. I pictured Father shaking his head and calling the letter writer *hysterical.*

I tapped the nib of my pen against the well to dispose of stray drops of ink, sampled ideas for two more minutes, and then wrote the wisest, most reasonable approach.

– *A Responsible Woman*

No. 1.  Upper and Lower Incisors and Canine.

No. 6.  Upper Incisors and Bicuspids.

No. 13.  Right Upper Molars.

No. 14.  Left Upper Molars.

No. 27.  Upper Wisdom.

No. 33.  Lower Incisors, Canines and Bicuspids.

# ROTTEN

I dreamt about the hypnosis.

The procedure again occurred in Father's downtown office, this time back in his operatory, at night. The stark wooden room glowed in the light of a bare bulb that reflected off the spittoon and the neat row of dental tools lined on a small oval table. Leather straps clamped my head and wrists to the operatory chair—an uncomfortable piece of furniture padded in worn mauve velvet and braced by four metal feet sculpted like the paws of a beast, as if the chair would one day spring to life and devour some poor, troublesome patient.

Father, his hands still bloody from a leeching, polished the sharp tip of his drill with a white cloth. Behind him in the shadows stood Henri Reverie in his dark suit and a black magician's hat that appeared to be a taller, more ominous version of his real-life hat, but his luminous blue eyes were the only parts of him I could truly see. *Oh, Lord*—those bright and haunting blue eyes.

"Shall we begin?" asked Father, and he leaned over me, reeking of blood and chloroform.

He pulled open my mouth with his thumb, which tasted like everyone else's saliva, and his ears turned as pale and as pointed as the Count's in *Dracula*. Bat ears made of human flesh is what they were—horrifying flaps sticking out from the sides of his pasty-gray head with its fierce and bulging red eyes. He pumped the drill's foot pedal to make the needle spin.

I arched my back and froze against the chair, and that drill buzzed against one of my molars until bitter flecks of tooth sprayed across my tongue. My nerves throbbed with pain. I screamed bloody murder.

"Good heavens, Olivia!" called Father over the grinding and the shrieking. "Your entire head is rotten." He stopped the drill and swiveled around to his little stand of tools. "Let's remove some of those troublesome spots."

"No!" I kicked my feet and tried to wrench my wrists free of the bindings. "Don't take anything away!"

Father picked up a silver instrument, a hybrid of a key and

a corkscrew, with a small metal claw at one end and an ivory handle on the other.

"Let me just get this dental key in there"—both his fanged face and the instrument rushed my way—"so we can break apart that problematic piece."

"No!"

He gripped my tooth with the metal claw and cranked the ivory handle. Pressure mounted on the molar, growing, pushing, squeezing, *CRACK!*—the tooth split in two.

I howled in agony, but Father muffled my cries by digging beneath the crumbling tooth, stirring up blood and more pain, stretching my cheek and lips with cold metal. He then grabbed hold of the shattered molar with a pair of long forceps and yanked each piece straight out of my gum.

"This rotten, broken tooth is your dream of attending a university," he said, and he displayed the decayed rubble on the palm of his hand. "Mr. Reverie, would you please be of assistance?"

*"Oui, monsieur."* Henri whisked his hat off his head and held it out for Father, who tossed my tooth pieces inside with the sound of rustling gravel.

Father loomed back over me and went in for another molar. Over the high-pitched din of my screams and the thumps of my thrashings he called out, "This is your dream of voting."

*Yank, plunk.* The second tooth landed in Henri's hat.

He continued onward.

"This is your dream of working for a living."

*Yank, plunk.*

"This is your dream of becoming 'A Responsible Woman' who publishes letters in newspapers."

*Yank, plunk.*

"This is your dream of wearing trousers while bicycling."

*Yank, plunk.*

The list went on and on, and my mouth grew emptier and emptier, until my wails weakened and my heartbeat slackened. My arms flopped over the armrests, my energy spent, and I witnessed Henri waving his gloved hand over the black silk hat with a graceful flick of his fingers.

"You see, Mademoiselle Mead?" He showed me the dark recesses of the hat's interior. At the very bottom lay a mirror that reflected my toothless mouth with blood spilling down to my chin. "If you stay with your father, he'll take it all away."

I awoke with a gasp, my gums sore, but all my teeth, thankfully, intact.

# CHAPTER EIGHT

# MR. RHODES

ather's fiendish visage did not return during breakfast, thank heavens. I munched my toast without
ever stopping to speak—a good, quiet girl—and
every few minutes Father beamed at me over his
newspaper, quite pleased with my angry silence,
which he clearly mistook for obedience.

He left for work, and I attempted to walk to school—I truly
did. My toffee-brown book bag hung off my shoulder, and
my lunch pail dangled from the crooks of my right fingers. I
made it a full block north before I witnessed a peculiar sight.

Our neighbor Mrs. Stanton exited the front door of her narrow green house on the corner of Main, followed by her three little ducklings: a pair of twin girls in white bonnets and a toddler boy in a navy-blue sailor suit. She sold preserves to grocers in the city, and she and her children often emerged from their house with a wooden pull wagon stocked with jars of brightly colored jams and vegetables swimming in pickling vinegar.

Obviously, all of this wasn't the peculiar part.

No, here was the strange thing that caused me to stop walking and gawk at the woman with my arms hanging by my sides: On this particular morning, Mrs. Stanton was a ghost.

The trees she passed, the white picket fence bordering her house—they were all visible through her skin and clothing and her tea-stain-colored hair, which looked as translucent as the layers of an onion. She was a cobweb woman. Barely there. Almost gone.

A nothing person.

"I FOUND THIS LYING ON THE SIDEWALK OUTSIDE THE building," I said to the statuesque receptionist manning the front desk of the *Oregonian*'s nine-story headquarters on Sixth and Alder.

The female employee, sporting half-lens spectacles and a thick black tie, sat with her posture so impeccably straight, I felt the need to stretch my neck a little higher. Rows of lady workers in tailored dress suits typed behind her in a commotion of clicking keys and high-pitched dings that signified the ends of typewritten lines.

I inhaled a long breath of inky air and handed the woman an unstamped envelope, addressed *Letters to the Editor Department*. "Someone must have dropped it," I said. "I thought I should bring it in." My fingers pulsed with nervous energy.

The woman took my envelope and studied the address through her half-moon lenses. Her hair was puffed so high and her sharp chin held with such confidence that I could have sworn I shrank six inches just from standing in front of her.

She lifted her face and offered a thin smile. "I'll deliver it to the correct department. Thank you for bringing it in."

A gleam in her eye told me she knew the handwriting on the envelope belonged to a seventeen-year-old girl with shaking hands, so I turned and left the building.

NOT ONCE IN MY LIFE HAD I PLAYED HOOKY FROM SCHOOL before that frosty-cold autumn morning. *Not once.* The temptation to be truant had never even occurred to me.

Yet instead of hurrying off to school, I found myself standing in front of the arched brick entrance of the Metropolitan Theater. A haunted sort of feeling squirmed around in my gut, but still I walked inside, my feet motivated by a will of their own.

The empty lobby felt like a hollowed-out husk compared to the hot and buzzing scene from Halloween night. My footsteps clapped across the black-and-white tiles, and the echoing, gilded ceiling above seemed a thousand feet high. I stopped and held my breath, worried I'd get caught trespassing. I probably shouldn't have even liked theaters so much—not after their allure had spirited my mother away one snowy December night when I was just four years old. When she told us she couldn't breathe in our house anymore.

The pipe organ started up in the auditorium, and my heart leapt into my throat. Beyond the open doorway, someone played "Evening Prayer" from *Hansel and Gretel*, the spellbinding melody Genevieve Reverie had performed when Henri invited me to float up to the theater's catwalks and bask in the warm electric lights. Whoever was attempting to play the song lacked Genevieve's passion and talent, but even the school-recital stiffness of the performance allowed the notes to melt inside my bones and ease my troubled soul.

With silent footfalls, I stole into the auditorium.

The music proved to be the work of a bottom-heavy lady organist with pumpkin-orange hair. She sat in front of the dark wood-and-copper pipe organ, all alone on the stage, her eyes fixed on the sheet music in front of her as if she were just learning the song that very moment. I hunkered down in a red velvet chair in the back row and listened to that mesmerizing melody that reminded me so of Halloween night. My eyelids drooped with each passing refrain. I remembered all the rows of lights hanging above the stage, beckoning me to them, and my cheeks and neck warmed.

Henri Reverie's pacifying voice rose to my ears: "And that's when I leap off the young lady's torso."

I opened my eyes with a start. There he was, on the stage, strolling over to the organist with three pages of notes in his hands, dressed in his midnight-black trousers and vest, without the coat.

*Henri Reverie.*

He pointed to one of his papers. "If you finish the song early, I recommend transitioning into 'Sleep, Little Rosebud.'"

The pumpkin-haired organist, who for some reason wasn't Henri's sister, withdrew her fingers from the keys and rotated toward the hypnotist. "Do you really stand on top of these ladies, young man?"

*"Oui,"* said Henri, nodding. "But I believe in equality, and I stand on gentlemen, too, depending on what I feel the audience would prefer to see. Haven't you ever heard of the great Herbert L. Flint?"

"No."

Henri stepped back. "You haven't?"

"Do you honestly think I've heard of every two-bit stage performer?" asked the organist.

"But he is not 'a two-bit performer.' He's a well-known and respected mesmerist. We adapted his use of the human plank for our show, and I always open with it. It is my most popular feat."

"And none of these stepped-upon volunteers ever complains?"

Henri shook his head. "None so far."

"Why do you think that is?"

"Well"—he lowered his papers and rubbed his smooth chin—"I never force anyone to come on the stage, *madame*. The volunteers join me up here because they want to, even if they initially demur. I think they want—need—to be seen. To be noticed."

The organist scowled. "And having a hypnotist stand on their torsos, while they're sleeping like pacified infants, is preferable to remaining shrinking violets?"

Henri shrugged. "As I said, they never complain, and the audiences adore viewing them up here. You should hear the applause. Americans gobble up magic and visual oddities, such as viewing a man standing upon a near-floating woman."

"It is scandalous. You may as well be in New York City, debasing yourself in *Sapho,* that *rrr*ibald"—she rolled the *r* in *ribald* with dramatic flair—"theatrical production I keep reading about in the newspaper. The one about the strumpet and her lovers."

"As I was saying . . ." He pointed to his notes again. "This is where you transition into 'Sleep, Little Rosebud.'"

"You ought to be ashamed of yourself."

"Start with an adagio tempo. The notes should be delicate at first."

"Youth these days will be the death of morality." The organist flipped through her sheet music to find the right selection. After a cough and an outward thrust of her chest, she blundered her way through a musical number that would have sounded quite pretty if it were being played by anyone else.

Henri wandered across the stage with his hands in his pockets, wincing and hunching his shoulders as the off-key notes assaulted his ears. His gaze turned to the (almost) empty auditorium, so I ducked my head down farther and inhaled a noseful of dust.

Before I could control myself, a sneeze exploded from my nostrils.

"Who's there?" asked Henri, which made the organist stop playing.

I froze at first, but then I felt like a fool crouching down on the dirty floor that way, my feet stuck in something sticky and my nose itching with the threat of another sneeze. I stood up and let myself be seen.

Henri squinted up at me. "Miss Mead?"

"Yes. It's me—I mean, it is I, to be grammatically—"

"Stay right there. Don't go anywhere." He leapt off the end of the stage and landed on his feet with a thump—a startling maneuver that made me think of illustrations of lions chasing down gazelles.

I turned and lunged for the door.

"No! I need to speak to you." I heard him bounding up the aisle behind me. "Don't go. For your own safety, don't go. I've been worried sick about you."

At those unexpected words, I stopped.

"Please . . ." He skidded to a halt a few feet away from me and held out his arms to catch his balance. "Please tell me—you have *got* to tell me—what terrified you so badly when you saw your father yesterday."

I bit my lip and hesitated.

"Please"—he braced his hands on his hips and regained his breathing—"tell me. I swear to God, you can trust me, Miss Mead."

"My name is Olivia. I have no intention of calling you anything as respectful as Mr. Reverie, so please stop this 'Miss' business."

"What I do on that stage, Olivia"—for some reason his accent suddenly sounded more American, less French—"all that showy stuff, it's just to earn money. I want to help people with hypnosis, not hurt them. I want to cure people of their addictions and fears and—and—"

"And dreams," I finished for him.

"No, not dreams." He swallowed and stepped closer. "Why did you react to your father the way you did? How did he look after the hypnosis?"

"Are you done flirting, young man?" called the pumpkin-haired organist from the stage. "I'm not being paid to watch you fraternize with girls."

"One moment, please, *madame*."

"I have a good mind to tell Mr. Gillingham you're wasting the theater's money—"

"Please—this is important." He turned back to me and

softened his voice to a whisper. "I'm going to tell you something I don't usually share with anyone."

"No! I don't want to become your confidante." I backed away. "I just want you to return my mind to the way it was."

"Listen—"

"No."

"Olivia"—he came to me and took hold of my arm—"my sister has a cancerous tumor the size of a goose egg in her bosom."

My jaw dropped with a gasp of shock.

"It's rare in girls her age," he continued, his eyes moistening, "but it's there. She needs surgery. There's a specialist in San Francisco. His fees . . . they won't be cheap."

"What? No." I wrenched his fingers off my arm. "You're lying. That's a cruel story to tell a person just to get your way."

"You can see the world the way it truly is, so be honest"—he straightened the bottom of his vest with a sharp tug of the black fabric—"do I look like someone who's lying about his sister's health?"

His eyes drew me toward them with a pull that tipped me forward onto my toes. I waved my hands to steady myself, and a second later, like a swift gust of wind, Genevieve Reverie emerged by his side in a white nightgown, her blond head slumped against his arm, her face thin and peaked. The rest of the theater rushed away into a vacuum, and all I saw was the two of them—Genevieve, ill, exhausted, supported by Henri.

I blinked, and she was gone. Her tousled-haired brother stood alone.

"For heaven's sake, Mr. Reverie," called the woman on the stage. "I've had enough of your dillydallying . . ."

"My father looked like the monster in Bram Stoker's novel," I told Henri. "Have you read *Dracula*?"

"Isn't that about a human vampire?"

"Yes, and that's exactly how you made him appear in his office. His skin lacked blood, and his teeth were the fangs of a ferocious animal. I'm witnessing other things as well—disturbing sights—so tell me, please, for the love of God, what in the world did you do to my head?"

"Mr. Reverie," bellowed the organist in a bone-rattling voice that consumed the entire theater, "throw that girl out of here this minute, or I'm asking Mr. Gillingham to cancel your performance. I know of two highly talented juggling brothers who would love nothing more than to take over your booking tonight."

"I'm coming, I'm coming."

He backed away from me, and a topsy-turvy feeling seized me again. My eyes insisted on seeing his hair as more ruffled than before, his dark clothing as frayed and worn. He suffered from fatigue. Distress.

"I'd very much like to discuss this matter with you more, Olivia," he said.

"I don't want to discuss this matter." I rubbed my eyes with the heels of my hands. "I want you to change me back. All is well!"

"I can't."

"You can't? All is well!"

"Not now."

I shoved my hands against my temples and swallowed down my anger so the right words would come. "Do you want to know how *you* truly look, Monsieur Reverie?"

He stopped in his tracks.

"You look like a shifty showman who doesn't really know what he's doing," I said. "And I'm willing to bet the remaining shreds of my sanity that *Reverie* isn't even your real last name."

He frowned and jogged back to the stage—back to his rehearsal with the glowering substitute organist who shook her head as if he were a misbehaving spaniel—and he seemed to ignore my words.

Before he reached the front row, however, he peeked over his shoulder.

He gave me my answer, in an accent that wasn't French in the slightest.

"You're right, Olivia. It's Rhodes. My name is Henry—with a *y*, not an *i*—Rhodes. But as I'm sure you've seen with your own eyes, I am *not* just a shifty showman."

# CHAPTER NINE

# DEAR, DARLING DAUGHTER

His dual names pulsed in my head all the way home.

*Henri Reverie. Henry Rhodes. Henri Reverie. Henry Rhodes.*

And then *cancer, cancer, cancer, cancer. Tumor, tumor, tumor, tumor. Genevieve.*

I quickened my pace and managed to find my way back to my house, despite the blurred and rippling sidewalks and the flashes of blue eyes from Henry's theater handbills, watching me from shop windows. Always watching me.

I tripped over the threshold of our front door, and Gerda

raised her head from dusting Father's antique denture collection in the parlor.

"What are you doing home from school, Miss Mead?"

I closed the door and inhaled a deep breath. "I have a headache." I parked my lunch pail on the marble-topped hall table. My book bag slid off my shoulder to the floor.

"*Ja?* A headache?" Gerda lowered the duster. "I left a note with the Acklens. It said that you would go with their boy to the party tonight. Should I not have done that?"

"Oh." I slumped against the wall. "Percy. How the blue blazes did I forget about him?" I massaged the aching bridge of my nose between my thumb and middle finger. "He's going to think I'm an absolute loon."

"Shall I send another note?"

"No. Thank you. I need some sort of reward for surviving this day." I pushed myself off the wall and headed for the staircase.

"Oh, Miss Mead—I almost forgot, your mother's birthday envelope arrived. I put it on your bed."

"Oh? Thank you." My stomach sank. "I suppose I had better go see what extraordinary adventures she's undertaken this year."

I clambered up to my room with the same withered-hot-air-balloon sensation I'd experienced when Henry pulled me down from the theater's ceiling.

Halfway across the bedroom floor, my feet stopped. There wasn't an envelope waiting for me on my pink bedspread.

It was a ticket, a pale brown one with curved edges and the words ONE-WAY PASSAGE TO NEW YORK CITY written across the center in block letters. My skin warmed, and my ears buzzed. I rubbed my eyes and willed away the delusion, for that's what it had to have been.

I lowered my hands. The ticket disappeared, and a plain white envelope came into view, return address New York City. I picked it up and ripped it open.

*October 10, 1900*

*My Dear, Darling Daughter,*

*Can you really be seventeen years old, my funny little lamb? You're more woman than girl now, which makes your poor mama feel like an ancient crone. My heavens, I was only three months younger than you are now when I became your mother. I hope and pray you don't follow my same path to early mother-hood. Don't rush into relationships with boys, even if they are as handsome as a certain young dental apprentice who wooed me off the stage eighteen years ago. You know as well as I do about the heartbreak that can result when two fools hurry to play grown-up.*

*On a much happier note, I'm giddy with excitement to announce I'm now established in New York City, playing Tita-nia in a little theater production of* A Midsummer Night's Dream. *"Thou art as wise as thou art beautiful." Oh, you should see my costume, my lamb—gold and purple silk, and a heaping crown of flowers upon my red curls.*

*I'm settled in an apartment near Barnard College, and I think of you every time I see those smart young women walking around with books tucked under their arms. I remember you trying to read your little collection of fairy tales to me when you were just four years old and how much I marveled at your intelligence. Does your father allow you to be bright? Or does he still insist young ladies ought to be silent idiots?*

*Oh, my darling, I would love to see what you look like as a grown-up young lady. As usual, I'm slipping a little bit of money into the envelope as a birthday present. If you'd care to come east and visit your wicked old mama, I would open my door to you with outstretched arms and hug away all the hurt I've caused you. I don't believe I did you any good when you were a wee little thing, and I still strongly feel our separation was the best for all of us. However, I certainly know a thing or two about being a young woman, and I could take better care of you now than I did back then. I would even let you take a tour of Barnard, and perhaps I'd allow you to watch that delicious play* Sapho, *if the moralists don't shut it down again.*

*Happy birthday, my Olivia.*

*Your Loving Mother*


A ten-dollar bill fluttered down to my lap.

*A Midsummer Night's Dream* must have been paying Mother well—or else she had found herself another wealthy suitor with a fat billfold. I crouched down on the floorboards and slid out one of Father's bright yellow cigar boxes from the dusty depths beneath my bed. Inside I kept my collection of Mother's birthday and Christmas gifts, delivered in little envelopes throughout the years, minus a few missing dollars and coins that had paid for books and hair ribbons.

I counted the cash, including my newest contribution.

"Holy mackerel, Mother," I said, followed by a long sigh.

One hundred twenty-three dollars now waited for me inside that old cigar box.

*One hundred twenty-three.*

I re-counted the stockpile and sat back on my heels, wondering how much tuition would cost at faraway Barnard College, where young women walked around with books tucked under their arms, as if in a marvelous dream.

# OLGA NETHERSOLE'S
## VERSION OF
# SAPHO
### BY CLYDE FITCH

# CHAPTER TEN

# "EYES UNCLEAN AND FULL OF HELL~FIRE"

F rannie stopped by for a rushed after-school visit.

"Are you unwell?" she asked from our front porch, where long shadows yawned across the scuffed red boards and the scraggly potted plants.

"I had a bad headache."

"I worried the hypnosis made you sick—or that your father sent you away." She hugged me against her chest. "You scared me to death with all that talk about asylums."

"I'm all right." I patted her on the back and let her squeeze me until my collarbones hurt. "In fact, I'm going to go to a party at Sadie Eiderling's house tonight. Can you believe it?"

She stiffened. "I beg your pardon?"

"Percy's taking me."

She dropped her arms and pulled away.

"Don't worry, I'm going to be quite careful of his"—I tipped my face forward and lowered my voice —"grabby hands."

"It's not a joke, Livie."

"He didn't grab you, did he?"

"No!" She blushed so hard, she went practically mauve. "No, I've just heard rumors . . ." She backed away. "I've got to go help Papa at the store. Please be extremely careful with Percy—and your father."

"Frannie?"

"Good-bye, Livie."

She scrambled down the porch steps, and for a moment I thought I glimpsed a white handprint on the back of her blue skirt, below her swinging brown braid.

A shudder and a blink, and the print was gone.

FATHER CAME HOME FROM WORK AROUND FIVE THIRTY that evening. I hid in my bedroom and pinned up my hair for the Eiderlings' party.

"Are you getting ready, Olivia?" he called up to me.

"Yes," I yelled through my closed door. "Gerda is boiling a ham for your dinner, and then she'll help me dress. I can't come down right now."

"Don't take too long. Young men don't like to be kept waiting."

"I won't."

I fussed with my hairpins in front of my mirror, my hands slippery and my mind squalling with fears about the visions. I kept expecting my mirror and my hairbrush to transform into nightmarish abominations—hissing creatures with snouts and needle-sharp teeth that would squeeze around my torso and take a bite.

My hair suffered from all that worrying. Most girls of Sadie Eiderling's caliber were wearing their long locks puffed high on their heads in enormous pompadours, like the fashionable girls in Charles Dana Gibson's drawings. On occasion, Frannie and I would try styling our hair in that manner, but our pompadours always turned out lopsided or collapsed like deflated soufflés—which was precisely the problem at the moment. My pinned-up mess of dark hair sagged as if I had just sprinted through the rain with Percy again. I hated it. Every strand.

"All is well!" I said, and I dropped my hands to my sides and growled.

*All is well? Balderdash! Bull dung!*

Even worse words entered my head, but they shall not be repeated.

I shoved more hairpins into my topknot, and my eyes drifted to a conjoined pair of silver picture frames that sat on top of my chest of drawers. In the rightmost frame sat a photograph of Mother, just sixteen years old, posed in a brocade Renaissance mourning costume in front of a backdrop of painted vines. A black veil draped over her thick ringlets, which looked brown instead of their natural red in the sepia image. I remembered her explaining to me that she had been playing Olivia, my namesake, in a traveling production of Shakespeare's *Twelfth Night*, and that's how she met Father. Her pretty face—rosebud lips, arched brows, almond-shaped eyes, long lashes—seemed nothing like mine, save for perhaps the round tip of her nose. She looked like the type of person who never lacked confidence about anything.

The accompanying photograph of my eighteen-year-old father, however—*my father*, Mead the Mad—was the spitting image of me, aside from his short hair and mustache, of course.

*Good Lord.* I was more like him than her.

*Good Lord.* What if I resembled him in behavior, too?

I snapped the frames closed, pinching a finger in my haste.

A minute later, Gerda joined me and helped button me up in an eggplant-purple gown I'd worn to the wedding of one of Father's cousins down in Salem.

"You look lovely this evening, Miss Mead."

"Thank you, Gerda." I straightened the satin poufs sliding off my shoulders. "I personally think I look like a giant purple bauble someone might hang on a Christmas tree."

She laughed. "No, no, no, you look like an elegant young lady. Your young man—"

"He's not quite my young man."

"*That* young man, then, will fall madly in love with you when he sees you dressed like this."

"Hmm." I chewed my bottom lip. "I'd feel a whole lot better knowing a person was falling in love with me because of me and not because of hypnosis or snug purple gowns."

Gerda tittered again. "You're so funny, Miss Mead. You'll make him laugh, if nothing else. And when men laugh, they feel happy and in love." She hooked the last button. "That's what *Mamma* always says about *Fader.*"

A knock downstairs made my shoulders jerk.

Gerda and I locked eyes.

"He's here," I said in a whisper.

"Put your shoes on." She scurried to my door. "I'll tell them you're almost ready."

Before I could say a word, she was gone, her footsteps padding down the stairs.

Down below the boards of my bedroom, the front door opened with its usual squeak. I heard muffled male voices. My pulse pounded in my ears in the same swift rhythm as the clock on my wall.

"Oh, please look normal," I whispered while facing my closed door. I folded my hands beneath my chin and scrunched my eyes closed. "Please, please, please don't turn out to be a monster."

"Olivia," called Father. "Young Mr. Acklen has arrived."

I opened my eyes, inhaled a deep breath, and dared to leave the safety of my room.

Below me, past the bottom of the staircase, Father and Percy chatted about the upcoming election—the impassioned battle between President McKinley and the Democratic anti-imperialist William Jennings Bryan. I only saw the back of Percy's head, and his auburn hair looked just as handsome and impeccable as usual, with a sheen of pomade glistening in the lamplight. He wore his wool outer coat over a pair of narrow-striped trousers, with a finely knit crimson scarf hanging around his neck. His silk top hat dangled from his right fingers.

Time seemed to freeze for a fraction of a moment. Hope for Percy swelled in my heart. Anything was possible, and if I had my way, we would have remained like that—suspended, innocent, unencumbered by my strange sight—for the rest of the evening.

But then Father's dark gaze—a bit too predatory for my taste—flitted toward me. His voice rumbled through the hall. "Ah, Olivia is here."

Percy turned around.

*Normal.* He was normal—well shaven and groomed and as beautiful as ever.

My legs gave way in relief, and I had to clutch the banister with both hands.

Percy stepped toward me, the ends of his scarf swaying with the lunge. "Are you all right, Olivia?"

"Yes." I gripped the handrail and proceeded down the steps. "I'm sorry. I got dizzy for a moment."

"Ladies and swooning," said Father with a roll of his eyes. "They can't help themselves, I'm afraid."

"All is well."

"The Eiderlings will have plenty to eat at their party," said Percy, "so you won't feel faint much longer." He fetched my coat from the wall hook and spread it open for me to enter. "Are you well enough to go?"

"Yes, I'm fine." I slid my bare arms inside the heavy sleeves, and a potent whiff of his cologne shot clear up to my sinuses.

Father beamed one of his hearty Santa Claus smiles and opened the door for the two of us. "Take good care of my girl, Mr. Acklen. I'll expect her home by ten." *And don't forget to propose to her*, I thought I heard him add, but he grinned, and Percy grinned, and nobody said a word about marriage.

MANDOLIN'S HOOVES STOMPED ACROSS THE MUD-CAKED street leading north of my neighborhood, and the buggy rocked me in a rhythm that might have made me drowsy if my spine weren't locked upright. Nerves thickened my tongue, and every conversation topic sounded jumbled and stupid in my head.

"How is your ear?" I asked when the silence grew too fierce.

"Better." He glanced my way. "I was only teasing about you owing me more than just a book, you know."

My cheeks warmed. "I know."

"You looked so frightened when I said that to you at school. What did you think I would make you do?"

"I don't know." I fussed with a loose pin in my hair and tried to persuade myself Frannie was mistaken about him. The word *grabber* loitered in my mind like an unwanted guest.

Percy steered Mandolin west, onto Irving. "I read all of it."

"All of what?" I asked.

"*Dracula*, of course."

"Oh." I tightened my coat around my neck. "Did you like it?"

"Yes. But why do *you* like it?"

"What do you mean?"

"Why do you like a horrific story involving so much blood and murder?"

"I don't know. Why does anyone like any literature?" I shrugged as if responding to my own question. "I love that books allow us to experience other lives without us ever having to change where we live or who we are."

He kept his eyes on the lamp-lit road ahead, which was disappearing into a gold-tinged mist that carried the scents of chimney smoke and rain. "You were right about there being certain . . . *scenes*." His mouth turned up in a smile.

My neck sweltered beneath my coat. "Yes, um, well, I warned you."

"And that Lucy character, with 'eyes unclean and full of hell-fire'—holy Moses." He shook his head. "Why would a girl like you want to read about someone like her?"

"The book was about far more than just Lucy."

"Oh, sure, there were also Dracula's lusty wives."

I snorted. "Why are you dwelling on the lewd women in the book? *Dracula* is more Mina's story than anything. Prim and saintly Mina. I'm sure you liked her all right."

"Oh, Mina was just fine. In fact, I think I fell a little in love with her and wanted to save her." He peeked my way. "She reminded me of you."

I met his eyes, which gave off a strange yellow cast in the darkness, the way a prowling cat's eyes appear when it's stalking through my backyard after nightfall. I shuddered and told myself I'd only imagined the phenomenon, even though a sideways sort of feeling washed through me again.

"Mina Harker reminded you of me?" I asked.

He nodded. "She was a lot like you."

"Oh." I took hold of the side of the buggy. "And who are you most like? Jonathan Harker? Dracula?"

"Arthur," he answered without hesitation. "Lucy's fiancé."

My blood chilled. Arthur was the character who had staked wild Lucy. Ferociously.

*He looked like a figure of Thor as his untrembling arm rose and fell, driving deeper and deeper the mercy-bearing stake . . .*

I wrinkled my brow. "Why would you want to be like *him?*"

"I didn't say I wanted to be like him. But this past summer there was a girl . . ." He straightened his top hat with a clumsy movement of his hand and hardened his jaw. "What am I saying? You don't want to hear about another girl."

"No, tell me. Did someone hurt you?"

"She . . ." He gave a little cough, as though his throat had gone dry. "Her name was Nanette. I met her in Los Angeles when my family was summering down there. She liked to listen to ragtime music and rode around the city on a bicycle. She wore bloomers that made old ladies throw rocks at her in disgust, and she called her parents *Lula and Pete* instead of *Mother and Father*."

"Oh?" My heart drummed with jealousy. Bloomers, no less. Beautiful bicycle bloomers.

Percy huffed a sigh. "I thought I could handle her, but she was a bit much. Her parents believed in free love. Her mother gave birth to her when she was living in some sort of utopian society that shunned marriage. Nanette's father may not even be her father."

He flicked the reins to bring Mandolin to a faster walk. The buggy swayed and bounced and thundered over the uneven road, and wind whistled across my ears.

"It turned out Nanette believed in free love, too," he continued. "I found out she was with two other fellows while I was courting her."

"Oh. I'm sorry." The buggy knocked me to the left, and my hand clutched his arm for support, my nails digging into wool. "And that's why you hate the Lucy Westenra character so much?"

"Olivia . . ." He shook his head. "You're supposed to hate Lucy, too. She drank the blood of children."

"But"—I let go of him and righted myself—"if she didn't have that bloodthirsty side, I'm guessing you still would have hated her. She was hardly a standard young lady with pure thoughts."

"I'm just saying that's why I feel like Arthur. I completely understand the burden of trying to love a devil woman." He eased his grip on the reins. "And that's why I'm more than ready to have an innocent girl in my life. Someone chaste and sweet and docile." He scooted next to me until our arms and hips rocked against each other, while the buggy rolled onward toward the grand mansions of Irving Street that rose up ahead like incandescent palaces. "Olivia . . ."

I waited for him to continue, but when he didn't, I fastened my top coat button and asked, "Yes?"

His foot nestled against mine. "It's my firm belief that you will be the savior of my poor broken heart. You're exactly what I need."

Shadows hid his face too much for me to get a good look at him, but the weight of his expectations—his overconfidence in my sweetness—bore down on my shoulders. I clamped my teeth together.

If he had my vision of the world, if he had seen me the way I truly was, he would have thrown me off the buggy right then and there and kept on driving into the mist.

# CHAPTER ELEVEN

# DELICIOUS

Percy slowed the buggy as we approached a sandstone fortress with a terra-cotta roof and a half-dozen turrets. Electric lanterns and chandeliers lit the entire building, and an arched wooden door, wide and thick enough to fend off both hurricane winds and invading armies, guarded the front entrance. Six other buggies stood alongside the curb in front of the castle, and the resting horses exhaled clouds of foggy breath through their wide nostrils.

"Whoooa." Percy tugged on Mandolin's reins and brought

the white horse to a stop behind an enclosed carriage with no driver. He must have been warming up with a mug of coffee in the Eiderlings' kitchen. "There's a good boy," said Percy. "Well done, Mandolin."

The horse nickered, and Percy tossed the reins to the ground and climbed out of the buggy.

I gazed at the mansion beside us, my stomach growling in anticipation of the awaiting feast inside. I remembered the words Kate had shouted up at me when I climbed onto the stage to meet Henry: *Go on, Livie. Don't be shy.* My blood thrummed with expectation.

"Wait until you taste the food here, Olivia." Percy tied Mandolin's reins to a black hitching post shaped like a horse's head. "Mr. Eiderling lets the boys sample his beer, so I always have a crackerjack time at Sadie's parties."

"Oh." I flinched, triggering a small whine from the buggy's springs. "I didn't know you'd be drinking . . ."

"Does that bother you?"

"I don't . . . Maybe."

He peeked over his shoulder with a crooked grin. "What are you, a temperance crusader?"

I threw up my hands. "Why is everyone so concerned about me and the temperance movement? I just don't want to be driven recklessly through the city by someone who's guzzled too much beer."

"Mandolin won't be squiffed, and that's what counts—

unless the butler brings out a bucket of ale for the beasts when we're not looking." He laughed at his own words, his chuckles cracking through the silence of the street.

I fussed with my white kid gloves and noted how every inch of fabric that I wore looked wrinkled and wrong. "Do I look nice enough to be here, Percy?"

"What type of question is that?" Percy strode over to my side of the buggy and offered his hand with a wiggle of gloved fingers. "Come on down, my pet." While supporting my arm and waist, he lowered me off the buggy onto the solid dirt ground and bent his face close to mine. "You have nothing to fear, Olivia. Do you understand?"

"Yes." I nodded, for I didn't see any sights that warned of danger.

Percy planted my hand on his arm and escorted me up the stone pathway to the broad castle door.

In response to Percy's raps with the round iron knocker, the Eiderlings' butler—a portly, gray-haired fellow with the sagging jowls of a bulldog—hoisted open the door.

"Good evening," said the butler, every letter enunciated to perfection.

Percy removed his top hat. "Good evening, Mr. Burber. Mr. Percy Acklen and guest for the supper party, if you please."

"Please step inside, Mr. Acklen. Miss Eiderling has already gathered the guests in the dining room."

"Thank you." Percy handed the butler his hat and scarf and slid his arms out of his overcoat, revealing a gray silk bow tie and a fine black tailcoat that complemented his striped trousers. "I hope we're not too late."

"Miss Eiderling likes to be prompt. I believe she's already asked for the first course to be served."

"Well, she is the birthday girl, after all."

Without responding to Percy, the butler took my coat and hung it on a tall cedar rack that reminded me of a scraggly old tree. An impressive collection of jackets and wraps already dangled from the crooked branches.

Percy offered me his arm again and led me across the grand entrance behind the butler. The soles of our shoes clopped on the polished marble floor that reflected our feet and the swishing hem of my purple skirt. Above us rose lofty, gold-accented walls and a sky-high ceiling that gleamed as white as fresh porcelain dentures.

"I smell oysters and salmon," said Percy, and his stomach rumbled. "And beer. Lovely, lovely beer."

We ventured down a mirrored hall the length of my entire house, toward the sound of laughter and the soft clinks of silverware brushing against dishes. Percy carried himself with grace, his head held high, his shoulders relaxed, his dark evening suit pressed and flawless.

"How do you know Sadie?" I asked before we reached the end of the hall. "Doesn't she go to Saint Mary's Academy?"

"My father helped her father avoid a lawsuit earlier this year. And"—he smiled, and that smile was reflected in the mirror beside us, magnifying his amusement—"I think she's secretly in love with me. That's why she invites me to her parties. I'm a toy she can't have, because her parents consider me beneath her."

I stiffened. "And do you love her?"

"No." He shook his head and lowered his voice to a whisper behind the butler. "She's another wild one. I've heard stories about her that would put both Nanette and Lucy Westenra to shame."

"But—"

"I told you, Olivia"—he pressed his gloved fingers around mine with a squeeze—"I want *you*."

I bit my lip, unsure how to respond.

We neared the swarming buzz of chattering guests that waited beyond the corner, and the scents of seafood and beer grew potent enough to taste the salt and the bubbles in the air. I gripped Percy's arm.

He patted my hand. "Don't be afraid. No one's going to gobble you up."

We rounded the corner.

My feet halted.

Percy was wrong. So utterly wrong.

Beneath a blinding crystal chandelier, around a lace-draped table, a dozen fanged young guests with ashen skin and lips like blue-black bruises chatted and gorged themselves on appetizers. I heard their voices as muffled nothingness, but I saw them—my word, how I saw them. With sterling silver forks, they scraped oysters from the half shells and devoured the mollusks' slippery gray flesh with slurps and swallows and ripples down their long white throats. Tall, gilded steins sat in front of each boy, but they were filled with blood, not beer. The young men wore black tails and vests the colors of fine jewels; the girls sparkled in dark silk gowns and bright diamond necklaces, but even they were savages.

A bespectacled redheaded creature with long yellow teeth and piercing eyes lifted his head and spotted us standing there. "Percy, you old bore! You're late."

A sea of deathly faces turned our way. All I could hear was the hammering of my heart against my chest.

"Mr. Percy Acklen has arrived, Miss Eiderling," said the butler, sounding bored. And then, as if in afterthought, he added, "And guest." The servant turned on his heel and left the room with footsteps that mimicked the quickening of my breath.

I turned to leave as well.

"Where are you going?" Percy grabbed hold of my wrist.

"I can't do this. They look like they want to murder me." I lunged toward the room's exit.

Percy tugged me back and pressed his mouth close to my ear. "This is embarrassing. Turn around and come back to the table."

"I can't."

"Please. What's wrong with you?" He scowled at me as if *I* were the monster in the room, his teeth so sharp. Fierce. *Oh, God.*

"No!" I gave a small cry and broke free of his grip, but then, with a sudden jolt, the world tipped upright. I leaned forward, regained my balance, and saw the room as a normal room, with more sound, fewer colors.

Fewer teeth.

The throng of faces at the table now belonged to a finely dressed assortment of regular young men and ladies who gaped as though they were encountering an escapee from the Oregon State Insane Asylum.

The girl at the head of the table breathed a curt laugh through her nostrils and scanned me from the top of my drooping hair to the toes of my three-year-old dress shoes. She had reddish-gold locks that rose at least a foot off the top of her head—an impressive soufflé!—and her dress was lined in black and cream stripes, with dizzying swirls on the curves of her bodice.

"Who is this, Percy?" she asked with a wrinkle of her small nose. "And what on earth is wrong with her?"

Percy cleared his throat and guided me toward her. "I'm sorry I was late. This is my guest, Olivia Mead."

Two of the girls snickered. The other guests leaned forward and studied me with watchful eyes.

"Oh! You're that hypnotized girl!" said a sunken-eyed blond fellow, raising his hand as if answering a question in a classroom. "The girl Henri Reverie stood upon at the beginning of the Halloween show. That was the funniest, bawdiest thing I've ever seen."

"*That* was the bawdiest thing you've ever seen, John?" asked the redheaded boy who had first spotted us. "Remind me to show you a certain deck of playing cards, my friend."

"Don't be crass, Teddy," said Sadie. "Even though the presence of certain individuals might suggest otherwise"— she glanced at me again—"this is a lady's supper party, not a North End saloon."

Next to Teddy, a dark-haired girl—a scrawny, bulging-eyed thing—burst into a peal of high-pitched laughter. "You brought the dentist's daughter, Percy? Why?"

"Yesss, why?" Sadie bared her bright white teeth. "Is this a joke, Percy? Did you somehow hear about my surprise guest?"

"What? No." Percy let go of my hand. "What guest?"

Sadie turned her attention toward the opposite end of the table. "Henri Reverie."

My heart dropped to my stomach. I craned my neck forward to better see where she was looking, and there he sat, down at the far end, his face turned toward his plate so I could only see a head of dark blond hair with a few uncombed tufts sticking up on top.

*Henri Reverie.*

*Henry Rhodes.*

"Before Monsieur Reverie leaves for his performance tonight"—Sadie shifted her sights back to me—"he agreed to dine with us and then to hypnotize me even more thoroughly than he hypnotized you, Ophelia."

"It's Olivia," I said.

"He's promised to help me sing like an opera ingénue."

"Like Svengali," I muttered without even thinking.

Sadie furrowed her brow. "I beg your pardon?"

"Um . . . I—I—I said"—I cleared my throat to summon my voice, which was retreating down my throat like a frightened rabbit—"he's . . . like the controlling hypnotist in the novel *Trilby*. Svengali hypnotized a girl into singing with the voice of an angel." *Doesn't anyone else my age read popular novels?* I wanted to ask, but I sealed my mouth closed to hide the anxious chattering of my teeth.

"I am not a Svengali, Mademoiselle Mead."

Henry—I could no longer see him as *On-ree*, even though he had slipped back into the counterfeit French accent—lifted his face. "Our hostess hired me of her own free will," he said, "so please do not suggest I am a demon sorcerer."

His eyes held mine, and, despite his defensive words and taut mouth, he brought a sliver of warmth to that cold, hostile room. *I've been worried sick about you,* I remembered him saying at the theater.

"Sit down, Percy," said Sadie with a nod to two empty chairs at the middle of the table, one of them next to Sunken-Eyed John. "There's a seat for your little friend beside you. Speaking of whom"—she took a sip of water from a crystal goblet before continuing, perhaps to create a theatrical pause—"is it true, Mr. Reverie, that dim-witted people are the easiest to hypnotize?"

More snickers erupted down the table, and all heads turned

again to Henry, who lowered his fork to his plate, a small smile on his lips.

"No, that's not true at all," he said. "A clever person, someone skilled at focusing on one subject at a time, is usually the most susceptible to hypnosis."

"A clever person?" asked Sadie with a giggle.

"*Oui*, Mademoiselle Eiderling. The cleverest."

I took the seat between Percy and John and gave silent thanks for Henry's defense of my intelligence, in spite of my Svengali accusation.

"Ah, I see." Sadie squeaked an index finger along the rim of her goblet. "Then I'm sure I'll be as easy to mold as soft putty when I'm in your skilled hands. I'm clever as can be."

"Too clever," said Teddy while chewing on an oyster.

"Thank you, Teddy."

"Tell me, Reverie"—Percy removed his gloves, his eyes locked on Henry—"now that you've hypnotized Olivia once, how quickly could you hypnotize her again?"

"Extraordinarily quickly."

"Really?" Excitement mounted in Percy's voice. "Could you do it in a minute? A half minute?"

"I could put her into a trance in less than one second." Henry dabbed the corner of his mouth with his napkin.

Silence seized the room. I bit my lip and worried he could do exactly what he boasted.

"No, you couldn't," said John beside me. "I think you're full of bunkum, Reverie."

"Am I?" Henry cocked his right eyebrow. "Perhaps I should put you into a trance in the same amount of time, *mon pote*, and set you crowing like a rooster."

The girls all laughed, including Sadie, whose cackles attacked my head like a swarm of screeching insects.

"Prove it by hypnotizing Olivia again, right here," said Percy, resting a wintry palm on the back of my hand.

The laughter quieted. I quaked, for Percy's hand looked as pale as death.

"The way you manipulated her the other night impressed me beyond belief," he continued, his face graying, his voice retreating into the distance. "I would love to witness how you do it—up close."

Anger roiled inside me. I shook Percy's hand off mine and cried out, "All is well!"

Percy wrinkled his forehead, but before that phrase could spew from my mouth again, Sadie clapped her hands and begged in a faraway echo of a voice, "Oh, do it, please, Monsieur Reverie. It'll be fun. We could prop her up next to the buffet table."

"Yes, put her next to the birthday cake, like a delicious tart," said a long-nosed fiend of a boy with a leer that turned my stomach.

"Yes, do it," the bulging-eyed girl chimed in, her canines sweeping over her bluing bottom lip. "How funny that would be."

I glared at Percy, who shrank back and pinked up to his

regular hue, as if he had just then realized he was failing at making me feel comfortable.

"I'll pay you to keep her asleep during the entire meal." Sadie stood to her full height and stared me down with irises that simmered bloody red. Her long black fingernails ripped into the tablecloth. "Name your price, and I'll go fetch my father's wallet right now."

I gasped for air and grabbed the arms of my chair while the room swayed and knocked me about worse than Percy's buggy. *Don't faint, don't faint!* I told myself. *Keep your wits about you. Don't show them you're weak—that's exactly what they're craving.*

"No," I heard someone say, but my tilting brain and failing ears couldn't figure out from where in the room the voice had emanated. I drew long breaths of sour beer fumes and willed the claws and the fangs to disappear, forced the black spots to stop buzzing in front of my eyes, until the room settled back into view. The partygoers ceased being demons once again.

Down the way, Henry peered at Sadie across the fine bone china and gilded steins. "Miss Mead is not an object to be laid out for your entertainment."

Sadie sank back down to her chair. "Prove to us you can put her under in less than one second, or we won't believe you. We'll call you a humbug and send you out the door before you eat another bite." She flapped her napkin across her lap. "You're our entertainer for the evening." She beamed with the smile of a victor. "Entertain us."

Henry backed his chair away from the table with a loud screech, and my heart jumped. He was going to do it. Sadie had harassed him to the point of obedience, and he would drop me into darkness before I could even think of springing out of my seat and fleeing the room.

The hypnotist indeed rose to his feet, seeming to follow her command—but instead of stalking toward me, he tossed his napkin onto his plate. "I will not be bullied into performing hypnosis."

Sadie laughed. "We're not bullying you, you silly, dramatic thing. I just—"

"What do they look like, Miss Mead?" Henry leaned his palms against the table. "What do you see?"

A soundless question—*What?*—formed on my lips.

"They don't look quite right, do they?" he asked.

"What is he talking about, Olivia?" said Percy with a nudge of my arm. "Is he hypnotizing you right now?"

"Is this part of it, Reverie?" asked Teddy. "Can you hypnotize her with just one look?"

A blush seared my cheeks and neck. I directed my eyes toward my empty Wedgwood plate with its swirls of blue flowers—no one had even served me any oysters yet—and squirmed under everyone's scrutiny. If only I could disappear into the wind and blow back through the streets and the darkness toward my own house. If only returning home early to Father wouldn't mean he'd blame me for ruining the evening.

"They look like vampires, don't they?" asked Henry.

I lifted my face, stunned he had asked that question in front of everyone.

"You knew the moment you came into the room that you should avoid them, didn't you?" he added. "I could see it in your eyes. This isn't a curse, Olivia. It's a gift."

I shook my head. "No, this is definitely not a gift. They've got pale flesh and horrifying teeth. I can't stand being around them. All is well!"

Silence befell the room again. I was about to stand and slink out to the hall, mortified, when Teddy slammed his hand on the table and made us all jump.

"Holy Mary," he said. "He did it. He hypnotized her from across the table. She thinks we all look like Count Dracula."

Sadie broke into her awful, screeching laughter again, and the other girls joined her.

"Bravo, Reverie," said Sunken-Eyed John, clapping his hands. "A swell magic trick. How'd you do it?"

"Olivia?" Percy poked my arm. "Wake up. You're babbling nonsense about that novel."

"What about *him*, Miss Mead?" asked Henry, nodding toward Percy. "What does he look like?"

I rubbed the sides of my head, and my whole body went hot and achy with humiliation. "Just hypnotize me, *On-ree*. She'll pay you well, and I won't have to be here anymore. Coming to this house was a mistake."

"Well, that's rude," said Sadie, and then she snapped her fingers and demanded, "Hurry up and make her go rigid as a plank, Monsieur Reverie. I'd like to see if I can stand on top of her myself."

"Oh, yes!" One of the boys applauded with loud smacks of his large hands. "I would pay good money to see *that.*"

"Do it, Reverie," said a husky-voiced fellow.

"Yes, do it!" others added.

I shot to my feet, but Sunken-Eyed John grabbed my wrist and pinned it to the table. His fingers squeezed against my bones.

"Let go of me." I struggled to break free, fire smoldering in my chest. "All is well. All is well!"

My ridiculous cries made everyone laugh all the harder, as if my fury were part of the show.

"Let go of her, John," said Percy over the obnoxious guffaws. "She's my girl, you louse."

"All is well!" White steam—the extinguished flames of my actual words—would soon gust from my mouth and nose. I was certain of it. "All is well! All—"

Out of the corner of my eye, I caught Henry approaching, which sent me further into a fit of angry panic. My legs and free arm thrashed about, knocking over my empty chair with a crash. "All is well!"

Henry's footsteps drew closer. The air thinned; my lungs hurt. Percy tugged on my elbow, while John kept my wrist pinned and pinched.

"All is well! All is—"

"It's all right, Olivia." Henry took hold of my flailing arm.

"All—"

"Stop panicking. I'm not going to hypnotize you." Henry yanked John's hand off my wrist, releasing the pain. "Let go of her. You're idiots, all of you. Spoiled brats. Find your own entertainment."

Before anyone could react, he guided me away from the table, toward the breath of freedom waiting beyond the dining room's entrance, and I choked on the fiery pain of embers lodged inside my throat.

"Hey! Reverie!" called Percy behind us. "Where are you taking her?"

We made it halfway down the mirrored hallway before I heard Percy's footsteps jogging after us.

"Where are you going?"

"Away from here." Henry steered me toward the wide front door that would lead to fresh air and escape.

Percy was on our heels. "Come back, Olivia. I didn't even get a chance to drink my beer."

Henry came to a sudden stop and turned on Percy. "Are you Miss Mead's suitor?"

"Yes." Percy pulled at his gray bow tie. "My name is Percy Acklen, and I am courting her."

"Then how the devil can you worry about beer at the moment, *bâtard*? Those people were treating her terribly. One boy called her a tart, and that ugly one next to her was pinning her down and hurting her. You just sat there like an imbecile."

"Now, wait a moment . . ." Percy stepped close. "Don't throw insults at me when you were the one hypnotizing my girl. We all thought you were giving us a show."

"Do you want me to take you home, Olivia?" asked Henry, ignoring Percy, his hand still cradling my arm. "I will explain everything to your father."

"No." I shook my head. "Please, no. My father will be furious if I come home early. He'll make everything so much worse than it already is."

"Oh, to hell with all of this." Percy marched over to our jackets hanging off the scraggly coat rack. "I'm hungry and grumpy and need a good supper. Let's go eat in the city and tell Olivia's father everything went well. Who needs catty birthday girls and overbearing daddies ruining our evening?" He threw his crimson scarf around his neck. "You, too, Reverie. I'm willing to bet you also have a father who's made your life miserable."

Henry lowered his hand from my arm. "No. Just an alcoholic uncle-guardian who got himself killed in July."

"Holy tripe. That's even worse. You're in." Percy clomped back over to us on the loud soles of his oxfords, my coat in hand. "Come join Olivia and me. I'm paying."

"Your buggy only holds two people, Percy," I reminded him.

"True. Well . . ." He helped me into my coat. "Do you have a hired carriage, Reverie?"

"No. Miss Eiderling paid someone to drive me here, but I don't think—"

"Then we'll all squeeze in together. It'll just have to be tight and cozy." Percy offered me his elbow and plunked his top hat on his head. "Come along. Let's get out of here and go toast to youth and vampires and rebellion."

# CHAPTER TWELVE

# YELLOW-RIBBON GIRLS

hree people did not fit comfortably into a buggy built for two.

Mandolin jostled us through the streets of Portland, and Percy, Henry, and I squeezed together on the padded green seat, my hips too wide to fit between the boys. I had to turn and sit sideways, facing Percy, while half my rump perched on Henry's warm leg behind me.

"Comfy?" asked Percy, shifting his face toward me, his nose an inch from mine.

"Somewhat," I said, and I gritted my teeth against a jolt from a buggy wheel slamming against a pothole.

Cologne and pomade and the scent of wool suits ruled the air around me. *Youth these days will be the death of morality*, I remembered the pumpkin-haired organist complaining earlier that day, and I wondered if she might be right. Wedged between the two young men like that, my chest shoved against Percy's arm and my backside bumping against Henry's femur, I must have resembled the heroine of *Sapho*, the play both the organist and my mother said was causing an uproar in New York City—*the one about the strumpet and her lovers.*

This was not the evening my father was envisioning for his newly tamed daughter.

Percy tipped his face toward mine again. "Is she still hypnotized, Reverie?"

"No," I said before Henry could even think of confessing that my father had paid him to cure my mind. "I'm fine."

Percy turned his sights back to the road ahead. "I'd like to learn a couple of hypnosis tricks."

"They're not tricks, *mon ami*," said Henry with a bite to his voice. "They're skills that require knowledge, compassion, and mastery. My uncle began training me back when I was just twelve years old, and he only did so because he believed I possessed both talent and responsibility."

"Your uncle? The rummy who got himself killed, you mean?"

I nudged Percy in the arm. "That's cruel, Percy."

"Yes. That uncle." Henry shifted the leg that rested below me. "He became the guardian of Genevieve and me after our parents died. And despite his weaknesses of recent years, he was once witty and kind and deeply in love with the arts of hypnotism and mesmerism."

Percy shot him a sideways glance. "You make hypnosis sound like a woman."

"It is like a woman. She's beautiful. She's mysterious." Henry's voice softened to a lush purr that made my stomach flutter. *"Une belle femme."*

"Risqué," said Percy with a chuckle.

"But you have to treat her delicately," continued Henry, ignoring Percy, "and with utmost respect. Or else you'll find yourself waking up in a cold sweat in the middle of the night, realizing"—he paused long enough for me to peek over my shoulder and catch him watching me through the darkness from beneath the curved brim of his hat—"you may have gone too far." He kept his eyes on mine. "You'll be deeply sorry if you've inflicted any harm."

Percy steered Mandolin around the bend to the right, and I forced my eyes away from Henry's.

"Well," said Percy, "despite how sacred you're making stage hypnosis out to be, I would really love to pay you to show me how to perform some of these *skills.*"

"That information isn't for sale," said Henry. "You're just going to have to mesmerize the world based on your own natural charms, Monsieur Acklen."

Percy barked a laugh that seemed to shatter something fragile in the air, and I rocked against them both, wondering if Henry Rhodes would put my mind back the way it was, if he was genuinely sorry for what he had done.

PERCY LED US INSIDE AN ELEGANT TWELFTH STREET establishment with frosted glass light fixtures twinkling over dark wooden booths and tables draped in ivory cloths. Waiters in white coats waltzed about with bottles of wine and steaming plates of fish and beef that made my hungry stomach moan. I'd never stepped inside the place before that moment. Father always preferred eating at home, so we seldom dined in restaurants.

Our host, a tall gentleman with a dusky walrus mustache, took our coats and the boys' hats and led us up two short steps to one of the dining areas. In one of the booths we passed, a woman in a lavender dress picked at a salad with soundless jabs of her fork.

Another vision approached—I could tell, for the air grew hard to breathe, and the colors of the woman's booth bloomed into shades that demanded my full attention. Her supper companion, a bony-faced old coot with a half-dozen gold rings, said something to her that made her blur and fade into fog and shadow.

I stopped in a daze and rapped my knuckles against Henry's arm behind me. "They're disappearing," I said. "Certain women."

"Who's disappearing?" asked Percy. "What's going on with you now?"

I sealed my lips, picked up the hem of my gown, and continued following the walrus-mustached host. The illusion passed. My lungs breathed with ease. Everyone now seemed made of flesh and bone.

The host seated the two young men and me at a round table, toward the back, with the flame of a white candle dancing in a silver holder at the center. We removed our gloves, and the host handed us thick red menus. I heard him describe the evening's specials in a friendly enough voice, but I could no longer pay much attention to the menu or the possibility of food. All I thought about was how I was going to convince Henry to put me back the way I was before I, too, faded like my neighbor Mrs. Stanton and that poor woman poking at her salad.

"Psst—look over there," said Percy in a whisper once the host had left us.

I craned my head toward the booth across the room that had caught Percy's eye. Four young ladies dined there in relative quiet, including redheaded and lovely Agnes Frye, my friend Kate's sister who had lured us high school girls to Wednesday's rally.

My skin prickled, warning of the arrival of yet another hallucination. The ladies' booth seemed to rush toward me for better viewing.

My eyes opened wide.

Lanterns switched on inside all the women's bodies. Their hair glistened with breathtaking luminescence—a light that reflected off the surrounding wood. Their skin flushed with a brilliance that rivaled our candle's flame. I sucked in my breath and watched in awe as they glowed—literally *glowed*—before my eyes.

"See the emblem hanging off their left shoulders?" asked Percy.

Agnes lowered her left arm and revealed a bright yellow ribbon.

My fingers tightened around my menu, and I slouched down in my chair with the hope that she wouldn't see me with the boys and come over. I shook my head to regain control of my brain, as mesmerizing as this particular illusion was. The prickling faded. The ladies' booth dimmed and retreated to its position against the wall. The world tipped back to its normal balance.

"What are the ribbons for?" asked Henry.

"Women's suffrage." Percy frowned. "My sister is like them. She used to wear yellow ribbons, roses, and buttons all the time without any of us knowing what the deuce they meant."

"You have a sister?" I asked.

"Yesss," hissed Percy. "I have two older, married brothers, both respectable lawyers, and a twenty-year-old sister who's no longer a part of our family."

"Because of the—?" I glanced back at Agnes and her friends.

"Yes." He swallowed beneath his stiff collar. "My father learned she helped run a banquet for Susan B. Anthony down in Salem last February, so he forced her to pack up and leave." He closed his menu with a solid *thwack*.

Henry wrinkled his forehead. "You're not allowed to talk to or see your sister anymore . . . just because she wants to vote?"

"That's right." Percy darted another quick peek at the suffragists. "After Father threw her out, she moved to Idaho so she could live the way she wanted and vote as much as she pleased. Mother nearly died from heartbreak and humiliation." He reopened his menu and pressed his lips into a hard line. "My sister is a spinster now, just like every woman in that booth."

"Agnes isn't a spinster," I said.

"Who's Agnes?" asked Percy.

"Shh." I held my menu over my face and slithered down another inch. "The redhead over there is my good friend's sister, and she has a loving husband."

Percy knitted his eyebrows. "How?"

"What do you mean, how? She got married in a church the same way your parents probably did. Her husband is a pro-suffrage man."

Percy snorted. "There's no such thing."

"I'm one," said Henry.

"Pshaw. You're just saying that to charm Olivia. All it does is make you sound like an effeminate French sissy, Reverie."

"Anti-suffrage men are the ones who sound like sissies and cowards," I said under my breath.

"I still want beer." Percy scanned one of the menu pages. "What about you, Mr. Suffrage? Are you drinking tonight?"

"No." Henry shook his head. "I'm performing. No one wants to be hypnotized by a drunk."

"Oh, criminy . . ." Percy laughed. "Can you imagine what that would look like? Oh . . ." He slapped his hand over his mouth. "I suppose you can, what with that sozzled hypnotist uncle of yours."

"I'm sure they serve Eiderling Beer at the bar here." I nudged Percy's arm and wished him away. "Perhaps you should go order yourself one."

Percy laughed again. "I thought you were a temperance crusader."

"You were the one who called me that, not I. If you want a beer"—my desire to catapult him away emboldened my voice—"go get one. You said we're here to toast youth and rebellion, didn't you?"

"Yes . . ."

"Then go." *Shoo*, I wanted to add, but he was already up and out of his seat.

"Don't hypnotize my girl when I'm gone, Reverie," he said with a wink.

"Wouldn't dream of it, *mon ami.*"

Henry and I watched Percy bound down the short flight of steps in his quest for Eiderling booze.

I slammed my menu shut. "Hypnotize me back."

Henry laid down his own menu. "I told you, I can't."

"Why not?"

"Your father only paid me a quarter of his promised fee for your treatment. I can't get the rest of the money until Tuesday evening, before I board a train for San Francisco."

"Why?"

"He wants to make sure the cure takes."

I winced.

Henry reached his hand toward mine on the tablecloth, not quite touching me but near enough to ignite a tingling sensation in my fingertips. "We're so, so close to affording Genevieve's surgery. Your father's payment will get us what we need. It'll give her a chance."

"You don't understand what people look like to me."

"No, I don't, but as I said at Sadie's table, it's not necessarily a curse."

"Of course it's a curse. You try living like this and tell me—" My anger flared; that blasted phrase threatened to shoot from my lips again. I smacked my palm against the table, which prompted two men next to us to turn my way and scowl.

"Hear me out before you get upset with me." Henry's fingers inched nearer. "When your father asked me to hypnotize you, he said he wanted you to *accept* the world the way it is."

"Don't you think I remember what he—?"

"But"—he scooted his chair closer to mine—"I didn't tell you to *accept* the world the way it truly is, Olivia. I told you to *see* it."

"No, you—"

"Think about it. I did."

I sank back in my seat.

"And you *can* see it," he continued, his French accent gone. "Maybe not at every single moment, but when it really matters to you or the person you're viewing, or during moments of intense emotion, you'll clearly see that you shouldn't be with poisonous jackasses like that vampire at the bar."

I sat up straight. "Percy doesn't look like either a jackass or a vampire."

"Yet."

I picked at the spine of my menu. "I want to see and say things normally again, Henry Rhodes. I've never had anyone like Percy show an interest in me before this week, and I don't want to spoil everything by acting like a lunatic."

"What do you mean, 'anyone like Percy'?"

"I know, compared to him, I'm plain and dull and—"

"Plain and dull?" Henry's voice rose to an embarrassing volume. "Is that what your father tells you?"

"Please"—I scooted my chair away from his—"you're talking too loudly."

"It makes me furious when people like that ninnyhammer Acklen make people like you feel inferior to them. Tell me, exactly what type of loving partnership is that supposed to lead to?"

"Please, be quiet. He's coming back."

Henry leaned forward again and grabbed my hand. "He's

not better than you, Olivia, and neither is your father. And you're far from plain and dull."

I pulled my hand away and sat up straight and proper.

"What's going on, Reverie?" Percy swaggered over to us with a mug of beer. "Why are you blushing, Olivia?"

"I should probably go." In his haste, Henry dropped his gloves to the floor. He leaned over to pick them up.

"What happened?" Percy plunked his mug on the table. "Did you say something lewd to her, Reverie? Or"—he bent forward with a grin—"are you attempting to court her by singing suffrage anthems?"

Henry got to his feet. "I can't stay. I'm performing soon and would like to check on my sister beforehand." He slapped his hand on Percy's shoulder and leaned close to his ear. "I said nothing lewd to Olivia, Monsieur Acklen. She's angry because I told her to run away from people who are poisonous to her."

"What?" Percy's brows pinched together. "Who's poisonous to her? What are you talking about?"

Henry fitted his gloves over his hands. "Thank you for the supper offer. *Adieu.* Good night."

And then he was gone, hustling toward the exit as if he couldn't get away from the two of us fast enough.

Percy plopped down in his chair, still wrinkling his brow. "What was all that about? Was he trying to hypnotize you?"

"No . . . he just . . . it's hard to explain. He . . ."

Out of the corner of my eye, I saw Henry returning to us. My neck muscles tensed. "Oh, no, here he comes again."

Henry approached our table and handed me something limp and white that I realized was one of my own evening gloves. "I must have accidentally picked this up when I was fetching my own gloves, *mademoiselle. Je suis désolé.* I am sorry." His eyes lingered on mine and then darted to the glove, as if he were trying to convey some sort of message.

"Thank you," I said, resting the glove in my lap.

"You're welcome." He left us again so swiftly that the air ruffled my hair and made the night feel even more out of whack.

"Criminy . . ." Percy peeked over his shoulder and watched him go. "My father always says theater people are eccentric and ill-mannered . . ."

I sighed. "You keep telling me what your father says and thinks, Percy. Weren't we supposed to be forgetting overbearing daddies right now?"

"I give my own opinions."

"Not really. For instance . . ." I kneaded the fabric of my glove between my fingers and was surprised to hear the rustle of a piece of paper inside the thumb.

"For instance what?"

"For instance"—I set the glove aside on my lap and attempted to ignore that peculiar rustling—"do you truly agree with your father that women shouldn't vote?"

Percy lowered his eyes.

I lifted my chin. "I read his letter in the newspaper yesterday."

He flashed a sheepish grin. "Oh, yes, that letter. Father's public opinion pieces always make me supremely popular with the ladies."

"But what is *your* opinion? Do you think women are inferior creatures to men?"

"I think . . ." He scratched the back of his neck, repositioned himself in his chair, took a swig of beer, and hesitated far too long. "I think volatile subjects are best avoided in fine dining establishments, Olivia. Let me call over a waiter and order you a nice meal, and then we'll talk about a lighter subject more suitable for a sweet little thing like you."

"But—"

"Waiter." He waved over a short server with large ears, who was just darting back to the kitchen. "We're ready to order."

The waiter scuttled over to our sides and asked what we wanted.

Before I could open my mouth, Percy told the fellow, "The young lady and I will have the salmon and a salad and a loaf of fresh bread, and could you cook the fish a little more than you normally would? So that the ends are charred and crunchy."

"Could mine be cooked the regular way?" I asked the waiter.

"Oh, you'll like it my way, Olivia." Percy handed the fellow our menus. "It's the only way to eat it."

"I don't even like salmon all that much . . ."

But the waiter was gone; my opinion hung in the air,

unacknowledged, while Percy dove into a story about his travels.

"Did I tell you we spend our summers down at the beach in California?"

"Yes." I cleared my throat. "You said so when you told me about Nanette."

"I'm a crackerjack swimmer, I've discovered. I've swum nearly a mile off the coast and never once tired from the waves smacking me around."

Percy yammered on, and my heart shriveled into a disappointed little prune. I didn't have to witness his true feelings by seeing any dangerous curved teeth or predatory gleam in his eyes.

I heard it in his voice, clear as church bells—and I'd probably even heard it and ignored it on Halloween night.

Percy thought me inferior.

# CHAPTER THIRTEEN

# PERCY'S TEETH

y the light of a streetlamp outside the restaurant, I found two tickets to Henry's Saturday matinee show stuffed inside the thumb of my glove. On the back of one of the tickets was scrawled a smudged note, yet I could still make out the message:

*Come to the side door of the theater after the show if you're able. I want you to meet Genevieve.*

I heard approaching hooves and looked up to find Percy driving his black buggy around the bend from the side street where he'd parked it. I crammed the tickets into the far reaches of the glove and slid the white leather over my hand, scraping my thumb on a rough edge.

Percy brought the buggy to a stop along the curb next to me and hopped out to the sidewalk. "You're blushing again. It seems you're always blushing."

I shrugged. "I'm just warm."

"It's freezing out here."

"The food warmed me up."

"Or the company, perhaps." He smiled and took my hand to help me into the seat above, but I didn't respond, which I'm sure made me seem like an unfeeling lump of stone.

The ride home started off uneventfully, and the message in my glove kept me from paying attention to our route. In fact, I didn't actually notice our surroundings until Percy directed the horse and buggy down the South Park Blocks, where wide expanses of moonlit grass separated the east and west sides of the street.

Strange, vaporous wisps of air rose off the damp park ground and drifted into the trees like steam rising from a pot—or spirits escaping graves. I'd seen such mist before; the effect wasn't one of my illusions, just a mixture of atmospheric warmth and cold and moisture. The sight unsettled me, though. Between the ghostly fog and Mandolin's footfalls across the soundless neighborhood, I felt like Ichabod Crane venturing through the depths of Sleepy Hollow upon the back of trusty Gunpowder.

"Why are you taking this route?" I asked, staring at the empty path that lay ahead.

"To stretch out the time and make it seem as if we didn't desert Sadie's party." Percy stole a glance at me. "I'm keeping you out of trouble, my pet."

"Oh. Thank you." I toyed with the little pieces of paper wedged beside my thumb. "But I'd prefer not to be called your pet, if you don't mind. It makes me feel like a cocker spaniel."

Percy didn't answer.

We came upon the corner of Park and Main, and he gave Mandolin's reins a firm pull. "Whoa, boy."

I stiffened. "Why are you slowing down?"

"Whoa, Mandolin."

The buggy came to a swaying stop alongside the rising mist. Cold air sliced across my cheeks. My shriveled prune of a heart pounded back to life with throbbing intensity.

"Why did you stop?" I asked. "We're still three blocks away."

Percy shifted his knees toward me, the upper half of his face masked by shadows, his eyes a knife slash of yellow. "Olivia . . ." His arm slid behind me, across the back of the leather seat. "I really want to kiss you." He leaned in close, and his sour Eiderling Beer breath flooded my nose.

"I . . . um"—I inched away—"I don't . . ."

"There's no need to be so nervous." He cupped my cheek with one soft-gloved hand. "I'll be gentle."

"I don't—"

"Do you want to play *Dracula?*" He lifted an eyebrow. "Would that make it more fun?"

My mouth went dry; I shook my head. "No! H-h-how do you mean?"

"I know you're a good little thing, but you have to admit"—his left hand found the crook of my waist, below my coat—"a girl who's read *Dracula* as many times as you have must be aching for the touch of a pair of lips against her neck." With that, he nestled his ice block of a cheek against my face. His breath tickled its way inside my ear. "Do you want to see what it feels like if I place my mouth against your bare skin? Do you want to be my"—he kissed my earlobe— "Mina?"

I closed my eyes and found my thoughts racing back to the Percy Acklen who had waved me down in the theater lobby with the lights glinting off his cuff links. I remembered those green-brown eyes and the mischief on his lips and the way we'd commiserated about our fathers before darting through the rain to my house.

"I d-d-d . . ." My teeth chattered. "I don't want to be with someone who thinks I'm inferior to him."

"I don't think that." His breath cooled the upper regions of my neck, below my ear.

"I don't even like salmon very much, but you never even asked me what I wanted before you ordered for me."

"Olivia . . ." He slid his bottom lip across an inch of my throat—not a kiss, per se, but a tease that gave me unpleasant shivers. "You're making too much of everything. Just have some fun. Play with me. Close your eyes and play."

"I don't—"

"Just play." He licked my neck, which almost made me laugh, if it weren't also kind of awful, but then he cupped his full mouth—wet and soft and warmer than the rest of him—around my neck and sank his teeth against my flesh. Blood rushed through my veins until I seemed to be made of nothing but blood and a pounding pulse—racing, anxious, beating, beating, beating blood he would taste if his teeth bit down any harder. His hand shifted to my posterior and gave a firm squeeze—*his grabby hands! Just as Frannie said!* Every part of him pressed down on me. His mouth, his fingers, his chest. I couldn't breathe.

I pushed him away, and his head smacked the buggy's overhang.

"Ouch!" He rubbed the top of his skull. "What did you do that for?"

"Did you ever grab my friend Frannie's backside?"

"What? Who the hell is Frannie?"

"Frannie Harrison. She goes to our school."

"Jesus, Olivia." He lunged toward me again. "Just close your eyes and let me kiss you. You owe me for what happened in class."

"But . . ." I gasped. "You said . . ."

He grabbed the back of my neck and squished his mouth

against mine. His lips were sloppy and wet, and the beer taste was so obnoxious, I gagged on the fumes.

"All is well!" I pushed him off, and his head clunked the buggy a second time.

His visage changed—oh, God, how it changed. His eyes sank into the blackened recesses of a gaunt and anemic face. His canines lengthened into the grotesque tusks of a wild boar.

"Why do you keep saying that all is well?" he asked, and his mouth seeped my blood.

"Oh, God!" I snatched his scarf from his shoulders and jumped off the buggy.

"Hey! Where are you going? And why'd you take my scarf?"

"I'm saving both our hides, you idiot." I wrapped the yarn around my bare neck and fled down the street. "My father will see your tooth marks if I don't wear your rotten scarf."

I heard the snap of reins behind me and the galloping rhythm of Mandolin taking off after me with the rattling buggy. I cut through side yards, even though the shortcut meant soaking my shoes and skirts with mud. My pulse hammered in my ears. My breathing turned ragged, but I pushed onward across the rain-soaked grass and dirt.

Percy was already parking the buggy by the time I sprinted up my own brick path. Our house's tall front windows stared me down—gawking eyes observing my frenzied arrival in the dark. I turned the doorknob but found it locked.

"No, no, no. You can't be locked. You can't be locked!"

I twisted the knob and banged on the door. My struggle to get inside allowed Percy to hustle up beside me mere seconds before my father swung open the door.

Father widened his eyes at my sweaty hair and muddied shoes. "What happened?"

"She fell out of the buggy," said my escort, who looked like Percy again.

"She fell out?"

I gasped. "All is—"

"She leaned over too far, trying to look at something"— Percy took my arm as if I were an invalid—"and tumbled into the grass. She muddied her dress, but I don't think she's hurt, sir. Naturally, I'll let you, a physician of sorts, make the final diagnosis."

I moved to enter the house, but Father blocked my entrance with his arms.

He nodded toward my neck. "The scarf, Olivia."

A wave of nausea rolled through me. "I—I—I beg your pardon?"

"Isn't that young Mr. Acklen's scarf you're wearing?" he asked.

"Y-y-yes."

"Shouldn't you be returning it to him before he leaves?"

I glanced back at Percy, who had gone pale again, although in a frightened way—an *I'm about to get dissected by dental tools* sort of way—with quivering lips and watery eyes.

"Um . . ." He stammered, "Well . . . th-th-there's no need for her to return it to me right now. She got cold out here and should keep warming up. I don't want her catching her death of pneumonia."

"Oh. Thank you." Father dropped his arms from the doorway. "How very thoughtful."

I leapt inside the house. "Good night."

Father shut the door, but before he could ask details about Sadie's party, I launched myself up the staircase, closed myself in my room, and unwound Percy's scarf until the crimson wool lay in a coiled heap upon the floor. With my head tipped to the right, I approached my oval mirror.

My reflection showed me two sore and bleeding puncture wounds on the left side of my neck—as vicious and angry-red as Lucy's wounds in *Dracula*.

*Not real.*

Two blinks later, the marks retreated and left a purpling bruise in their stead, which was almost worse.

"But unlike Lucy and Mina," I said to my solid face in the mirror, and I braced my hands around the curved wooden frame, "you will *not* be returning to your vampire for a second bite, Olivia Mead. You will not." I swallowed and nudged Percy's scarf away with my toes.

"[Bicycling] has done more to emancipate woman than any one thing in the world. I rejoice every time I see a woman ride by on a wheel. It gives her a feeling of self-reliance and independence the moment she takes her seat; and away she goes, the picture of untrammeled womanhood."

—SUSAN B. ANTHONY, 1896

# A RESPONSIBLE WOMAN

The following morning, my plaid wool winter blouse, buttoned clear up to the top of my throat, hid Percy's bite mark from view. On my way downstairs to breakfast, I tested the durability of the top button by twisting it about until I felt confident the little pearl fastening would remain in place. A thin edging of lace tickled like a gnat beneath my chin, but the discomfort was minor—well worth the trouble of avoiding the topic of my virtue with my father.

Father sat at the breakfast table, his face a concealed mystery behind the newspaper, as usual.

"Good morning." I took my seat and unfolded my napkin.

"Good morning, Olivia." The newspaper didn't budge.

"Are you playing billiards today?"

"It's Saturday, isn't it?"

"Yes"—I fluffed the napkin across my lap—"it is."

"Then I'll be playing. What are your plans?"

"I'll probably go to Fran—"

A headline caught my eye and paralyzed my tongue:

### OLD MOTHER ACKLEN FOR PRESIDENT?

My heart stopped. Nervous sweat broke out beneath that strangling straitjacket of a collar. I pulled at the lace to breathe.

"What's the matter?" Father lowered the paper. "Why did you stop talking mid-sentence?"

"Is—is . . . ?" My eyes refused to budge from the newsprint. "I think I see a headline about one of the Acklens."

Father closed the paper to get a better view of the front. "Oh, yes. That."

"What does the article say?"

"It's nothing to fret about." He folded the paper in half so I could no longer see the article. "Some silly woman wrote to the editor, suggesting Judge Acklen's mother would make a far better president than either McKinley or Bryan."

I pressed my lips together. "Really? They printed a letter like that?"

"Surprisingly so. They usually keep suffragist drivel out of the *Oregonian*." With a grunt, he unfolded and readjusted the newspaper so that it lay next to his plate with the second page on top. The only items left viewable from my seat were a political cartoon involving President McKinley and an article about the Socialist Eugene V. Debs.

Father raised his steaming mug of coffee to his lips, but before taking a sip, he added, with a quick glance at me, "Please, Olivia, don't even think of reading the letter. It was probably written by a man, anyway."

He sipped his drink.

I raised my eyebrows.

"Why do you think a man wrote it?" I asked.

He lowered the mug to the table with a smack of his lips. "It's too well written for a woman."

Before I could respond, Gerda glided through the swinging kitchen door on a bacon-and-egg-scented breeze.

A smile wiggled across my face. *It's too well written for a woman*, Father had said. *Well written*. He believed my work to be well written.

Gerda set my breakfast plate in front of me. "Good morning, Miss Mead."

"Good morning, Gerda." My smile stretched to an unmanageable width.

She nudged my elbow below the table. "A lovely party last night?"

"Oh. Yes." I lowered my eyes. "Lovely."

"Good. More coffee, Dr. Mead?"

"Not at the moment. Thank you."

"Then I'll let you two eat." She wiped her hands on her apron and made her way back through the door.

I reined in my smile but longed to ask Father more about why he thought the letter was so well written, and if he felt swayed by the argument, and if the writer seemed to live up to her name: *A Responsible Woman.*

Instead, I buttered my toast with a rhythmic *scrape, scrape, scrape, scrape.*

"What did you say you were doing today?" he asked between bites of food.

"I'm bicycling over to Frannie's."

He swallowed the last bite and cleared his throat. "You're getting a little too old to be riding around the city, don't you think? Especially now that a young man is courting you."

"I don't care for Percy as much as I thought. Please don't consider us courting."

"You don't care for him?"

"I learned his reputation isn't as spotless as he made it out to be. I'm a good, chaste girl, so you should be proud of me resisting his charms."

"He tried to"—Father coughed up crumbs—"*charm* you?"

"And what do you mean about me getting too old to bicycle?" I stopped buttering. "I see plenty of women cyclists."

"I don't know why that is, when there are so many households to run."

"Are you saying I can't ride anymore?"

"I'm saying we should perhaps only hire Gerda on the week-days when you're in school. You're more than old enough to be taking care of the cooking and cleaning on Saturdays."

"Gerda is relying on her employment here."

"I'm sure she can find a family who needs a girl to clean only once a week."

"But—"

"It's time you took on more duties, Olivia. You're not a child anymore."

I dropped my knife to my plate with a clank.

"Or are you a child?" he asked. "Am I mistaken?"

I eyed the stack of newspaper pages piled up beside him and thought of my published letter to the editor buried inside. *A Responsible Woman* was what I had claimed to be.

"No, I'm not a child." I dragged my teeth against my bottom lip and tried to still the wanderlust in my legs. "But can the change of her schedule wait until next week? I was planning to offer to help Frannie's mother with preparations for tomorrow's anniversary party."

"Well . . . ," Father grumbled. "I suppose Gerda is already hard at work for the day . . ."

"Thank you."

"But next week, this new schedule must start. And I must say, I'm sorely disappointed by this turn of events with Percy."

"I am, too." I picked at my eggs with my fork.

Father returned to the newspaper and grinned at the political cartoon, his dark eyes sparkling, a chuckle shaking his torso, while I ate my breakfast and rid my head of Percy.

I TIGHTENED THE LONG PINS THAT SECURED MY GRAY felt bicycling hat to my hair, hitched up my black skirt, and mounted the padded seat of my vermilion-red bicycle. Before Father could run outside and change his mind about letting me ride, I took off and pedaled down Main Street, amid horse-drawn wagons delivering fresh Saturday produce to the city's grocers. Nearly a year before, the *Oregonian* reported that the city now boasted one automobile, owned by a German immigrant named Henry Wemme, but I hadn't yet seen the contraption. I'd only heard stories about how it caused horses to rear and bolt when it charged through the city with its motor howling.

Ruts and stones in the uneven road jostled my shoulders, but the ground was dry and firm, aside from the occasional pile of horse dung. Gunmetal-gray clouds loomed over the city, threatening rain, yet they were merciful and withheld their showers.

I turned left on Third Street, before getting anywhere near the sewage stink and unsavory characters of the waterfront district. Feeling the need to go faster, I leaned forward and powered the pedals with all my strength. My calf muscles burned, the bicycle chain whirred below my flapping skirts, and I caught enough speed to lift my feet and cruise past the towering brick buildings and streetcar tracks. Air rushed across my tongue; the wind fought to whip the hat off my head. The company names written on the buildings—INDE-PENDENT STEAMSHIP CO., E. HOUSES CAFÉ, EMBERS PHOTO STUDIO, THE J. K. GILL CO., FUNG LAM RESTAURANT, and even METROPOLITAN—streaked into a blur.

To avoid the saloons and gambling dens (and Father) in the North End, I steered left and zoomed up Washington, my heart racing, heat fanning through my face, my arms, my legs. I veered down Sixth and rode three more blocks before turning right onto Yamhill. McCorkan's Bicycle Shop's forest-green awnings came into view, and a Christmas morning sense of elation stirred inside me. My feet slowed on the ped-als. The chain *click-click-click*ed to a stop, and I planted my shoes on the road in front of McCorkan's display window.

There they were, prominently displayed on two dress forms.

Bicycle bloomers.

Rational garments.

Turkish trousers.

Whatever one wanted to call them, the garments—so vibrant compared to our black physical-education pants, which were meant for female classmates' eyes alone—resem-bled beautiful, billowing hot-air balloons that could lift a girl off the ground. One pair matched the blue of the American flag swaying in the wind outside the shop. The other was as shocking red as the bicycle I straddled. The pants swelled wide enough that they would make the future owners appear to be wearing skirts—if the young ladies kept their legs pinned together.

But as everyone knows, bicycling ladies don't keep their legs pinned together.

The shop door opened with the soft tinkle of a bell, and out stepped Kate and her sister Agnes. Both of the Frye ladies had flushed faces and wore the American-flag-blue version of the bloomers. They headed toward two parked bicycles alongside the curb. Kate carried a little satchel tool bag meant for cyclists embarking upon longer rides.

"Oh." Agnes squinted at me through the glare of the sun behind the clouds. "Look, Kate, it's Olivia. Was that you I saw at the restaurant with two boys last night?"

"Um . . . well . . ."

"Are you looking for bloomers?" asked Kate.

"Just admiring them for now."

"You should ask your father to buy you a pair," said Agnes, putting her hands on her bloomers-clad hips. "Turkish trousers don't get caught in bicycle spokes like that dangerous skirt of yours. Besides"—she winked at me—"today's a day to celebrate if you're a Portland woman."

"It is?" I scratched my chin and tried to recall if we celebrated any famous Oregon women's birthdays . . . or if there *were* any famous Oregon women, for that matter. "Why?"

Agnes lifted her chin. "Because that *damned* editor"—she didn't even flinch when she swore like a sailor—"Mr. Harvey

Scott, finally found the courage to print a suffrage letter in the *Oregonian*."

"Language, Agnes," said Kate with a twinkle in her eye.

I gripped my handlebars and tried not to topple over with my bike. "I read that letter, but I—I—I . . . I don't . . ."

"I know, this historic occasion is enough to make a person speechless." Agnes mounted one of the awaiting bicycles—a canary-yellow beaut with a silver horn attached to the handlebars. "I don't know if you realize it, but Mr. Scott's sister is our local suffragist leader, Abigail Scott Duniway. Up until this morning, that stubborn old mule has refused to print anything pro-suffrage in his paper. We blame him for the failure of the referendum."

I shook my head. "But . . . I don't understand. Why do you think he printed this particular letter?"

Agnes shrugged. "Perhaps he thought it was a joke. The headline tried to poke fun at the letter writer, but it failed miserably. Mother, Kate, and I all received telephone calls from friends who read the letter and want to personally toast this mysterious 'Responsible Woman.'"

"Oh." Prickles of both fear and pride crawled across my skin like hundreds of sharp-clawed insects. *What have I done?* I thought. *What the blazes have I done?*

Kate straddled the other bicycle with a swing of her right leg and pumped her pedals into motion. "Well, I'll see you at school, Olivia."

"Ask your father to buy you bloomers," added Agnes,

following her sister into the street. "Tell him you're asking for trouble if you don't adapt to modern safety advances."

The young Frye ladies rode away, their bloomers flapping and billowing in the breeze like the sails of a schooner.

I know it was my eyes deceiving me again—a strange side effect of my awe over my letter's publication, perhaps—but halfway down the next block, the wheels of both the Frye girls' bikes lifted an inch off the ground, and the ladies careered down the street on the wind.

I FOUND FRANNIE PERFORMING HER FAVORITE BOOKSHOP duty: arranging new arrivals in Harrison's display windows. I rapped on the glass, gave her a quick wave, and hurried inside the store. The jangling bell above the shop door announced my entrance.

"Good morning, Livie." Frannie stood up straight with a book in each hand. "Is everything all right?"

I poked my head around shelves to check for eavesdroppers. "Where's the rest of your family?"

"Carl is out delivering a rare book, and the rest of the children are at Grandmother's. My parents took a riverboat ride to celebrate their anniversary."

"I thought they were celebrating with a fancy supper tomorrow."

"They are, but Papa wanted to treat Mother today, since she'll be cooking the meal tomorrow."

I sighed. "Such a good man. Such a beautiful man."

"I beg your pardon?"

I darted my head behind another bookshelf. "There aren't any customers here, either?"

"No, it's just me here at the moment. Why? What's happening? More hallucinations?"

I approached her and lowered my voice, just in case anyone should emerge from out of nowhere. "Frannie . . ."

"Yes?" she whispered back.

I swallowed and summoned a burst of courage. "I'm 'A Responsible Woman.'"

"Yes, of course you are, Livie." Her tone and nod were patronizing. "Except for when it comes to your relationship with Percy Acklen."

"No." I scowled. "I'm talking about the pro-suffrage letter printed in today's newspaper. I'm 'A Responsible Woman.'"

Her brown eyes swelled as round and bulgy as my largest prized marbles. She exhaled with the sound of a deflating bicycle tire. "Egad, Livie. Really and truly?"

"Did you read the letter?"

"Of course I read it. It was the talk of the breakfast table this morning, and every woman who's walked through the shop door has asked for publications by Abigail Scott Duniway or Susan B. Anthony."

"They have?"

She set down the books she was holding and pulled me toward General Literature. "We've sold every single copy of Duniway's women's rights novels in the past two hours. See the gap?" She pointed to an empty space toward the end of the *D* section. "People think she's the one who wrote the letter."

"Holy mackerel." I breathed a sigh that whistled through my teeth. "Maybe this will mean women won't give up the fight. Maybe there'll be another referendum."

"Maybe." She raised her eyebrows. "But does Percy know you're the one publicly making his father sound like a buffoon?"

"Oh. Percy." I growled and held my head between the tips of my fingers.

"The party didn't go well?" she asked.

"Tell me honestly, did he touch you?" I asked in return.

Frannie turned her face away and ran a knuckle across Charles Dickens's spines.

"Frannie?"

"Are you still in love with him?" she asked.

"Not anymore."

"Then, yes." She dropped her hand from the books. "I admit, he grabbed me last year when I was retying the lace of my shoe in the school stairwell. He came up the steps behind me, gave me a spank and a squeeze, and then continued up the stairs without even looking back. I hated myself the whole rest of the day."

"Oh, Frannie. Why didn't you tell me?"

"I was never sure if he simply confused me for someone else, or . . ." She fussed with the end of her braid. "I don't know. It happened a whole year ago. I hoped he might have matured a little."

"No." I folded my arms over my chest. "He's still a grabber . . . and a biter . . . and a terrible kisser."

"You kissed him?"

"He kissed me, and it was awful."

The shop door opened, and a woman and her twin daughters—girls no older than twelve or thirteen—strolled into the store.

"Do you have *The Awakening* by Kate Chopin?" asked the mother.

"I believe so," said Frannie in a professional tone. She reached up and took hold of a tan book with green grapevines laced around the title. "Yes, ma'am. Here it is."

I wandered to one of the front-window displays and thumbed through a Kipling book while Frannie proceeded with business. In addition to Chopin's novel, the woman and her daughters purchased *The Yellow Wallpaper* by Charlotte Perkins Gilman and *A Vindication of the Rights of Woman* by Mary Wollstonecraft. I hadn't read *The Yellow Wallpaper*, but I knew all three of the texts questioned the subordination of women.

After the sale, each of the customers retreated with a book wedged under her left arm, and before they reached the door, a transformation occurred. The little family brightened. Their faces, like those of Agnes and the other suffragists at the restaurant, shone with some sort of internal brilliance, and their hair—fluffed and pinned beneath a small straw hat in the case of the mother, long braids for the daughters— became the bold yellowish orange of firelight.

The door shut behind them, and the little bell punctuated their exit with a jingle. The illusion ended.

"You see what I mean?" asked Frannie, coming toward me. "You stirred up something remarkable with that letter. What does your father think?"

"He doesn't know I wrote it."

"If he finds out . . . do you think . . . what about the hypnosis?"

"I wrote that letter after he mandated that hypnotism *cure*"—I spat out that last word—"so, clearly, it did nothing but push me into trying things I never would have dared before."

"You're not saying you like being hypnotized, are you?"

"No! It's just . . . Look here . . ." I squatted down and fished around in my right shoe. Henry's theater tickets, along with some quarters I'd brought in case I got hungry, were hidden between the stiff leather and my thick stocking. "I've seen Henry—"

"I thought it was *On-ree*."

"His real name is Henry Rhodes, and he gave me these tickets so we could stay in contact with each other." I pulled out the tickets and stood upright. "I begged him to end the hypnosis, but he needs my father's money for his sister. She has a tumor that requires surgery. It's cancerous."

Frannie took the tickets from my hand and, with her lips pursed, read them over.

"He can't change me back," I continued, "until my father gives him his full payment on Tuesday. That's when he'll be taking his sister to San Francisco for her surgery."

"He's about to leave town?"

"In three more days."

"Are you still seeing strange sights?"

"Yes." I grabbed for the tickets, but Frannie hid them behind her back. "Frannie?" I tugged on her elbow. "Give those back."

"You're telling me"—she swung her arm away and inched backward—"you're going to keep viewing your father as a vampire, and doing whatever other horrible things that hypnotist is making you do, for three more days?"

"I've got no other choice. That poor girl might die if she doesn't undergo her surgery. The cancer's in her bosom."

"How do you know he's not making up her illness?"

"Don't be mean."

"How do you know, Livie?"

"I trust him."

She stopped and thrust the tickets at me. "Fine. Trust a traveling, mind-altering showman."

"There's no need to get upset." I took the tickets from her.

"I bet he smells terrible, too."

"Frannie!"

"I'm just worried about you. Wait . . ." She squinted at the backside of the tickets and snatched them straight back out of my hand. "What's this?"

"What?"

"This note. 'Come to the side door of the theater after the show—'"

I grabbed the papers so hard, one of them ripped. "Never mind what that says."

"You're going to meet him in private?"

"I don't know." I slunk toward the exit. "I'm not sure what to do about any of this, but I know whom to trust and whom to avoid, so stop frowning at me like I'm an idiot."

"I didn't say you were an idiot, Livie."

"But you're looking at me as if I am one." I turned and pushed open the door.

"Wait! Livie . . ."

The door slammed shut behind me before she could say another word.

I climbed aboard my bicycle and pedaled away, toward the Metropolitan.

CHAPTER FIFTEEN

# ALL IS NOT WELL

enry's matinee performance wasn't scheduled to start until one thirty in the afternoon. To bide the time, I stopped for a ham sandwich across the street in a smoky café with a pressed-tin ceiling and theater posters hanging from knotty-pine walls.

Halfway through my meal, one of the other diners plopped himself across from me in my booth.

"What's a good little girl like you doing all by herself in the city?" he asked, and when I raised my face, I found Sunken-

Eyed John from Sadie's party, grinning at me. "Does Percy know you're not a respectable woman?"

I set the second half of my sandwich aside on the bone-colored plate. "I don't care what Percy does or doesn't think of me."

"Is that so?"

"Yes. I am not his sweetheart."

"Well, that's unfortunate for him." He leaned forward on his elbows, his breath stinking of cheese and ale. "I learned a little secret about you."

I knitted my eyebrows together. "What secret?"

"Well . . ." He ran his tongue along the inside of his cheek. "I told my father about your odd behavior with that hypnotist last night, and he said he knew who you were. Your father used to work on his teeth—before last Wednesday."

My skin went cold. "Who is your father?"

"John Underhill Sr., owner of the city's largest shipping firm. My mother is the president of the Oregon Association Opposed to Women's Suffrage—or whatever the devil that thing's called."

"Oh." My voice cracked with too much of a quaver for the heroine of the morning's newspaper.

A smirk inched up the side of John's face. "Your daddy telephoned my father to brag about a hypnotism cure. It sounds as if Monsieur Reverie has you on the end of a leash, performing tricks like a trained little monkey."

"Why did my father tell him that?"

"I just said, to brag." He leaned back with a broad smile and spread his arms across the upper ridge of his side of the booth. "So, you say you're not Percy's girl anymore?"

"No, I'm not."

"Are you a lesbian?"

"A what?"

"Are you in love with women, not men?"

"No, I—"

"Why don't you come home with me right now"—he slid his shoe across the floorboards and wedged it between my feet—"and I'll thrust the masculinity straight out of you myself. I'll break you like the wild filly you are."

Without even thinking, I raised my right foot and stomped John's toes with my heel.

"Ouch! Christ!"

I tried to stand up with some semblance of dignity, but I banged my knee on the table, which sent my water spilling into the cretin's lap.

He jumped up. "Hey! You little—"

"All is well."

"Oh, God, not that again."

"All is well." I grabbed my hat and pushed my way through a crowd of other young men piling into the restaurant with hunger shining in their eyes and growling in their bellies. Clouds of tobacco smoke and spiced colognes blew in my face, telling me, *You don't belong here . . .*

"Hey, watch where you're going, girlie," cried one of the

men, grabbing my elbow and smiling as if I were part of a bawdy joke.

I shoved his scratchy tweed arm aside and made my way past all the plaid coats and derby hats and waxed mustaches, out into the sweet fresh air.

A MIDDLE-AGED COUPLE WITH ACROBATIC TOY POODLES opened Henry's show, and their yippy little dogs and gaudy sequined costumes sucked every breath of enchantment from the Metropolitan Theater. I could now see that the stage floor was streaked in sawdust and filthy trails of footprints, and the pipe organ appeared shorter and duller than the tower of copper and beauty from Genevieve's ethereal rendition of "Danse Macabre." *Cheap* was the first word that came to mind when I sat in the sparse audience that Saturday afternoon. Cheap. Gaudy. Disappointing. It wasn't even the hypnosis showing me the way the theater truly was. All it took to sour my belief in magic was a lack of Halloween glamour and that disgusting encounter with Sunken-Eyed John.

The poodle couple took their bows to overly generous applause, and after they pranced off to the wings, the organist with the pumpkin-colored hair swaggered across the stage without any special introduction or fanfare. She plunked down on the bench in front of the pipe organ and embarked upon a slow and lumbering rendition of "Sleep, Little Rosebud"—not even "Danse Macabre."

I couldn't stand sitting there, subjected to her ruckus, and

I couldn't bear the thought of Henry's appearance in the show looking fake and lusterless—not when I required him to possess the power to set my world right. I got to my feet and fled to the lobby, where I asked a gray-whiskered gentleman in the box office for a piece of paper and a pen.

At the counter next to the ticket window, while the organ music plodded along in the background, I scribbled down my frustrations on an ivory sheet of theater letterhead.

*Dear Henry,*

*I am writing down my thoughts for you, because yelling at you will only make me say that "All is well," and I am tired of that damnable phrase spouting from my lips. I am not sure if I can last three more days. That meaningless sentence you have forced me to say is turning me weak and putting me in danger.*

*I just came across that ogre of a boy, John, from Sadie's party, and he got uncomfortably flirtatious with me—but all I could say was "All is well." Someone else left unwanted bite marks on my neck last night (please do not ask why or mention this indiscretion to anyone), and I am sure you can guess which three words shot from my mouth when I tried to shout, "Stop!" I may be able to tolerate my strange visions until Tuesday evening, but I fear I will be allowing myself to become the victim of something even more heinous if my shouts of anger and distress continue to be silenced.*

*I know you love your sister dearly and fear for her health. I believe your story about her tumor to be true and not a ruse to keep me from complaining about this "cure" of yours. Yet you must imagine what her world would be like if she could never complain about her discomfort or cry out to protect herself. You would never wish such a dangerous fate upon her, would you? If not, then please take pity on me and allow me to stop saying that all is well.*

*Let me speak my anger again—please! I swear upon my grandparents' graves I will hide from my father my ability to say what I mean. You must change me today. Do not leave me like this.*

*All is NOT well.*

I waited with my letter on the cement steps leading up to the theater's side entrance, ten yards down from the streetcar tracks. The gray clouds continued to do nothing more than hang over the city, teasing of rain but refusing to spit a single drop. I stretched out my legs on the stairs and enjoyed a small sip of sunlight that managed to steal across the sidewalk. My bicycle rested against the rails beside me—my horse awaiting the getaway.

One of the city's electric-powered streetcars whirred to a stop down the way, its brakes squeaking in the damp air, the wheels clenching against the tracks. Only its rounded front end was visible from where I sat, but I assumed departing theatergoers were climbing aboard around the bend.

Behind me, the theater door swung open, and the substitute organist exited. She tramped down the stairs with a gold and green carpetbag hanging over her left arm, and she screwed up her lips when she saw me sitting there, perhaps remembering me from the day before, when I had kept Henry from rehearsing. Her newtlike eyes studied me, as if she were evaluating an apple for bruises and wormholes, finding more bad spots than good.

The wind shifted—or maybe it was just my brain switching directions. In any case, the organist tipped her head a certain way, and her orange hair careened down to her waist in plump curls. Her face slimmed and softened with youth. The carpetbag transformed into a German hurdy-gurdy instrument with strings and a crank, and her frumpy brown dress blossomed into a ruffled blue slip of a gown, like the shocking costumes of lady entertainers in North End saloons.

Without a word, her regular fussy, sharp-eyed looks reappeared, and she wandered around the corner, toward the streetcar. I stared at the place where she had vanished, my mouth hanging open, for I felt I'd just encountered a person much like my mother—a beautiful entertainer trapped in the body of an aging woman. Not an easy place to be, I'm sure. I wondered if my mother also shot bitter glares and unkind words at the young theater people around her.

The door opened again, and I got to my feet when I saw Henry stepping outside in the dark coat from his Halloween performance. He wore his black square-crown hat pulled down over his eyes, as if to conceal his identity, and he chewed on something crunchy that sounded like hard candy.

"Henry?" I asked, and I gripped both the rail and the letter.

He looked up, revealing familiar blue eyes that brightened at the sight of me.

"Olivia, *c'est toi*." He galloped down the stairs until he landed in front of me, smelling of peppermint. "You came."

I slammed my letter against his chest.

He gulped down the last of his candy. "What's this?"

"Just read it. Please."

He unfolded the letter.

I chewed my bottom lip and watched his eyes shift back and forth over my writing. The longer he read, the more his brow puckered in a frown.

He blew out a sigh that rustled his hair and lowered the letter to his side. "Did Percy really bite you?" he asked in the American version of his voice.

"Why do you have two accents?"

"I asked my question first."

Before I could gather enough breath and courage to answer, the pack of squeaky show poodles exited the side door, their exhausted-eyed owners following in a web of leather leashes. Henry and I both stepped away from the theater, and I grabbed my bicycle by the handlebars. Side by side, we headed toward Third Street with the barking ruckus trailing behind us.

"I'd like to see your neck," he said over the commotion of the dogs and the hum of the streetcar breezing off in the opposite direction.

"Are you off your rocker? I'm not going to expose my neck in public." I held fast to my bike, which I walked by my side up Third.

The streetcar's bell clanged at an intersection in the distance, and the poodles yipped to the south while we trekked north. Our section of Third lay empty at the moment, aside from Henry and me.

"Why did he bite you?" he asked. "Was it a romantic bite?"

"No." I blushed with such intensity that my eyes watered. "I'm . . ." I fanned my face with my hand. "I'm trying with all my might not to say that all is well, so please don't ask any more questions about it. The point is, I couldn't tell him no when I was alone with him in the buggy last night."

Henry stopped. "Did he make you do anything else?"

I stopped, too. "As in what?"

"As in . . . um . . ." He nodded as if I should know what he was thinking, his face pinking up. "Hasn't anyone ever told you about . . . ?"

"I don't . . . he didn't . . ." I pulled at my collar and cringed at the memory of one of Mother's detailed letters that instructed how to avoid becoming in the family way. "I'm not sure if you mean . . ."

"Um"—he scratched his cheek—"never mind. Were you able to get away from him after he bit you?"

"Yes. I pushed him off me twice, and both times his head whacked the top of the buggy."

I resumed walking my bicycle.

Henry stayed behind for a moment, but when I glanced over my shoulder, he grinned and caught up.

"*Mon Dieu*, Olivia. You're much stronger than you look. I took you to be a frightened little bird when you came up on the stage with me on Halloween."

"Now, there you sound French again. Are you French or American?"

"My mother was born in Paris and grew up in Montreal. My father was from Toronto. My uncle took guardianship over us in Cleveland."

"And French sounds more mysterious and exotic than a Cleveland accent?"

"*Oui.*" He smiled and slipped his hands into his pockets. "Uncle Lewis asked me to sound French whenever I appeared on the stage. I was always good at imitating my mother's accent, and I speak both languages fluently."

"Hmm." I stole a glance at him. My fingers gripped the handlebars.

I summoned a vision of my own accord.

Large rips formed in the underarm seams of his coat and revealed glimpses of a striped shirt underneath. His red vest—the same dazzling garment from Halloween night—drained to the color of underripe cherries, and the black of his suit faded to gray. On his head, his felt hat deflated until it looked battered and squished and as well traveled as an old railroad car. His eyes turned puffy and red.

I shifted my attention to the sidewalk ahead.

"You don't look like the mesmerizing Henri Reverie any-more," I said. "Not when I get a good look at you."

"I don't?" He turned his face toward me. "What do I look like, then?"

"Tired. Desperate. A little like a hobo."

He responded with a weary smile. "That's exactly what I am."

The commotion of the city—the wagons, the workers, the Canada geese honking across the sky toward the Willamette River—filled my ears again. The vision passed.

Henry, back in his regular, intact clothing, hopped into the street at the corner and waved for me to follow. "Come along. Genevieve is in here."

I followed him across the intersection, my bicycle chain spinning as I hustled to avoid a horse-drawn milk cart jangling our way.

On the other side of the street, Henry stopped in front of the four-story Hotel Vernon, which had fuzzy strips of bright green moss growing between the walls' red bricks. I saw two boarded-up windows on the third floor, and a round hole that could have been made by a bullet gaped from a piece of glass on the second story.

I kept hold of my bicycle and craned my neck to look up at the building. "Is this where she is?"

"Yes."

"I can't go into a hotel with you."

"Genevieve isn't feeling well enough to come outside."

"If any of my father's patients see me—"

"Go in ahead of me." He nodded toward the entrance. "We're in room twenty-five on the second floor."

"What about my bicycle? If he passes by, Father might recognize it."

"Here . . ." He took hold of the handlebars and the frame. "I'll take it inside for you and ask if we can park it in the lobby. Go on up and wait by the door to the room. I'll be there soon."

I scanned both sides of the street, and when I didn't see anyone I recognized, I ducked inside the hotel. A sign at the back of the lobby said STAIRWAY, so I made a beeline toward it, passing Grecian pillars, plush armchairs, and emerald-green rugs laid over a diamond-tiled floor. Despite the attempts at finery, a worn and decaying look—and odor—clung to every article in the lobby, including the customers. A woman in a beaver-fur stole sank back in an armchair, and her clothes blended in with the moss-green upholstery, as if she and the chair were becoming one. A hotel clerk with a devilish Van-dyke beard was belittling two well-dressed black men who were trying to check in at the front—and I could have sworn I saw the polished counter straight through the guests' striped trousers and coats.

I headed up to the second floor, my heart skipping, and tried to ignore the stink of the place and the nervous twisting of my stomach. Henry's voice echoed down below, asking the clerk if he could park my bicycle in the lobby, his voice smooth and as exquisitely French as fine wine. Less than two minutes later, he was upstairs, coming toward me down the hallway, tugging a gold key out of his coat pocket, while I stood in front of the closed door of room twenty-five.

He moved to insert the key into the lock, but before he could click the metal into place, I blurted out, "Let me see your teeth first."

Henry's hand stopped in midair. "Pardon?"

"Show me your teeth."

"Why? Because you're a dentist's daughter?"

"No, because I want to make sure I can trust you."

I lifted my hand toward his face, but he flinched and shrank back against the gold wallpaper.

"I'm not a vampire, Olivia."

I stepped closer, which made him blink and flinch again.

"Then why are you acting so suspiciously?" I asked.

"Because . . ."

"Because what?"

"I'm worried I'll—" He sidestepped away from me, but I pinned his arm to the wall, lifted his lip past his gums, and wished to see the truth in his teeth.

Normal.

Harmless.

Clean.

His spotless incisors, canines, bicuspids, and molars were actually quite beautiful, perhaps even brushed on a regular basis. His breath still carried the Christmassy scent of his peppermint candy, and his lip felt as soft as a petal against my thumb. Our eyes met, and I dropped my hand from his mouth.

"What were you going to say you were worried about?" I asked in a squeak of a voice while retreating two feet backward.

"I was worried that . . ." He removed his hat and ran his fingers through his hair. "I'm sure there's part of me you still won't be able to trust."

My heart sank. "You're not going to fix me, are you?"

"Come meet Genevieve. We'll discuss what we're going to do after you've spoken to her."

"Of course I'm going to agree to go along with everything when I see your sister."

"Olivia . . ." His voice softened. He took my hand. "Please don't get upset. I'll consider altering the hypnosis if I can figure out a way to keep everyone safe."

"You've got to swear you won't leave me like this." I gripped his fingers. "Swear to me you won't run away to San Francisco without helping me."

"If you help Genevieve, I swear upon my life I'll help you."

A hot tear escaped my left eye before I knew it was even coming.

"I promise, Olivia." He squeezed my hand. "I won't leave you like this. We're partners, not enemies. *Oui?*"

I nodded and wiped my cheek with the back of my hand, tasting salt on my lips. "Yes. *Oui.* Partners."

He turned the key in the lock and led me into a small room

with amber curtains pulled back to expose the dwindling late-afternoon sun. The flowery burgundy paper peeling off the walls soaked up most of the light, but the place wasn't quite the woeful retreat of a dying girl I was expecting. A twin bed, a lime-green sofa made up as a second bed, and an elegant ivory washbasin lent the room a homelike atmosphere. The smell of lilac soap, not fever, sweetened the air.

Something on the far corner of the bed caught my attention: a short blink of candlelight that faded the second after I spotted it, as if someone had snuffed out a flame. I tensed, for I saw a pair of eyes watching from the darkness.

Before I could ask Henry what I'd just seen, the light brightened again, illuminating the face of a girl. A moment later, it flickered away, and the bed lay empty.

"Olivia, this is my sister, Genevieve." Henry came around my side and walked toward the waxing and waning figure on the sheets. "Genevieve, I present to you Olivia Mead."

I couldn't move. One moment, she was clear and vibrant—a golden-haired girl in a white nightgown, crawling toward me across the covers—the next, she was sputtering out, and the bed looked abandoned, save for the indentations of hands and knees on the mattress.

"What's wrong?" asked Henry, his face paling. "What does she look like?"

I gave a shiver. "I see things the way they are, but I can't predict the future."

"What does she look like?" he asked again, his voice taking on a tinny phonograph quality as his sister consumed my attention.

I swallowed. "A candle flame that can't decide if it has the strength to keep burning." I shifted my eyes away from her.

Henry's bottom lip trembled. His arms hung by his sides like two useless extensions of his body. I felt compelled to hug him, but Genevieve spoke before I gathered the courage to do so.

"Henry told me what he was paid to do, Miss Mead," she said. "Please come sit by me so I may talk to you. Don't be afraid to look at me."

I turned and ventured over to the bed while clutching the sides of my skirt. Genevieve continued to flicker and fade, as if she were sitting in a blackened room, illuminated every few seconds by a soundless flash of lightning. My brain went dizzy and fuzzy from watching her come and go like that, and I half expected crashes of thunder to rumble across the walls and make sense of the phenomenon—yet none ever arrived. I sat beside her and steadied my breathing.

"Henry told me you're not allowed to speak your anger anymore," she said during a moment of illumination that revealed the concerned arc of her eyebrows, "and you can see people's true selves, sometimes in frightening forms."

I nodded, still speechless. I discovered that blinking a few times in a row almost made her stay in place. "Are you in pain, Genevieve?" I asked her.

"No." She placed her hand over her upper chest. "The

tumor is simply something I know shouldn't be there, which, I admit, does make me feel a little sick. And tired."

"I'm so sorry."

"And what about you?" she asked, scooting closer with a rustle of sheets. "Are you staying safe?"

"I'm healthy, so I can't complain."

"No, be honest with me. Are you suffering because of Henry's hypnosis?"

"Well . . ." I averted my eyes from hers again, choosing to gaze instead at the wrinkles in my black skirt and the spots of dirt flecked across the hem. "I've just asked him to alter the part about . . ." I shook my head and sighed. "I can wait, Genevieve. It's just three more days. You're a little bit younger than me, aren't you?"

"I'm almost sixteen."

"Sixteen?" I clasped my hand over my eyes. "No, I'll just keep saying that all is well."

"You hinted you weren't safe," she said. "What's happened to you?"

"Someone bit her," said Henry.

Genevieve gasped. "Bit her? Why?"

"It was the boy—the cocky one—who escorted her to that party last night." Henry sank down on the sofa with an uncomfortable sigh. "That type of behavior happens sometimes . . . when, um, *gentlemen* get . . . romantic."

"I assure you, I'm not a loose girl," I said to Genevieve. "I tried to tell Percy to stop, but all I could say was—"

"'All is well,'" Henry finished for me.

Genevieve flickered into view with greater wattage. "Where did he bite you?"

"On my neck."

"Like Dracula?" she asked.

I smiled. "You've read *Dracula*?"

"Of course. It was *magnifique*."

"When did you read it?" asked Henry.

"I borrowed it from the library last year, when you were so busy reading your hypnotism books and fussing over your hair for the girls." She brightened even further, remaining solid and steady for seconds at a time. "How bad of a bite was it, Miss Mead?"

I squirmed and didn't answer.

She shifted her legs over the side of the bed. "Please show me."

I looked to Henry, who pursed his lips as if he didn't know what to say.

"Oh, I don't know about that," I said. "It's an awfully embarrassing thing to share . . ."

"No need to be embarrassed," said Henry. "If I'm an honest hypnotist, which I like to think I am, I should see how much harm I've caused."

I sipped two calming breaths through my lips—*in, out, breathe, deeper*—and lifted my hand to the topmost pearl. Henry stood up from the sofa and trod toward me with hesitant footsteps, making my fingers shake and slide around on the pearl's slick surface before I could twist the clasp loose from the buttonhole. I undid the second button, which allowed the air in the room to cool the skin of my throat, and I exhaled, as if I'd just freed my neck from the embrace of a noose.

The blouse remained taut over the lower half of my neck. I unbuttoned the third clasp and pulled the plaid wool aside to expose my bare skin.

Genevieve whimpered and sputtered out of view. Henry's eyes widened. He came closer and peeled the fabric farther down.

"Is that . . . is it . . ." I attempted to smile away my mortification. "Is that the normal look of a bite from a gentleman who's feeling romantic?"

Henry tucked my blouse back over my skin. "I don't think romance had anything to do with that mark."

"Perhaps . . ." Genevieve surged back into light. "You could maybe consider hypnotizing her father into paying your fee, eh? Then you could immediately end her hypnosis and—"

"What? Genevieve!" Henry froze. "You know full well I can't hypnotize people into giving me money."

"But—"

"Look what happened to Uncle Lewis when he tried that sort of thing. What good would I be to you if I'm lying in some gutter, bleeding to death?"

"But that was all because of a gambling debt," said Genevieve. "This is different."

"Something would go wrong, and I'd end up either in jail or in a coffin." Henry tottered over to the window and scratched his forehead. "I don't know what to do, Olivia. We really can't change any part of the hypnosis before your father sees satisfying results."

"But he's already seen results," I said. "He knows I can't get angry with him. What more proof is he waiting for?"

Henry rubbed his face, but he did not answer.

"What is it?" I rose from the bed. "What do you know, Henry?"

He dropped his hands to his sides and faced me. "I have an appointment to go to your house in an hour. He's asked me to make adjustments to the hypnosis."

"What? More mind control?"

"He wants to show you off to members of some sort of organization—the Association of something or other."

My mouth went dry. "The Oregon Association Opposed to the Extension of Suffrage to Women."

"That's the one." Henry leaned his shoulder blades against the window. "He wants to demonstrate your treatment to some woman who's in charge of the association."

*Oh, Lord. Sunken-Eyed John's mother.*

"What else did he say?" I asked with my hands balled into fists.

"He mentioned it's the millionaires' wives who are the strongest anti-suffrage voices, and he's terrified of losing his rich customers if these powerful women think you're a suffragist. If he can convince this lady that I've removed your 'unfeminine' beliefs, he'll be invited back to her election-night party, where I'm to demonstrate to an entire crowd that suffragists can be cured."

I stepped back, my breath tight in my lungs. "Am I the suffragist you'll be curing in front of everyone?"

"You'll be there," he said with a grim nod, "but you might not be much of a suffragist by then."

I dropped back down onto the bed with a force that jarred my neck.

Genevieve's hand nestled against mine. "Surely we can get money some other way."

"After both the theater and Dr. Mead pay me Tuesday night," said Henry, "we'll only be two dollars short of the rest of the surgeon's fee. Just two measly dollars! How else am I supposed to legally find that sort of money? Before it's too late for you?"

I sniffed back tears and buttoned up my blouse, nearly forgetting I had left my neck exposed and cold.

"Olivia." Henry stepped toward me on the hard soles of his shoes. He cupped a warm hand over my shoulder. "Please, look up at me."

I did as he asked, my teeth clenched, my every muscle tense and on the defensive.

His eyes locked on to mine. The force of his skills shattered all my barriers. "Close your eyes. Think of nothing but sleep."

I did exactly that, for sleep swept its numbing, dark cloak

over my face and chest and legs—down to the smallest of my toes.

"Relax. Melt down, melt down, until all you hear is the sound of my voice. Calm your breathing."

My lungs relaxed, along with the rest of me.

"Yes . . . that's good. Very good. Let your breathing grow slower. And slower. And slower. Melt all the way down until you feel the utter bliss of deep relaxation."

I collapsed into a heap at the bottom of a cozy black box.

"Now," he said near my ear, "imagine a lamp switching on and finding the two of us seated in the safest room you can imagine."

Gaslight whispered to life, and Henry and I were sitting together at Frannie's kitchen table. A vegetable soup bubbled on the stove, and the Harrisons' bright yellow wallpaper, as well as the children's pinned-up drawings and poetry, surrounded us. Henry reached across Mrs. Harrison's home-embroidered tablecloth and took my hand.

"You no longer need to say that all is well when you are angry." He bent his face toward mine. "You are free to speak your mind, but you will do so with caution around your father. For now, in front of him, you will limit your volatile words only to moments when someone is about to get hurt. Do you understand?"

I nodded.

"Good. You will keep seeing the world the way it truly is so that you may remain alert for danger, but I will give your mind entirely back to you after the election-night show. For it will be just a show, Olivia. This is all merely a temporary spectacle to make your father happy." He squeezed my hand and lifted his head. "Now, I will count to ten, and you will awaken and return to your home, where I will see you in less than an hour—*ma partenaire.*" He squeezed again. "My partner."

"My only doubt was as to whether any dream could be more terrible than the unnatural, horrible net of gloom and mystery which seemed closing around me."

—BRAM STOKER, *Dracula*, 1897

# CHAPTER SIXTEEN

# THE WHITEHEAD GAG

The hour before Henry's arrival at our house moved with the excruciating slowness of twelve hours. I passed the minutes on the bench in front of my late grandmother's high-backed Beckwith parlor organ. My song of choice: "Evening Prayer" from *Hansel and Gretel.* My fingers lacked Genevieve's skill, but, oh, what a glorious relief when I thrust my troubles into the black and white keys and pumped my anxieties into the foot pedals.

I must have played the song at least five times in a row; I lost track after the second or third round. Halfway through the fifth or sixth go, someone knocked on the front door. My fingers slipped, and the lowest keys belched a deep grumble.

Gerda passed the parlor's entryway on her way to the front door.

"I'll get that, Gerda," said Father from down the hall.

Gerda stopped and tightened her apron strings. "Are you certain, sir?"

"Yes." Father walked into view. "Return to the kitchen. Immediately."

"Yes, sir." Gerda's shoulders slumped, and for a hiccup of a moment, before she bustled back to the kitchen, the poor woman faded before my eyes. Our brown wallpaper behind her bled through her wavering wisp of a body. Her footsteps retreated to the back of the house.

I rose up from the organ bench and approached the hall, my pulse ticking in the side of my neck. Father opened the door, revealing Henry on our front porch, his short black hat in hand.

"Come in, Mr. Reverie." Father pulled the door farther open and clapped the hypnotist on the back as he made his way across the threshold. "Thank you for coming out to my house this afternoon. I know you must be a busy lad."

Henry shrugged. "It is no trouble, Monsieur Mead. I am happy to help if you feel the cure is not to your satisfaction." The French accent was back in place.

Father shut the door and puffed up his chest. "As I said when I telephoned, I require more results." He took Henry's hat from his hand and plunked it on one of our brass wall hooks. "Come to my office for a moment and—"

"Father, I've learned something tragic about Mr. Reverie," I said, and I clasped my hands behind my back to hide the terrible trembling that results when one deviates from the plans of a tyrant.

Father lifted an eyebrow. "'Tragic'? That's an awfully dramatic word, Olivia."

"H-h-his sister . . ." I swallowed and averted my gaze from Henry's startled eyes and gaping mouth. "She requires a surgeon to remove a tumor. It's cancerous. Perhaps you know a local physician who could help her as soon as possible."

Father cocked his head at Henry. "Is this true?"

"I really wish it weren't, sir, but . . . she is sick."

"I'm terribly sorry to hear that." Father tugged at his beard and seemed to search his brain for the name of someone who could help. His eyes softened. The quest for Genevieve's well-being nudged aside his urgency to fix me. I held my breath and prayed this version of Father would remain with us.

"Well," he said, "I don't believe I know any cancer surgeons, unless you're discussing an oral tumor . . ."

"No, it's not that," said Henry. "I appreciate you even considering the matter, but you don't need to—"

"Wait a moment." Father turned abruptly toward me. "How do you know this about his sister?" He placed his hand on Henry's shoulder—not in a firm way, but enough to make my neck sweat beneath my collar.

"I b-b-beg your pardon?" I asked.

"I said, how did you suddenly find out he has a sick sister?" Father squeezed down on Henry, who seemed to shrink an inch. "Mr. Reverie didn't once mention her during your treatment in my office. I doubt he'd announce something so private at his Halloween performance."

"There was a . . ." *Oh, hell.* I hadn't concocted an excuse for that particular detail. *Damn! Damn, damn, damn!*

Father's eyes narrowed. "Have you two spoken with each other since the hypnotism on Thursday?"

"No, sir," said Henry.

"N-n-no, sir," I agreed. "I just—"

"How did you become privy to his family troubles, then, Olivia? Why on earth do you have the intimate details of this stranger's personal life?"

"Father . . . please, don't get upset. The point is, his sister needs help, and I thought—"

Father grabbed Henry's wrist. "Come with me. Do not say a word— No!" He raised a finger with a nail sharp and black. His eyes burned scarlet, and his cheeks sank into the skull of his graying face. "Don't even open your mouth and think of hypnotizing me into giving you extra money."

"I'm not asking for extra money, sir." Henry pulled back and tried to wrench his arm out of Father's grip. "I didn't ask her to say anything about my sister—I swear to God!"

"That's true!" I said. "He didn't ask that at all."

"Quiet! Both of you!"

An awful buzzing rang in my ears. I pushed my hands over them and let out a cry of shock as Father paled even further and sprouted fur on the backs of his hands—part wolf, part corpse, part red-eyed demon.

"If you want me to pay you for your services, boy"—he yanked Henry down the hallway, toward his home office, which he used for drinking and for nighttime emergency treatments—"then shut your damned mouth."

Henry's feet skidded and tripped across the rugs and the floorboards.

"Don't hurt him!" I chased after them. "Please—I didn't mean any harm. I just thought you should know in case you could help . . ." I followed them into the office and braced my hands on the door frame. "His sister isn't even yet sixteen. What would you do if I were the one dying of cancer?"

"You're not dying of cancer, Olivia. Don't be so melodramatic," said Father, but he was no longer anything like my actual father. A clawed devil with spiked teeth and a sharp, hairy chin slapped Henry down into the office's wooden dental chair and buckled his left wrist to an armrest.

"Let me go!" Henry pushed at the creature with his free hand, but Father managed to pin down and shackle his other wrist, too.

"Stop!" I rubbed my eyes, but Father refused to look normal. "Are you really forcing him into that chair? Am I really seeing this?"

"I've offered you a large sum of money, Mr. Reverie." With

one hand planted on Henry's chest, not far from his throat, the horrific version of the man with whom I lived squeaked open a cabinet door. On the shelves gleamed his home collection of dental tools—forceps, clockwork drills, pelicans, chisels, tooth keys. He pulled out a Whitehead gag, a beastly contraption that resembled a bear trap with leather straps. "If you truly do have a sick sister, then I assume more than anything that you'd like me to pay you that money."

"Father! Let him out of that chair!"

"Yes, sir, b-b-but . . ." Henry bent his legs and hovered over the seat, not quite landing his posterior on it. His knees wobbled everywhere, while his wrists stayed strapped to the wood.

"Relax." Father pushed on his knees. "Sit back." He shoved him down by his collarbone, which made Henry's feet pop up on the footrest. "There's no need to panic. I'm just going to fit this gag into your mouth"—he shoved the metal trap between Henry's lips with terrible scraping sounds—"to make sure you aren't verbally manipulating my mind while I give my instructions to you." He yanked the straps around Henry's head, stretching his jaw both vertically and horizontally until Henry groaned in wide-eyed terror.

"Stop it!" I pulled on Father's shoulder and arm. "This is terrible. What type of monster have you become? Just look at yourself."

Father elbowed me away. "Get out of here, Olivia. You're not supposed to be able to argue with me."

"But—"

"Silence!" He pushed me so hard, I banged my lower back against his desk. "Tell me the God's honest truth," he said over Henry, "have you and my daughter spoken since Thursday's hypnosis?"

Henry panted and glanced my way. I nodded, so Henry did the same. He managed a "Yes" that sounded like gargling.

"Is she trying to persuade you to reverse the hypnosis?" asked Father.

Henry nodded again.

Father tipped the dental chair back, raising Henry's feet as high as his hips. "My Olivia isn't the greatest beauty in the world, I admit, but she can break your heart a little, can't she?"

Henry's chest contracted with each shallow breath.

"But, despite feminine wiles," said Father, "we gentlemen must be strong. We must protect the women from their own foolishness. They're fragile and ignorant and need our constant care. I think, if you stuck by my side and ignored my daughter's passionate pleas"—he bent down close to Henry's face with bared yellowed fangs that hung down to his chin—"we could show the world that hypnosis is the key to keeping these modern young women in their proper places. No man will lose a sweet loved one ever again."

"Father"—I held my throbbing head—"you look disgusting."

"Get out of this office, Olivia."

"Take that barbaric thing out of Mr. Reverie's mouth."

"I said, get out!" Father grabbed me by both arms and steered me toward the door.

"No, don't hurt him." I thrust out my foot to try to catch it on the door frame. "Please! Don't hurt either of us."

Father unhooked me from the doorway and pushed me out into the hall. The door slammed shut in my face, and the lock latched.

"Father!" I slammed my fists against the door. "Please, open up!"

"Go wait in the parlor," he called through the wood. "And if you're not sitting there patiently when we both come out, Mr. Reverie will never see a cent of my hard-earned money. You're supposed to be tamed, for God's sake. I was led to believe you were cured. What happened to you saying that all is well?"

I backed away, and the whisper of the gas feeding into the lamps merged with the wheezing of my lungs.

"Is everything all right, Miss Mead?" asked a small voice behind me.

Down the hall, Gerda's blue eyes peeked out from the kitchen doorway.

"If you can find a position with a kinder employer," I told her, "I recommend doing so as quickly as possible."

I turned and staggered into the parlor and clutched my side, which cramped like the dickens from breathing too fast.

. . . . .

THE OFFICE DOOR OPENED WITH A LOW CLICK.

I stood up from my slumped position on our mustard-yellow settee and endured each approaching footstep as if someone were digging his heels into my heart.

Father came into view from around the bend, and as hard as I blinked, I couldn't stop seeing him as a monster—I simply couldn't. Behind him emerged Henry, rubbing his red wrists, his lips bleeding.

"What did you do?" I asked.

"Silence, Olivia." Father held up a hand with the long, rotten nails. "I've said this before," he said through his teeth, "and I'll say it again: This is all for your own good. You do not need to be burdened with impossible dreams."

I wrapped my arms around myself and stared at Henry's bleeding mouth.

*Genevieve,* I reminded myself. *She's waiting for him in that moldering hotel room.*

"Fine." I swallowed and rocked myself for comfort. "Hypnotize me, Mr. Reverie. Let's get it over with."

Henry stepped forward. "Do not be afraid," he said in a French-tinged voice that possessed a sharp edge.

He held out his hand to mine, and I saw that his nails were as black and hooked as Father's. He heaved a sigh that revealed a pair of canine teeth fierce enough to sever his own tongue.

I pulled my hand away, but his fingers shot out and grabbed

my wrist. He jerked my arm toward him and plunged me into darkness with the firm command, "Sleep!"

"WHEN YOU AWAKEN, YOU WILL HAVE NO MEMORY OF this session."

Henry counted from one to ten in a dreamy rhythm that reminded me of skipping rope with my braids jumping on my shoulders, and then, with his hand on my forehead, he told me, "Awake."

My sandbag eyelids blinked open. I found myself on the settee again, my back slouched against all the scratchy needlepoint pillows my grandmother had sewn decades before.

Henry jumped off the cushion beside me, rustling up a breeze of dusty parlor air, and he exited the room in a streak of black clothing and blond hair. The front door slammed shut, and I wondered if he had even remembered to grab his hat.

Father loitered next to his armchair, his hands stuffed in his pockets, his face turned to the parlor's exit.

"What did you make him do to me?" I asked from the settee.

"Everything was done with your best interest in mind, Olivia." He tugged his handkerchief out of his breast pocket and dabbed his shiny forehead. He looked more man than monster again, but I had seen what he was capable of, and I still believed him to be a fiend. "If all goes well," he continued, "then I'll be satisfied, and young Reverie will get paid. That girl will get her surgery."

A pair of solid footsteps marched toward us from down the hall. Gerda stopped in front of the parlor and untied her white apron. "I'm afraid I must give my notice, Dr. Mead."

"I beg your pardon?" Father straightened his neck. "You're quitting?"

"*Ja.*" She pulled the apron over her head. "I cannot work for a man who pays a stranger to harm his daughter."

"What happened during the hypnosis, Gerda?" I jumped to my feet. "Did you hear them?"

"Were you eavesdropping?" asked Father.

Gerda slung her apron over the parlor rocking chair. "I'd like my final wages, Dr. Mead. I've worked a week and a half since you paid me last."

Father huffed and muttered something under his breath about everyone wanting to take his money. Gerda stepped aside and let him pass. His feet made an awful tromping ruckus all the way back to his office.

"Miss Mead . . ." Gerda grabbed my hands with shaking fingers. "There are certain topics you won't be able to talk about anymore."

"What topics?"

"Please, don't even attempt to say words that feel as if they shouldn't be spoken. And cover your ears if you hear those words uttered."

"What words? What topics?"

"I can't say them out loud to you, either." She glanced over her shoulder. "They'll hurt you."

Father plodded back into view with three floppy dollars in hand. "Here are your wages. Mark my word, as soon as you come to your senses, you'll regret this ridiculous decision."

"Thank you for the wages." Gerda took the money with a polite nod. "There's cold ham and carrots in the icebox. Fresh bread is cooling on the kitchen table. You should be just fine for tonight's supper." She darted a quick glance at me. "I'm sorry, Miss Mead. *Lycka till.* Good luck."

# CHAPTER SEVENTEEN

# VILE SUFFRAGE

G o numb, I told myself from the far corner of my bed, in the crook of my cherry-pink walls. *Don't move. Don't think.*

I pushed the palms of my hands against my temples until my head was as clamped as those of Father's patients in his wicked operatory chair. Moving even the smallest muscle would bring memories and, with them, an anger that burned through the lining of my stomach.

*You will submerge yourself in a depth of relaxation such as you have never experienced before . . .*

Father knocked on my closed bedroom door. "Olivia? I've prepared supper for us."

I still didn't move, but I asked, "*You* prepared supper?"

"I've lived without a wife for thirteen years now. I have been known to assemble a meal or two." He rapped against the door again. "I know you're angry, but you need to eat."

"What terrible thing am I going to do if I speak the wrong words?"

"I don't want to say."

"Why not? Because you realize how horribly you're behaving?"

"No, because it's for the best if you don't even envision the subjects I've asked you to forget. Now, come down and eat your dinner."

"I'd rather not."

"Olivia . . ."

"No."

"You're not supposed to be arguing with me."

"I'm not supposed to be saying volatile words, which I'm not. I'm speaking quite calmly." I turned on my side, away from the door, and made myself go stiff again.

"Very well. I'll place a plate of food outside your door."

"Like a jailer," I said under my breath as his footsteps creaked down the stairs.


AROUND EIGHT O'CLOCK, WHEN THE GAS LAMPS GLOWED and my stomach growled too much to bear, I brought the plate of food into my room. I sat down on the floor and ate cold ham and carrots. All the while, the yellow cigar box stuffed with money peeked at me from beneath the ruffles of my bed.

*I'm settled in an apartment near Barnard College,* Mother had said in her letter, *and I think of you every time I see those smart young women walking around with books tucked under their arms.*

And then . . . *I would even let you take a tour of Barnard, and perhaps I'd allow you to watch that delicious play* Sapho, *if the moralists don't shut it down again.*

The box was just sitting there, waiting for me to lift the lid and dip my fingers into the stack of bills both limp and crisp. A train ticket. Rent money to use while finishing my requirements for my high school diploma. A typewriter to help me start a journalism career. College tuition. Textbooks. The possibilities were all there, within my grasp. All I had to do was reach out, grab the thick wad of bills, and escape out the window.

*Yet . . .*

One hundred twenty-three dollars might also pay for Genevieve's surgery.

It might allow Henry to release me from my treatments that very night.

Before my fingers could stretch forward and touch the smooth lid, Father swung open my door without knocking.

"We have guests arriving."

"What guests?"

"The Underhills." He took hold of me by one elbow and jerked me to my feet. "Do not ruin this for me."

Father steered me out of my bedroom and down the stairs just as someone was clanging our brass knocker. The closer we got to the door, the more the knocking deteriorated into muffled thuds that sounded strange to my ears.

Another vision neared. I sucked in my breath and prepared for the worst.

Father lunged for the door and opened it up to a startling collection of sideshow oddities:

Sunken-Eyed John with his long, crooked teeth.

The bulging-eyed, dark-haired girl with the scrawny neck and blue lips from Sadie's party.

The lady carnival barker in the red-striped coat and straw hat.

A Draculean man with a white mustache, oddly arched nostrils, and teeth that protruded over a ruddy lip.

"Welcome to my house," said Father, and I half expected him to quote the rest of Count Dracula's first spoken lines to the fellow who resembled Stoker's character: *Enter freely and of your own will!* Instead, he uttered a nervous-sounding, "P-p-please, c-c-come inside."

The Underhills passed across our threshold, and my eyes readjusted. The delusion ceased. Our guests became a normal family of four, albeit a garishly wealthy one, with plush silk jackets for the ladies and solid-gold cuff links and pocket-watch chains for the gentlemen. The lady barker again transformed into the brunette woman who was handing out pamphlets in front of the headquarters for the Oregon Association Opposed to the Extension of Suffrage to Women.

The dark-haired daughter snickered. "You were so funny at Sadie's party, Ophelia."

"It's Olivia," I said.

The girl stiffened her arms straight in front of her, and with her eyes wide and dazed, she droned, "'All is well. All is well.'"

"That's enough, Eugenia," said Mrs. Underhill, slapping her daughter's hands. "We're only here for a brief visit. Let Dr. Mead proceed with business."

"Yes, very good." Father closed the front door and lifted a metal bucket from the little hallway table. "As I already discussed with you, Mr. Underhill, sir, I have found an innovative solution to our state's peskiest problem. Imagine, if you will, your lovely wife no longer needing to manage the Oregon Association—and spending her precious time in more enjoyable pursuits."

Mrs. Underhill arched her slender eyebrows.

"Imagine," continued Father, "never having to worry about your dear daughter choosing the path of social impurity, or your son accidentally getting trapped with a shrew of a wife—a shrew who is only after your money so she can try to buy the vote."

Mr. Underhill's white mustache twitched.

"All of these worries will disappear," said Father, "and

become ancient relics of the past, with Henri Reverie's Cure for Female Rebellion and Unladylike Dreams."

Father pushed the pail into my sweating hands, and I half expected the preposterous name for the treatment to materialize on the side of the container, scrawled in the curved black lettering of traveling hucksters' tonics and cure-alls.

Father lifted a piece of plain white paper from the bottom of the pail. "Mrs. Underhill, will you please do me the honor of slowly reading the words on this page so I may demonstrate the fruits of young Mr. Reverie's work?"

Mrs. Underhill took the paper and again raised her brows. She cleared her throat and looked between me and that bucket, while Sunken-Eyed John and his tall, mustached father blocked my path to the door.

*To escape or not to escape . . .*

Mrs. Underhill drew in her breath and spoke the first word. "Suffrage."

My stomach moaned loudly enough to make John chuckle. He scratched his nose and muttered, "That's what happens when you dine where you shouldn't."

Mrs. Underhill ignored her son and inhaled another short breath.

"Women's rights."

I gagged and dropped the bucket to the floor with a clank.

Mrs. Underhill's next three phrases pelted my stomach like white-hot bullets.

"Suffragist. Votes for women. Susan B. Anthony."

I covered my mouth and shoved my way to the door.

"College," called Mrs. Underhill after me, and I tore out to the front porch, leaned my chest over the rail, and vomited into the bushes. Sweat dripped off my forehead and nose. Shivers racked my body. I just hung there, my ribs pressed against the rail, and let the fresh night air swim inside my head.

The soles of fine leather shoes pattered out to the porch behind me, but no one spoke a word until I turned around and slid down the splintery rail to the ground with a thump.

"You are most definitely coming to my election-night party, Dr. Mead," said the missus, whose face blurred and wavered before my eyes—veering from slick carnival barker to silken society queen. "It'll be held at the Portland Hotel at seven o'clock. Bring that hypnotist. Bring this girl. And let's end this ridiculous fight for the vote."

"You put me in here a cub, but I will go out a roaring lion and I will make all hell howl."

—SALOON-SMASHING TEMPERANCE FIGHTER
CARRIE NATION, from jail, 1900

# CHAPTER EIGHTEEN

# TRANSGRESSIONS

I slammed my bedroom door shut behind me. Shelves rattled, wall lamps flickered, and wide-eyed china dolls smacked to the floor. A new sort of growl roared up from the pit of my stomach—not a moan of nausea, but a primal howl.

"I hate this!" I yanked on my hair and pulled out the tight pins. "I hate my life!"

I lunged toward the window and pulled back the curtains, ready to fling up the sash and climb down the trellis, despite my shoeless feet.

Bars blocked my exit. Thick copper bars that shone in the

moonlight, secure as jail cell barriers—or the rungs of an enormous birdcage, as in the popular song.

*She's only a bird in a gilded cage* . . .

"You're not real." I backed away. "I know you're not real. Stop looking like you're actually there."

I grabbed my shoes and house key, shut my bedroom door, and stole downstairs to our tiny wood-paneled bathroom, a pine-scented closet added behind the kitchen when I was thirteen. Father—probably already sloshing about in a brandy-induced stupor—didn't make a peep from his closed office hideout.

I gave the sink's stiff spigot a twist, and the pipes trumpeted their usual high-pitched racket before water squirted into the cast-iron basin. I washed my face, scrubbed my teeth, and gargled with Holmes's Sure Cure Mouth Wash until my tongue and cheeks burned.

My feet then swished back down the hall, silent as spider-webs, while I carried my shoes in my left hand. In his office, Father began singing some old ditty from before I was born.

I held my breath and opened the front entrance.

More bars—fat steel ones. I shut the door and bang-bang-banged my forehead against the wood.

*You will* see *the world the way it truly is—not accept it. You will not accept it.*

I lifted my smarting head with gold specks buzzing before my eyes.

*You will not accept it.*

I reopened the door. The bars vanished.

Without even grabbing my coat or hat, I closed up the house and leapt into the night.

Out in the side yard, my red bicycle waited for me against the house's chipped planks. After buttoning up my shoes, I hopped onto the saddle like a dime-novel cowboy, wobbled my way across the front yard's sparse and lumpy patches of grass, and pedaled toward the city with legs propelled by wrath.

The streets lay empty and silent, with rows of white arc lamps dangling from wires overhead, guiding the way, whispering, *This way, this way, kill him, kill him.* I pedaled faster, faster, faster, faster, hopping aboard smooth sidewalks to avoid getting slowed by ruts in the streets. A man stumbled out of a tavern and tottered into my path, but I swerved to avoid him and felt the graze of his arm against my elbow. He shouted a curse word, so I shouted it right back at him, even though I'd never cussed aloud in my life.

Outside the great Henri Reverie's hotel, I tossed my bicycle to the ground and threw open the establishment's front door. I marched straight toward the staircase sign at the back of the lobby with my nails sharp and poised to fight.

"Olivia?" asked a voice from one of the lobby's chairs.

I stopped and whipped my head toward the sound.

Henry set aside a newspaper and rose from an armchair with a baffled expression that grew even more perplexed when I walked over and pushed him three feet backward.

"You made me vomit! In public!"

"I told you to trust me."

I pushed him again. "You humiliated me."

"You made your father torture me."

"I threw up in the bushes in front of those people." I kept shoving. "I got sick as a dog."

"Olivia, stop. Be quiet."

"Don't tell me to be quiet. Who do you think you are?"

"Please—"

"You made me vomit, Henry. You're as horrible and controlling a jackass as he is." I raised my arm. "I could kill you!"

My nails sliced down his cheek, and to my horror, blood rose to the surface of four long gashes that stretched from his eye to his mouth.

He cradled his skin and staggered backward, dazed and whey-faced.

"Take your lovers' quarrel outside, you animals!" yelled the hotel clerk with the Vandyke beard, and other voices joined in the commotion—those of concerned guests, a hotel employee in a round cap, and then Henry, who took hold of my arm and tried pulling me away while telling the clerk that everything was fine.

But my feet wouldn't budge.

In a gilded mirror across the lobby, a red-eyed devil stared me down, her dark hair hanging in her face like poisonous black asps, her teeth bared and clenched, the dagger nails of her right hand dripping fresh red blood that stained the green rug below her. Every muscle in my body stiffened at the sight of her—of me—yet I couldn't pull my eyes away.

"Olivia, please! Come outside." Henry gave my arm a good yank and guided me out of the hotel.

The crisp blast of autumn air snuffed out some of the fire blazing inside me. With a whimper of exhaustion, I collapsed against a brick wall beyond the front window and leaned my cheek into a fuzzy blanket of moss. My legs quivered, the muscles and tendons straining to keep me upright.

Out of the corner of my eye, I saw Henry pull a handkerchief out of his breast pocket and cover his bleeding face.

I squeezed my eyes shut and sucked in my breath. "How much blood is there?"

"Hardly any. It mainly stings."

"It looked as if it could turn into gallons."

"You're probably seeing it worse than it is." He stepped closer. "Olivia, I promised you we were partners, not enemies. Why'd you have to bring up Genevieve and let it slip that we've seen each other?"

"I was trying to appeal . . . I just . . . he's still my father. I thought . . ." I rubbed my forehead. "We're not partners. A partner wouldn't allow me to retch in front of strangers."

"Your father gave me those orders when he had that medieval contraption wedged in my mouth."

"But he took out the gag eventually."

"We signed a contract back there in his office. A mutual agreement, saying if I completed the tasks asked of me, he would give me the full remainder of Genevieve's surgeon's fees."

I closed my eyes again. "I'll give you one hundred twenty-three dollars if we end everything tonight and send you on your way right now."

Henry didn't answer, and for a moment I thought he might have run away.

"Are you still here?" I raised my head and found him in the same spot as before, his mouth hanging open, the cloth pressed against his face.

"What are you talking about?" he asked.

"My mother has been sending me birthday and Christmas money ever since she left us when I was four. I've been saving the cash in a box in my room all these years."

"What have you been saving it for?"

I shrugged. "I don't know. I used to imagine heading out on great adventures, circumnavigating the world like Nellie Bly."

"But"—he lowered the handkerchief—"what had you been planning to use it for before Genevieve and I came to town?"

"It doesn't matter."

"Yes, it does."

I hugged my arms around my middle. "I can't tell you what I've imagined doing with the money. You've made sure I'll be sick if I say the word out loud."

"Does it have to do with education?"

"Yes, but I'm not even sure it's enough for one year's tuition. I'd probably have to apply for a scholarship, anyway."

"Olivia . . ." He stepped in front of me. "Look at me."

I peeked up and saw pink fingernail marks on his cheek in the lamplight shining out through the hotel window.

"Listen to me," he said, and his wounds and his lips and his nose blurred away. Only his eyes remained. "Listen carefully, for what I am going to tell you is extremely important. You will no longer feel nauseated and vomit when you hear or say the following words: *Suffrage. Women's rights. Suffragist. Votes for women. Susan B. Anthony. College.* In fact, you feel healthy and fully recovered from what happened to you this evening."

The disgusting tempest in my stomach settled into peaceful seas. The clouds in my head cleared away.

"However," he continued, "you will feel compelled to cover your mouth and make a gagging sound whenever you hear or say those words. *Suffrage. Women's rights. Suffragist. Votes for women. Susan B. Anthony. College.* You will not suffer any pain or nausea. You will simply cover your mouth and make a sound. Do you understand?"

I nodded.

"Good. Now, slowly, gently"—he pressed his hand against my forehead—"awake."

I blinked and wobbled.

Henry lowered his arm and cleared his throat. "I would have liked to do that before, but I couldn't with him watching."

"Thank you."

"I'm not taking your money."

"But . . . election night . . ." I braced my hand against the wall. "Genevieve . . ."

"We have three days left to figure out a way for it to seem that I'm hypnotizing you in front of that election-night crowd—without doing a single thing to you. I want to give a performance that will somehow end up teaching your father and all those antis a lesson."

"How on earth would we do that?"

"I don't know." He leaned his back against the bricks beside me. "But you're obviously smart, and I've had years of experience in putting on a good show. I'm certain we can think of something."

"What about Father?"

"Well . . ." He tucked his hands into his pockets. "Subtlety will have to be the key to this performance. We've got to make him think we're following his directions."

"And then you'll leave and take care of your sister?"

"Yes. I promise. We'll catch the last train south that night." He turned his head my way and pressed his lips together. His forehead puckered, suggesting a flaw in the plan.

"What is it?" I asked.

"You should come with us."

I blinked as if he'd just flicked water into my eyes. "I beg your pardon?"

"You could finish getting your high school diploma in San Francisco. Stanford's not far, and I've heard they allow women."

I pushed myself off the wall. "I can't go with you. I hardly even know you."

"My father's cousin Anne lives in the city, and she'll be housing me while Genevieve undergoes her surgery. She doesn't have the money to help us with medical payments, but she's able to provide a roof over our heads. I'm sure she'd welcome you, too."

"I cannot run away with you." I walked over to my tossed-aside bicycle and hoisted it onto its wheels.

"You have money." Henry followed me to the bike. "You wouldn't have to rely on me or any other man for income. But I'd be there for you, as a friend, if you needed anything."

"I told you"—I hiked up the bottom of my skirt and swung my right leg over the bicycle's red bar—"I don't even know you."

"Think about it, at least. Please, consider joining us."

I tried to roll forward, but he pushed against my handlebars and blocked my escape with his body.

"I don't want to leave you behind," he said, "when I know I caused your life in Portland to crumble before your eyes."

I scratched at a small bump on my turtle-shaped bicycle bell and mulled over the idea of my life crumbling before my eyes. An entertaining thought struck me during the mulling. A highly entertaining thought that led to an embarrassing snort.

Henry shifted his weight. "What's so funny?"

Another snort erupted, one that progressed into a full-blown laugh that made my shoulders shake.

"What's so funny, Olivia?"

"I just realized all the things I've done since I've met you and undergone your Cure for Female Rebellion and Unladylike Dreams—in bold, capital letters. Think about it, Henry." I counted off each transgression by lifting my fingers on the handlebars. "I walked out on a formal dinner party. I rode in a two-seater buggy with two young men—and sat on your lap, no less. I accompanied you into your hotel room. I played hooky. I published a suffragist letter in the newspaper—"

"You what?"

"Read the front page of today's *Oregonian*." I tilted my head at the nail marks on his face. "I scratched you up like a wild woman. I caused a terrible uproar in a hotel lobby. Oh, I even cursed at a drunkard I almost ran over with my bike. And I rode through the city by myself after dark, while my father imagined me sulking in my bedroom. We're not curing *my* dreams."

He arched his eyebrows at the emphasis on *my*. "Are we curing someone else's?"

"My father's. His life is the one that's crumbling, because he's doing exactly what he wanted to avoid—driving me away." I kicked up my foot to find the right pedal and rang my little bell. "Now move, *s'il vous plaît*. I need to ride home before my empty bedroom gets discovered."

I pedaled toward him, but he pushed me backward by the handlebars again and said, "I'm going to escort you home."

"How are you going to keep up with me while I'm riding?"

"You can't ride through the dark streets on your own. If you fall and hit your head, who would know?"

"As I just said"—I steered the handlebars out of his grip—"how are you going to keep up while I'm riding?"

"I'll sit on the handlebars if I have to." He lifted his knee as if he were going to climb aboard.

"No, Henry!" I laughed and managed to back the bike out of his reach. "You'll tip me forward."

"Then let me sit in front of you so I can pedal while you hang on."

"Ha!" I rode the bicycle off the curb with a jolting bump that startled more hair out of pins. "That would be a laugh."

He leapt into the street behind me. "I'll bet *you're* strong enough to pedal us both."

"I don't know . . ." I rode around him in a wide circle. "I'm only a girl."

"I'll just chase after you, then, and try to keep up." He laughed, a throaty chuckle—an enjoyable sound I don't think I'd ever heard from him before. "Stop riding circles around me, Olivia. Let me get on. I'm willing to sit in back."

"You'll probably fall off." I planted my feet on the ground. "I ride fast."

"I bet you do."

I hopped down from the saddle while still holding the handlebars, and—adding yet another transgression to my growing list of sins against my father—allowed Henry to climb onto the seat behind me. He tried putting his hands on the bars, next to mine, but I nudged them away.

"I'll need to steer. You'll make us fall if you're hanging on, too."

He held up his palms. "What should I hang on to, then?"

"I don't . . ." I laughed and blushed and couldn't believe I was letting him sit on my bicycle behind me, pressed up against my back, his mouth so close to my neck. I got chills just from the thought of him breathing against me. "Oh, just put your blasted hands around my waist. Help me push off, and if we somehow stay balanced, put your feet on the mounting pegs on the rear wheel."

I pressed my right foot against the top pedal. "I'll count to three, and then we both need to give a big push. Ready?"

He squeezed his arms around my waist and answered, *"Oui."*

"One, two, three."

He pushed, I pushed, and both of my feet left the ground. We wobbled and tipped, and he had to shove the soles of his shoes against the road more than once to keep us from falling on our sides like a capsizing ship. My legs pumped and strained, and somehow, one block south of the hotel, we managed to gain speed. Balancing became easier; the act of pedaling turned smooth and as simple as riding on my own. Our chances of serious injury increased, but my legs no longer ached from powering us along.

We cruised onward, past the slumbering businesses on Third. My hair streaked behind me and probably smacked Henry in the face, but he never complained—in fact, he chuckled the whole time, and, when I steered us around the corner to Yamhill, he whooped like a French Canadian cowboy.

"You're not going to fall off, are you?" I yelled into the wind.

"Not unless you do."

"In a few more blocks," I called again, "you need to look in the window of McCorkan's Bicycle Shop on our right."

"Why is that?"

"They sell bicycle bloomers. Buying a pair is yet another one of my unladylike dreams."

"I could get you a pair from backstage."

"Really?"

"Really. I've seen them in the costume room."

That grand possibility inspired me to pedal faster, and the

chain buzzed like a mighty industrial machine beneath our legs. Overhead, the moon peeked between the clouds, washing the road before us in swaths of silver. "Beautiful Dreamer" waltzed through my mind, especially the line "Starlight and dewdrops are waiting for thee," which seemed particularly lovely in the lamp-lit splendor of the nighttime streets of Portland.

Henry's arms tightened around my waist.

"I'm not going to stop," I yelled over my shoulder, "because I don't want to fall, but there they are. Turkish trousers."

We sped past the red and blue beauties, which were mere poufs of shadow in the unlit store, and Henry asked, "Is it because you want to dress like a man?"

"Pfft. No. I want to dress like a woman who drives men around on her bicycle."

He snickered near my ear, and we both laughed like grammar school children all the way back to my street, drunk on moonbeams and speed and the incomparable exhilaration of hanging on to another person as if one's life depended on it.

The descent wasn't half as graceful as the flight. Two blocks from my house, we hit a bad bump, and the handlebars jostled in my hands like a thing possessed. Henry dragged his feet across the dirt to skid us to a stop, kicking up dust and tiny pebbles, but the bicycle fought his efforts and dumped us on our sides one block away from home. We landed with a thump in a tangle of arms, legs, fabrics, and metal.

I pushed myself up to my elbows and unwound my feet

from Henry and the bike. A sore spot, bound to become a bruise, formed on my hip.

"Are you all right?" I asked.

My now supine passenger sat up with a dopey grin and wiped dirt off the sides of his coat. "Mademoiselle Mead, I had no idea you were a daredevil."

"My father would call me a scorcher."

"What's that?"

"A reckless bicyclist."

"Olivia 'Scorcher' Mead." He nodded his approval. "I like it." He climbed to his feet and lent me his outstretched hand.

I let him pull me upright, and we faced each other with our hands entwined. A pine tree bobbed a shadow across his scratched-up cheek, and the nail marks faded and glowed with the peekaboo moon.

His smile faded, and his dark-blond eyebrows turned serious. "What will your father do if he catches you sneaking in?"

I shrugged. "What more can possibly happen?"

"That's what has me worried."

"I'll just say I desperately needed fresh air after getting sick." I slid my fingers out of his. "Don't worry about me, Henry. Go home and take care of your sister. How is she tonight?"

"Exhausted. That's why I was reading the newspaper in the hotel lobby. I didn't want to bother her."

I nodded. "Well, you're a good brother. I'm sure she greatly appreciates you."

"I don't . . ." He turned his face downward and grimaced as if his ribs ached.

"What's the matter?" I asked.

"Nothing." He ran his fingers through his hair and tried to smile away whatever was bothering him.

"Tell me, Henry." I inched closer, my soles stirring up bits of gravel in the road. "Are you hurt? Was it the crash?"

"No, it's just . . ." He swallowed with a loud bob of his Adam's apple. "This isn't the life I ever expected to lead, Olivia. I'm beginning to think I'm bad luck."

"Why?"

"I'm certainly not good luck to you. Look what I've done by agreeing to tinker with your mind. And look at my family. Every single person I love dies on me. I feel as if I'm being punished, but I don't know what I could have done that's so indescribably awful."

"I'm sure your parents' deaths had nothing to do with you."

He swallowed again. "My mother died of cancer, the same kind as Genevieve's. My father lost his life to a bad typhoid outbreak when I was twelve. And . . . well, I already told you about Uncle Lewis and his poor choices."

I nodded. "I agree—all of that is bad luck. But it has nothing to do with you."

He released a long wheeze of a breath that had to have hurt his lungs, and he smoothed down the hair he'd just tousled. "Thank you. You're really far too kind to me."

"The scratches on your face don't look kind."

"I know, but . . ." He reached out and wove his fingers through mine. "Thank you."

Another breeze nudged the needles of the rustling pine and toyed with my hair, tickling stringy strands across my cheek. My skirt billowed around my legs and flirted with the knees of Henry's trousers.

"Henry, do I look like a monster to you?" I asked with a squeeze of his hand. "I saw myself in the mirror in the hotel lobby . . ."

He shook his head. "No, you look like someone who's been on a wild ride and could use a rest—that's all. Go get some sleep, and on Tuesday we'll figure out a way to set everything right. And if you let me, I'll take you away from all your troubles."

"I still don't—"

"Olivia," he whispered, bending his face toward mine. "Pieces of me have been dying with each loved one I've lost."

"I'm sorry . . ."

"But that ride through the city"—a grin burgeoned at the corners of his lips—"that daredevil, bicycle scorcher ride, reminded me what it's like to be wide awake and alive. Please, let me do something for you."

I nodded. "All right. I'll think about it."

"Good. I hope you do."

He kept his face close—close enough to kiss—and I wasn't sure if I should give him a peck on the cheek or back away.

"Are you waiting for me to kiss you?" I found myself asking in a voice too high-pitched.

He gave a startled blink and lifted his head. "What? No."

"You were so close . . . I didn't know if . . ." I lowered my eyes.

"No, I couldn't kiss you if I wanted to."

I peeked up at him. "Why not?"

"It's not easy for me."

"What do you mean? Is something wrong with your mouth?"

"No." He gave a strained smile. "Ladies have a habit of saying the only reason they're kissing me is because they're under my spell. They especially say that if they seem to like it but feel guilty about liking it, and if they're a bit older than me."

"Oh." I loosened my hand from his. "Is this a common problem?"

"No, but it's happened twice. A hazard of the profession, I suppose, but it makes me nervous about kissing anybody."

"Oh. Well"—my voice faltered; I tried not to stare at those red lips of his—"I certainly don't want to complicate this odd relationship of ours even further."

"No." He tucked his hands into his coat pockets. "It's for the best if we stick to simpler pleasures, like bicycle rides . . . and buggy outings."

I laughed and brushed my hair out of my face. "Yes, that's much simpler and far less intimate."

"Oh, definitely."

"And we don't need any more transgressions going onto my long list of post-hypnosis sins," I added.

"No, absolutely not. You don't want—"

I placed my hand on his shoulder and kissed him, just to try it with someone who wasn't drunk and Percy—and only because my heart was still thumping so rigorously from the bicycle ride—and because he fascinated me—and because it seemed as if we both desperately needed a kiss. His mouth felt so velvety soft that I let my lips linger. He tilted his head and held on to my waist and returned my kiss in such a way that lovely little prickles tingled across my stomach and down the backs of my legs.

Our lips parted, and I marveled at how hard I had to work to catch my breath. Henry brushed his thumb across the line of my jaw, but I stopped him by taking hold of his hand.

"I need to go home," I said.

He withdrew his fingers from mine, and the absence of their pressure left my hand empty and cold. "All right."

"Henry . . ."

"Yes?"

I smiled. "I had ridiculous amounts of fun on that bicycle ride, too."

His face brightened clear up to the golden tips of his hair. "We'll figure out a way to make Tuesday work," he said. "I promise. Let me know if you concoct any ideas."

I nodded and grabbed hold of the bike.

Without a single other word—or kiss—he slipped his hands back into his pockets and walked away into the shadows, whistling a song that sounded both sad and lovely, like a Pied Piper who pitied the children he was luring out of town.

FATE WAS KIND TO ME THAT NIGHT. DESPITE THE AWFUL creaks that accompanied my footsteps when I snuck up the staircase, Father's bedroom door remained shut, the light within extinguished. I believed I'd made it safely back to my bedroom by the grace of the brandy swimming through his veins.

In the darkness of my room, I hurried to shed my day clothes, climbed into my long nightgown, and threw an extra quilt over the mirror to hide my reflection from myself. My plate of half-eaten supper still waited on my floor, so I hustled it down to the kitchen in fear of mice sneaking into my room to feast.

Back upstairs, I tucked myself beneath my cotton sheets and the piles of autumn blankets that warmed away the chill of the house. My legs still experienced the fluttery sensation of whooshing through the streets of the city, and my just-kissed lips spread into a smile.

On the brink of sleep, when my mind hovered in that strange off-balance twilight between wakefulness and dream, I envisioned a ballroom inhabited by anti-suffrage ladies with Whitehead gags silencing their mouths. Below the peculiar image, like the suffrage caricatures printed in the *Oregonian* most weeks of late, ran a caption:

A TASTE OF THEIR OWN MEDICINE.

My eyes blinked back open.

A grin stretched to my ears.

*A taste of their own medicine.* The solution to the dilemma of our election-night performance.

CHAPTER NINETEEN

# A PLAN

F ather distributed Sunday morning's heaping spoonful of bad news, quite appropriately, in the kitchen.

"Now that Gerda is gone," he said from behind me at the sizzling griddle, "you'll need to manage the housework every day of the week."

The flapjack I had been flipping dropped to the floor.

"What about school?" I asked.

"The house needs tending, and we have no one else."

"But you said you worried about leaving me home on my own."

"Your industriousness will keep you active and out of trouble, and the hypnosis will prohibit you from attending any unsavory rallies. But fear not"—he bent over and picked up the crumbling pieces of oatmeal from the floor—"I have a strong inkling you're going to be in high demand Tuesday night. If we find you a young society gentleman, which I'm certain we will when those boys witness your demure personality, you may not ever need worry about cooking and cleaning again. You'll likely acquire a maid and a cook with your future husband. You'll be able to devote your full attention to my grandchildren." He nodded with an optimistic arch of his eyebrows.

An argument rushed up my throat, but the fight wilted at my lips.

*You are free to speak your mind, but you will do so with caution around your father,* Henry had instructed me in his hotel room. *You will limit your volatile words only to moments when someone is about to get hurt.*

Father moved to leave the room.

"Father," I said before he could go. "Frannie's family invited me over for Mr. and Mrs. Harrison's twentieth anniversary dinner tonight, remember?"

"Yes, I remember."

"Am I allowed to go? I'd prepare your meal before I left."

He picked at the ends of his beard. "I would have to escort you to their front door and pick you up. No bicycling."

"Because it's unladylike?"

"Because I don't want you conspiring with that hypnotist. He's signed a contract with me."

"I—" I bit down on my tongue, for I was about to slip and say, *I know.*

"You what?" asked Father.

"I'm glad you signed a contract. It's a sensible thing to do."

He cleared his throat. "I've forgotten—what time did Frannie say they're serving dinner?"

"Three thirty, I believe." A lie—the dinner was set for five o'clock.

"Then I'll walk you over at three and pick you up at six."

"Thank you, Father. That's very kind of you."

He retreated from the kitchen, and my mouth hissed a gust of white steam—my snuffed-out arguments.

AT THREE O'CLOCK SHARP, FATHER DELIVERED ME TO Harrison's Books, which was closed for Sunday.

"I'll fetch you at six, Olivia," he said with a peek at his pocket watch, as if he were already counting down the minutes.

"Can you make it seven o'clock, Dr. Mead?" asked Frannie from the bookshop's doorway. "Martha and I baked a cake. We'll need time for dessert."

"Well . . . I suppose." Father crinkled his brow. "If you think the festivities will last that long."

"At least that long. Eight might even be better. Papa will likely play his fiddle."

Father frowned. "Eight at the latest."

I patted his arm. "Thank you, Father."

Frannie shut the glass door behind me with a jingle of the bell, and Father retreated down the street with his gray derby bobbing up and down on his thick hair.

I grasped Frannie by the shoulders. "I'm here early because of a plan."

"A plan?"

"I need to go to the theater and speak to Henry."

"But—"

"Wait before you try to talk me out of it. Gerda quit yesterday. Father won't let me go to school anymore."

"What?" She reached up and gripped my elbows.

"Father hired Henry for a second treatment that was even worse than the first, but Henry is helping to alter the effects. Father got himself invited to an election-night party hosted by the Oregon Association Opposed to the Extension of Suffrage—" I involuntarily covered my mouth and belched a horrid, gagging sound.

Frannie grimaced. "Are you all right?"

"Yes." I let my hand flop down to my leg. "Anyway, at this party, in order to receive Father's payment for the hypnosis, Henry is supposed to hypnotize me in front of everyone and prove there's a cure for suffragists." Again, I smacked my hand over my mouth, and I hacked like a cat.

"Why are you gagging?"

I rolled my eyes. "It's all a part of the hypnosis."

"Livie! This is terrible. Are you still seeing terrifying sights, too?"

"Oddly enough, that's the least of my troubles." I clutched her hands. "But never mind that. Here's where I need your help. First, please let me borrow your cloak."

"But—"

"Second, talk to Kate on Monday at school. Let her know that the antis are congregating for some election-night hoopla at the Portland Hotel at seven o'clock. It would be splendid to have a team of suff"—my right hand slapped my mouth again—"ragists, *ack*"—I spat up another foul sound—"standing out front, singing anthems, wearing yellow ribbons. But tell them they must leave the hotel grounds no later than seven fifteen. That part is vital."

She stared at me with unblinking eyes.

"Please, Frannie." I pulled her against me and squeezed my arms around her.

"Livie, what's going to happen to you when the party is over?" she asked into my hair. "How in the world can you keep living with your father?"

I closed my eyes and pulled her so close, her shoulder dug into my throat. "I'll likely leave for New York Tuesday night."

"What?"

"My mother lives there. Near Barnard."

"Your mother has been an absent fool all these years."

"But she doesn't want to transform me into a creature who doesn't even resemble me." I pulled free of our hug. "Please,

Frannie. Help me. I need you. Genevieve needs you, too. I've seen her in her room in the Hotel Vernon. She's fading. The cancer will kill her if it's not removed soon."

Frannie's nose turned red and sniffly, and her chin shook. "I don't want to see you escape clear across the country." She wiped her eyes with the back of her sleeve. "But . . . if you genuinely believe you need to endure all of this rubbish to save this person's life, then, my goodness"—she heaved a heavy sigh—"let's help that girl."

# CHAPTER TWENTY

# DES PARTENAIRES QUI S'EMBRASSENT

The stage door was locked. At first all I could think to do was grumble and pace about the sidewalk while holding the brown hood of Frannie's cloak over my head. Just as I was about to run to the theater lobby and spin a story about needing to deliver an urgent item to Henry, fate intervened in the form of a few small beasts.

The side door opened. The middle-aged dog trainers and their half-dozen curly-haired poodles burst from the theater in a gust of high-pitched barks.

"Let me hold open the door for you," I said over all the

yipping, and I sprinted up the stairs, nearly tripping over my skirt.

"Thank you, dear," said the man of the group with a tip of his hat.

The flurry of fur and leather leashes and pitter-pattering feet traveled down the stairs, and I slipped inside the theater.

A heart-seizing note from the organ beyond the curtains soldered my feet to the ground. I stood there in the half dark, rooted to the floor, while the force of a loud waltz reverberated up my calves and knees. Laughter boomed from the audience. Lights poured through the black curtains separating the stage from the wings, luring me over . . . *Come see, come see.*

I rounded a small table topped with a pitcher of water and a bowl of peppermint-scented candies and came to a stop in the wings.

My eyes widened.

Three couples were dancing a waltz on the stage, but the women—not the men—were leading, with their hands on the gentlemen's waists. The gentlemen followed, their left fingers lifting invisible skirts off the ground. The peculiar pairs glided around the dusty floorboards with silly smiles on their faces, paying no heed at all to the wild shrieks of laughter from the audience.

*"Mesdames et messieurs"*—Henry strutted into my view, his red vest shimmering in the stage lights—"let us give a warm round of applause for the Reversed Portland Dancers."

The audience clapped and chortled, and I slithered farther into the backstage shadows. The silhouettes of stagehands in caps and suspenders rushed toward the wings.

Henry guided his subjects out of their trances, and an even grander applause swelled for the great Monsieur Reverie. A smoky-smelling fellow showed up a few feet away from me and pulled on a long rope that clattered the main curtain closed.

I held my breath and crept out of my hiding spot.

Henry staggered off the stage, and my eyes beheld him falling apart. Literally. The bottom half of his coat unraveled at astounding speed, and the seams of his pants stretched and ripped from his ankles up to his knees. He grabbed hold of one of the wings' black curtains and rested his forehead against the cloth, inhaling deep breaths that made his shoulders rise and fall.

"Henry?" I unclasped Frannie's cloak from my neck and approached him. By walking and blinking I stopped the illusion of his fraying garments, but he still hunched over as if he might collapse. "Are you all right?"

He lifted his head. "Olivia?"

"I'm sorry I snuck backstage . . ."

"No, it's fine." He let go of the curtain and took my hands. "It's nice to see you back here. Is everything all right?"

"I'm fine, but how are you?"

"I didn't sleep well last night."

A stagehand brushed past us, so Henry led me away from the wings and toward the table with the water and candies.

He poured himself a glass with shaking hands. "Genevieve has a fever."

"Oh, no!"

"The doctor thinks it might just be a regular cold, not her illness, but she's supposed to take a pill and stay in bed."

"Does it seem like a cold?"

"She's sneezing and coughing, but I don't know . . ." He guzzled the water like a man downing whiskey.

I wriggled Frannie's coat off my shoulders. "I'm so sorry, Henry."

He came up for a loud breath. "It reminds me too much of the typhoid—and my mother's illness. I really hate this. Why can't she just be healthy?"

"Is there anything I can do?"

"No." He shook his head and wiped his lips. "Nothing besides what you're already doing."

"If it's of any comfort, I have an idea for Tuesday evening."

"You do?"

"I—" I held my tongue, for the substitute organist lumbered toward us from the wings with stacks of sheet music poking out of her carpetbag.

"Here." Henry gestured with his head toward the back of the theater. "Let's go speak in private. There's something I need to give you, anyway."

He set down the glass, popped a candy into his mouth, and took me by the hand again, while the organist frowned at us and fished her hand into the candy bowl.

Henry and I wound our way through a dark maze of set pieces and sawdust and down an echoing stairwell that smelled of fresh paint and cigarettes. We arrived in a large underground space crammed with props and extra stage pieces packed onto shelves and crowding the passageways. Bare bulbs dangled from the ceiling, casting a yellow light that produced hulking shadows shaped like masks and trombones and Wild West pistols.

Henry led me down a narrow walkway, toward the opposite end of the room, and the feathers of a dangling pink boa tickled across my cheek, making me think for a moment we were walking through a labyrinth of spiderwebs.

"The wardrobe mistress isn't here today," he said. "We all wear our own clothing for this show, but we've been allowed to come back here in case we want to add anything to our outfits." He opened a back door and pushed a switch on the wall that illuminated a room filled with costumes on coat hangers, bolts of fabric, sewing machines, bobbins, and millinery head blocks. He let go of my hand and walked to a rack of clothing both colorful and drab. "I received Mr. Gillingham's approval to give this to you."

My stomach leapt. Henry pulled something off a hanger and returned to me with a pair of garnet-brown trousers.

Bicycle bloomers.

*For me.*

I dropped Frannie's cloak, covered my mouth, and burst into tears.

"What's wrong?" he asked, but all I could do was hurl my arms around him and tip us both off balance.

He grabbed hold of my back. "Are you all right?"

"They're beautiful. I'm sorry . . ." I wiped my face with the back of my hand. "I don't know why I'm crying. I love the bloomers. But it's so hard. Oh, criminy, I love them so much." I blubbered like a madwoman against the soft lapel of his coat.

"Here, sit down with me," said Henry, and he lowered us both to the floor, which was scattered with threads of blue and white. He fetched a handkerchief from his breast pocket and gave it to me.

I blew my nose and watched tears rain down on the glorious trousers. Henry stroked my arms until my breathing slowed, and his face gradually grew less hazy through my drying eyes. My scratch marks on his cheek were but thin, hidden streaks beneath a covering of greasepaint.

I hiccupped. "I'm so sorry. I don't know why I reacted that way. It's hardly the behavior of a modern woman with bloomers, is it?"

"Don't worry about how you reacted. Who cares? Now"—he bent his head close—"tell me your idea for Tuesday."

I cleared my throat and drew a long breath. "Well, at the election-night party . . ." I coughed into the handkerchief.

"Tell the audience you can cure more than just one rebellious woman. Tell them you can cure a whole crowd of us." I spread the bloomers across my lap and toyed with the buttons on the hems. "When we first arrive, there will likely be women singing and chanting about the vote outside the hotel. Ask the men to go fetch them to prove your abilities."

"All right . . ."

"If all goes well, when the gentlemen come back, they'll say the women are gone. Inform the audience you'll use the ladies at the party as an example instead. Invite them all in front of the crowd, with me included if it helps"—I met his eyes—"and hypnotize them all into silence. Take away their voices."

His face went still. "Permanently?"

"Long enough to scare them. Show them the dangers of living without the ability to have a say in the world. And then, when they panic and beg in writing to speak again, point out the beautiful irony of a group of antis hating the idea of silence."

He cracked a wry smile that gleamed in his eyes. "It's brilliant."

"Do you really think so?"

"It's well worth a try." He laced his fingers through mine in my lap. "We'll definitely need to make sure you're up there with the crowd to make your father happy, but I have a trick to avoid getting hypnotized if you don't want to lose your voice."

"There's a trick?"

"It's easy. Take your tongue"—he showed me the pink tip of his between his teeth—"and wedge it against the roof of your mouth."

I pushed my tongue to my palate. "Is that all?"

"Theoretically, yes. When I'm hypnotizing you, all I'm doing is putting your conscious mind to sleep so I can communicate directly with your subconscious. When you distract yourself with your tongue"—he closed his mouth and seemed to test out the effect in his own mouth—"or when you mentally will yourself against the hypnosis, your conscious mind stays awake. I can't get into the deeper parts of your brain."

"But what if . . ." My face warmed. "What if my subconscious mind . . . enjoys the relaxation part of hypnosis too much?"

"Well . . ." He slipped his hands out of mine. "You've got to ignore that impulse to be relaxed. Be strong. Push me out. Imagine slamming a door in my face."

"You're awfully good at soothing a person, Henry . . ."

"Even if you like it, you've got to block me. Even if your father's standing right there, keep yourself alert. Force me away."

I squirmed. "Now I'm worried."

"Let's practice. Come on." He sat up tall. "We'll try it right here."

"All right." I rolled back my shoulders. "I suppose if you just use your usual techniques, and—"

He retook my hands and looked me in the eye, and I flopped forward and banged my temple against his shoulder.

"Awake! No, Olivia, you weren't even trying."

I shook my head and straightened my posture. "You don't understand. Relaxation is precious to me. And you're talented."

"Be strong—forget the soothing parts. Slam the door in my face." He squeezed my hands. "Look into my eyes."

I did, and my forehead tipped forward as if it were made of a sheet of slate.

"No. Awake."

I righted myself again.

He sighed and furrowed his brow. "My job, Olivia, is to catch you off guard. Your job is to be alert and strong at all times. I don't want him to force me to do anything despicable to you ever again. And I don't want to think that last night . . ."

He stopped and rubbed his hand over his mouth.

I pinched my eyebrows together. "What about last night?"

"The hazard of the profession I was telling you about." He scooted backward on the floor and stared at his folded legs. "Women saying they're under my spell. I don't want to think hypnosis had anything to do with . . . *anything* . . . last night."

"I was in a fully conscious state, Henry. I may be an overly susceptible subject, but I can tell when I'm hypnotized and when I'm not."

"I wasn't sure. I started to worry when I got back to the hotel."

"I kissed you because I thought it would be fun." I pushed my hands against the floor and slid myself toward him. "I thought we could both use a kiss. It had nothing to do with hypnosis or female equality or anything else but the simple fact that we were having a grand time."

"Well . . . good . . . and, well . . ." He scratched his neck. His eyes met mine. "You were right."

"About what?"

"I did need it." He played with the pucker of my skirt above my knee. "I didn't even realize how badly I needed it until it happened."

I gave a soft breath of a laugh. "I understand."

He took my hands again—a tender gesture, not another hypnosis test. A hush came over us. Footsteps moaned against the wood above our heads, but the rest of the world seemed miles and miles away, as if we were holed up in our own private burrow at the center of the earth. Our interlocked fingers nuzzled against one another. Our seated bodies fidgeted until our knees touched and stayed together. The ethereal spell of our moonlit bicycle ride settled over the hats and the costumes and our tipped-together heads, which seemed to be drawing closer on an invisible thread.

This time, Henry kissed me first, his lips soft and warm, even more so than the night before. I set the handkerchief and the bicycle bloomers aside and reached up to his neck, not caring if the gesture seemed bold. The harder we kissed, the faster the demons in the crooks of my mind slipped away. A better escape than hypnosis. Almost better than bicycling. I reached up to his soft hair and pulled his whole body to mine.

He eased me backward to the floor, and my head rested amid remnants of lace and scattered snippets of fabric. I thought I heard the distant music of the pipe organ playing "Beautiful Dreamer," or maybe even "A Hot Time in the Old Town." It didn't really matter. Nothing mattered except for lips and gentle hands and the coarse texture of a black woolen coat beneath my fingertips.

A mirror stood over us—I had seen it when we first entered the room but tried to ignore its intimidating slab of reflective glass. It watched us as we lay there, tasting and feeling each other, like Sapho and her lovers.

I kept my eyes closed. Henry's fingers slid between the buttons of my blouse, and I worried my reflection would show me a ghost of a girl, fading, oppressed, and ruined. My hand strayed to the firm spread of his lower back, below his coat, his vest, and even his shirt, and I feared I'd look like one of the North End prostitutes I'd always heard about, with their rouged cheeks and low-cut gowns. My mouth strayed to the sweet taste of his neck, and I thought of Lucy Westenra and her unclean lips and eyes.

Not knowing how I looked became too much to bear.

I turned my head to the side. My eyes opened. I saw her. Olivia Mead.

Just me—and Henry Rhodes—evading our troubles in the farthest corner of a theater.

Henry lifted his head, his cheeks flushed, his breaths uneven. "What are you looking at?"

"Us."

He peeked at the mirror and met the reflection of my brown eyes. "Why?"

"To see if we look wicked."

He tilted his head against mine. "And?"

"We just look like Olivia and Henry."

He brushed my hair out of my face. "Do you feel wicked?"

"I didn't until I started thinking about it."

He leaned forward for another kiss, but I touched his chin before his lips brushed mine.

"Here's another worry," I said. "I think I may have gotten my start in the world in the back of a theater, just like this."

He snuck in a soft kiss to my cheek. "What do you mean?"

"My mother came to Portland with a traveling theater company when she was barely sixteen. My father was an eighteen-year-old dental apprentice. For all I know their relationship started in this very same theater. Oh . . . good Lord." I cringed and sat up. "I hadn't even thought of that before."

"I'm sorry you did think of it." Henry sat up, too, and removed his coat.

"My mother lives in New York City now." I bit my lip and glanced at him out of the corner of my eye. "I'm thinking of going to live with her after everything's over Tuesday night."

A shadow darkened his face. He dropped his coat to the floor beside him, and the movement reminded me of a rosebush weeping petals.

"I want to be with family," I said. "I know you asked me to go with you and Genevieve, but . . ."

"No." He swallowed and nodded. "I understand."

"Do you?"

"I do." He nodded again, but I could see disappointment dimming the sparks in his eyes.

"Will this change any of our plans we just discussed for Tuesday night?"

"No." His brow creased. "Of course not. No matter what happens, I'm going to help you."

"We're still partners, then? *Partenaires?*"

*"Oui."* A small smile rose to his lips. *"Des partenaires qui s'embrassent."*

"What does that mean?"

"It means you should learn more French if you're going to partner with me, *ma chérie.*"

"No, be honest"—I nudged his knee—"what does it mean?"

He smirked and blushed a little. "Partners who kiss."

I snickered. "Partners who kiss?"

*"Oui."*

"What a marvelous concept."

He smiled, and I smiled, and we both broke into a fit of tipsy-sounding laughter.

Our faces gradually sobered. Silence stole over the room again, aside from those footsteps shuffling above.

I leaned toward Henry and his lovely mussed-up hair and peppermint-scented lips, and for a little while longer, we enjoyed our lives as *des partenaires qui s'embrassent.*

# CHAPTER TWENTY-ONE

# INNER WORKINGS

I thought I saw Father on my journey northward on Yamhill Street.

I spun around, and with my back to Fourth, I stood with Frannie's hood pulled over my head—a deer freezing to blend in with the trees. None of it seemed right: me hiding from Father, Father fearful for me—or maybe even *of* me. In his view of the world, I likely resembled a fairy-tale witch who baked children in pies. Or, even worse in his eyes, a witch who could destroy both his home and his right to drink.

I strode to Harrison's Books on unsteady legs, looking over my shoulder every few seconds.

Frannie let me inside after I knocked on the glass door. "Is everything all right?" she asked, and she locked the shop back up behind me.

"Well . . ." I sighed and unbuttoned the cloak. "I think we might be ready for Tuesday."

Phonograph music drifted downstairs—a piano song that sounded as old and romantic as the Harrisons' twenty-year marriage.

She took the cloak. "Is this to be a farewell supper, then?"

I couldn't meet her eyes.

"It is, isn't it?" Her voice cracked.

"I'm not sure. I'm worried everything will go terribly wrong."

"Just be careful, no matter what happens. Please promise me that."

I nodded and rubbed my knotted-up stomach. "I promise."

She wiped her eyes with the cloak. "Let me know when I should properly say good-bye, all right? I don't want to suddenly find out you're in New York without me realizing you're gone."

I fussed with the folds of my skirt, which was hiding the bloomers I had slipped over my legs in the theater. "The world is getting smaller, you know. A train ride across the country is so much easier than before."

Frannie sniffed and nodded. "I suppose that's true."

"It is."

Without another word, we linked arms and headed upstairs

to a celebration of two people who had learned to be kissing partners long before Frannie and I were born.

For a short while, all was indeed well.

Bittersweet, but well.

FATHER FETCHED ME AT EIGHT O'CLOCK, AND WE WALKED through the dark streets in silence with the soft swish of the bloomers brushing beneath my petticoat. Near the Park Blocks, I saw our shadows drifting ahead of us in the lamplight and, in them, the silhouette of a little girl with braided hair, sitting on the shoulders of a trim young man in a tall hat. Two steps later, the image shifted, and all that was left were the regular shadows of Father and me, walking three feet apart from each other.

"I miss when you used to carry me on your shoulders," I said, still watching the sidewalk ahead of us.

"Yes, well . . ." Father cleared his throat. "I think you might be getting a little too big for that nowadays."

I couldn't help but laugh, and I could have sworn I heard a low chuckle rumble from above his thick beard.

The wedge soon formed between us again. Our shadows spread farther apart, and they looked hunched and cold and lonely.

OUT IN THE BACKYARD ON MONDAY MORNING, WHILE MY classmates wrote compositions and solved algebraic equations in school, I scrubbed brown soap and Father's undergarments across the zinc grooves of our washboard in the steaming double boiler. Hair fell into my face from the force of all the rubbing, and my hands reddened and absorbed the smell of lye.

After the washing, I pinned the laundry to the clothesline, and little flecks of rain flew at my eyelids and cheeks. "Don't pour, don't pour," I begged of the sky, for I had come too far to lug everything down to our drying racks in the dark basement, where mice skittered about. I rushed to clip every garment to the line, and our backyard became a white wonderland of undershirts, petticoats, and drawers. Ghosts without bodies, just hovering in the mist.

I closed the door on that chore and climbed upstairs to pen a short note at my desk.

*November 5, 1900*

*Dear Madam,*

*Please accept my deepest thanks for delivering my letter to the editor this past Friday. I was delighted to see the article's publication in Saturday's edition of the newspaper. The reception to the piece far exceeded my expectations, and I am now strongly considering a career in journalism because of the pure joy I experienced in sharing my words with the people of this city. May ALL women one day gain a voice.*

*Sincerely,*

*A Responsible Woman*

THE TEAM OF FEMALE TYPISTS IN DARK DRESS SUITS AND ties clicked away at their tidy rows of desks in the *Oregonian*'s headquarters, and the same spirit of adventure I had felt on Friday coaxed me farther inside the building.

I noted one striking difference from the week before: a freckled young man with black hair sat at the front desk instead of the statuesque receptionist.

"May I help you?" he asked while unscrewing the cap of a fountain pen.

"I'm looking for the woman who worked at this desk last week."

"She no longer works here." The fellow set to scribbling a note on a sheet of company letterhead.

"She's not here?"

"No, she's been dismissed."

"May I ask why?"

"Yes"—he grinned and peeked up at me—"you may ask, but I will not answer."

"Does it have anything to do with that letter that was printed on Saturday's front page?"

The young man stopped writing. "Oh, Lord. You're not bringing another note of thanks, are you?"

"There are notes of thanks?"

"And violent hate mail threatening to set fire to both that letter writer's house and our building. But mostly ghastly letters of thanks." He reached down beside his desk and hoisted up a canvas sack spilling over with envelopes. "Ladies stuffed them through the mail slot all weekend long. One of our workers slipped on the piles when he first opened the office this morning. Nearly broke his neck. And then an hour ago, another batch"—the young man gestured with his head toward a bag slumped against a wall like a rummy in an alleyway—"arrived from the postman. Our editor, Mr. Scott, is fuming."

My fingers itched to grab all those beautiful stuffed envelopes and rip them open, one by one. "Would you like me to burn the letters for you?" I asked.

The fellow lifted his eyebrows. "Burn them?"

"I'll gladly take them and toss them into an incinerator. I'm opposed to the vote myself."

"You are?" He plopped the rustling sack back on the ground. "I don't come across many middle-class young ladies who oppose the vote."

"Are the bags heavy?" I asked.

"I don't think I entirely believe you're an anti-suffragist."

I covered my mouth and gagged against my palm.

The man gave a start. "What was that?"

"My reaction to that terrible word that starts with an *s*."

He lifted his chin and seemed to squint down his nose at me, even though he was sitting and I was standing. "Who are you?" he asked.

"Who are *you*?" I asked, just to be as impertinent as he was.

He stiffened at my question, and the typists behind him disappeared into ink-colored smudges. The clicks and dings of their typewriters drifted miles away. The man was suddenly dressed in a white lace tea gown, as relaxed and comfortable as can be—as if he thought himself to be more woman than man.

"Oh." I lowered my face, and the typewriters clacked back to life.

"What is it?" he asked, suited again in brown tweed and a necktie.

"I just . . ." I laid my letter for the fired receptionist upon his desk. "Will you please give this note to the woman who used to work here? It's very important."

"Are you a responsible woman?"

I sank back on my heels. "I—I—I like to think of myself that way."

"You know what I mean." He tapped the base of his pen against the desk. "'A Responsible Woman.'"

"Oh . . ." I pushed my envelope his way. "So, you can see straight through me. Well, that . . . that simply makes us equal, Mr. . . . ?"

"Briggs."

"Mr. Briggs. Believe it or not, I can see through you, too."

"I seriously doubt that."

I leaned my palms against the desk and dropped my voice to a whisper. "Deep inside, you're not so different from me. Are you?"

He gazed at me with a face unnaturally rigid—the paranoid

stare of a person whose inner workings were thrust on display against his will. His reaction made me feel cruel, so I stood and turned to leave.

"Here," he said from behind me.

I shifted back around.

He lifted one of the mail bags. "Go burn them, Responsible Woman."

"I will. Thank you." I took the dense bag and dragged it across the smooth tiles, hearing the future jostling about in all those packed-together papers inside.

THE FIRST THING I DID WHEN I GOT HOME WAS TO GO TO my bedroom. I had hardly sat down before I began tearing open the envelopes.

> *Dear Responsible Woman,*
>
> *You put into words exactly what I wanted to say to Judge Percival Acklen . . .*

> *Dear Responsible Woman,*
>
> *I wouldn't be old enough to vote in this year's election, even if women were enfranchised, but I want to thank you for giving hardworking, unsung females like my mother a voice . . .*

> *Dear Responsible Woman,*
>
> *Who are you, and are you already part of the Oregon State*

*Equal Suffrage Association? If not, please join us at our next meeting . . .*

*Dear Responsible Woman,*

*I'm a pro-suffrage man, and although I'm cautious about discussing my sentiments among my colleagues at work, I applaud you for your bravery . . .*

*Dear Responsible Woman,*

*As you may already know, in June of this year 3,473 "gentlemen" of Portland contributed to the failure of the state-wide women's suffrage measure. Please write more editorials to awaken the obtuse males of this city.*

*PLEASE!*

Dozens of people thanked me. Even men praised my eloquence. Other people felt I should be horsewhipped and chained in my kitchen, but for the most part, the handwritten and professionally typed reactions set my hands trembling with gratitude and hope.

I widened my curtains to invite in more light for rereading some of the letters, and even fragile Mrs. Stanton and her wagon filled with pickling jars seemed to shine a little brighter out on the sidewalk.

That afternoon, I fetched my canvas Gladstone bag and packed my clothing—bloomers included—along with the one hundred twenty-three dollars. I then shoved the luggage under the pink ruffles of my bed.

*In barely twenty-four hours*, I realized, my knees still on the ground, my eyes locked on my hidden belongings, *A Responsible Woman and the Mesmerizing Henri Reverie—Young Marvels of the New Century—will be venturing to the Portland Hotel and putting on one hell of a show.*

# CHAPTER TWENTY-TWO

# THE LOWEST FLAME

L ess than an hour after school would have been dismissed, Frannie showed up at my door with a basket smelling of chicken looped over her arm.

"How are you doing?" she asked.

"Well . . ." I raised the Fannie Farmer cookbook I was carrying. "I'm mastering the fine art of housewifery."

She frowned. "Is that even a word?"

"I looked it up once, after Father used it."

I dropped the book on the hall table and opened the door wider.

Frannie stepped inside. "How are you really doing?"

I shut the door and leaned my back against it. "My bags are packed. I'm ready for tomorrow."

She nodded and bit her lip.

I nudged her basket with my knuckle. "What's this?"

"We had leftover food from the anniversary party, and I thought"—she cleared her throat—"if you wanted to come with me, we could deliver it to Genevieve."

"That's terribly kind of you."

"To be honest"—she closed one eye and cringed—"I want to meet her."

"You mean you want to see if Henry is lying about her."

"That's not what I said."

"But it's what you mean."

"All right"—she lowered her shoulders—"maybe that's a little bit true. But as I said yesterday, if you're concerned enough about her to put up with your father, then I'd like to see what I can do to help. And I asked Mama about that sort of cancer, and she said she'd be surprised a girl could have it that young."

"Henry's not lying."

"No, let me finish. She said if a fifteen-year-old girl did indeed get diagnosed with it, that girl would certainly need extra support and encouragement."

I glanced down the hallway, toward the kitchen. "I'm not sure if I can go. I have to light the stove for supper . . ."

"We'll be quick. I'll even pay for the streetcar so we can get there faster."

"Hmm. I wouldn't mind seeing how she and Henry are doing." I grabbed my coat off the hook. "It has to be extremely quick. Nothing can go wrong."

I KNOCKED ON THE DOOR OF ROOM TWENTY-FIVE AND tried not to breathe too much of the stale cigar smoke filling up the hall.

"I hope I'm not waking her," I whispered to Frannie. "She's had a fever, and Hen—"

The door opened a crack. Henry's blue eyes peeked out. "Olivia. Hello. I thought you might have been the doctor again."

"No, it's just me. I'm sorry if we're disturbing Genevieve's sleep, but this is my good friend Frannie, and she's brought some food."

Henry opened the door a foot wider. "That's awfully nice. Thank you."

"You're welcome." Frannie handed him the basket, which dipped toward the ground during the transfer, for it was heavy—I'd helped her carry it down the street. "There's chicken," she said, "fresh vegetables, bread, and two slices of cake. You can keep the basket until Olivia next sees you."

"That's far too kind."

"Olivia told me what she's doing to help, so I thought . . ." Frannie pulled her coat tighter around herself. "I wanted to do something, too."

"How is Genevieve?" I asked.

"Um . . ." Henry scratched at his ear. "She's, uh . . ." He peeked over his shoulder. "What did you say, Genevieve?"

His sister called something from inside in a voice too soft for me to hear.

"It's Olivia and a friend," said Henry. "They've brought food." He shifted back to us. "A doctor was just here. She's still running a fever. He's still not sure if it's a cold . . . or if . . ." He grimaced. "He's not a cancer expert by any means, but he thinks . . . the tumor . . ."

He rubbed his hand across his forehead, and a vision attacked without warning.

Buckling knees.

Listless arms.

Sickly pallor.

Henry—not Genevieve.

I closed my eyes and kept my voice steady. "Is there anything else we can do?"

I opened them again to see Henry—normal Henry—shaking his head and swallowing.

"I don't think so," he said. And he dropped his voice to a whisper to add, "She's been crying. She always gets upset after doctor visits. I was just about to go down to the lobby so she can sleep and recuperate."

"I should have brought you some books," said Frannie.

"No need for that." He managed a small smile for her. "I'm sure you probably hate me a bit, if we're being honest. But I appreciate your help with my sister."

"I'd like to see Olivia," called Genevieve, loud enough for us to hear.

Henry turned toward her, one hand on the door, the other on the picnic basket. "Are you sure about that?"

"Her friend, too. I want to thank them."

"All right." Henry stepped back and maneuvered the basket out of our way. "Come inside, ladies."

We entered, and I immediately saw her. A weak blue light on the bed. The lowest flame of a gas lamp. Hope seemed to be vacating her body.

Frannie and I walked toward her, and even Frannie, who didn't see what I did, stiffened.

"I'm so sorry you're not feeling well." I cupped my hand around Genevieve's arm, which felt solid, despite its unsubstantial appearance. "This is my friend Frannie."

"It's nice to meet you." Genevieve gave a polite smile, but she remained a low blue glow. "Thank you for the food. I'm sorry I'm such a mess. The doctor was just here . . . and . . ." She turned her face away. Silent tears rushed down her cheeks. "I'm sorry."

"It's all right." I squeezed her arm. "It's all right to cry. Don't be sorry."

"I don't want to worry Henry . . ."

"Neither of you need to worry," I said. "You'll soon be with a physician who knows how to help you. Just get some rest for now. That's all you need to do. Please don't lose hope. Don't be afraid."

I heard sniffling beside me and caught Frannie—who always managed to cry whenever someone else was crying—rubbing the back of her sleeve across her face. She lowered her arm when she noticed me looking at her.

"He's not eating," said Genevieve under her breath.

"What?" I leaned closer to the bed.

Genevieve licked her chapped lips. "Henry's not taking care of himself. I know he's not."

I glanced back at her brother.

"Please tell him to eat and sleep," she said. "I think he'd listen to you."

"Are you not eating, Henry?" I asked.

"I haven't been hungry. But"—he lifted Frannie's basket—"we have good food now."

"Then eat it." I turned back to Genevieve. "And please make sure you try to eat, too. We're almost there."

"I know."

"Get some good sleep." I tucked her blankets over her shoulders. "You'll be on your way to San Francisco soon."

"Thank you. I'm glad you came."

Frannie and I headed back to the door, where Henry still lingered with the basket.

I reached for his hand but remembered we had an audience, so my fingers fumbled and latched on to the cuff of his shirtsleeve instead.

"Please take care of yourself," I said.

"Don't worry." He grinned, but his eyes lacked their persuasiveness. "Everything will be perfect tomorrow night." He tugged on my own sleeve, and his finger brushed across the side of my thumb.

We parted ways. The door closed behind us with a low thud that traveled through my bones.

Frannie and I journeyed down the hotel stairwell, side by side, our feet slow and plodding in the echoing quarters.

By the time we reached the bottom, she was holding tightly to my hand.

"I may not be here to witness the full fruition of his balancing of the sexes, but already we see the promise of its coming, and future generations will reap its blessings."

— SUSAN B. ANTHONY, "The New Century's Manly Woman," 1900

MODERN.

MRS. NEWGIRL *(to* DAUGHTER*)*. — Goodness me, Kitty! Don't stand there with your hands in your pockets, that way; — you don't know how ungentlemanly it looks!

# CHAPTER TWENTY-THREE

# ELECTION DAY

NOVEMBER 6, 1900

Tuesday morning, an hour and a half after Father left for work in his operatory, I lugged the canvas Gladstone to its next hiding spot, across the city.

Every neighbor's house I passed filled me with pangs of nostalgia for my life in the city. Each familiar street sign disappearing over my shoulder jabbed at my conscience and chipped away tiny flakes of my heart.

Yet I kept walking.

I passed a brick firehouse with a ballot-box table set up

next to a black and red steam pumper engine in the garage. Out front, a line of men—a hodgepodge of hats and caps, coveralls, dungarees, and smart black suits—waited to exercise their democratic right and paid no attention to me strolling behind them with my overstuffed bag.

Two blocks later, a wagon led by a handsome pair of chestnut horses rolled past me with flags waving and cornets and trombones blaring "Yankee Doodle." Banners hung off the wooden slats in the back, shouting, WILLIAM JENNINGS BRYAN! and ANTI-IMPERIALISM!

"Tell your father to vote for Bryan, little lady," called out a man around Father's age in red-striped suspenders that looked more like Henry's peppermint candies than the American flag.

"I'm not supposed to have any say in politics," I called back, but then I squeezed my lips shut and eyed the nearby pedestrians. My heart jumped around in my chest until I assured myself Father hadn't just witnessed me sassing a political campaigner while wandering the streets with my worldly possessions. I kept my head down and my mouth closed until I reached the front desk at the Hotel Vernon.

"I'd like a room, please," I said to the hotel clerk with the devilish Vandyke beard—the same terrible little man who had belittled the Negro customers and yelled at Henry and me to take our lovers' quarrel outside.

"A room for one?" he asked.

"Yes, a place of my own." Oh, how I loved the sound of

that! "And I'd like to pay in advance to ensure there will be no trouble finding you if I need to check out early."

Even if the clerk did remember me as the screeching lunatic from three days before, he made no complaint about my presence once I plunked a dollar bill onto his desk.

"Room eight," he said with a smile above his pointy umber beard, and he slid a golden key across the polished mahogany.

I left my suitcase in the first-floor room with a quilt-covered bed that appeared to be collapsing on one side. Another whiff of the establishment's mold met my nose, but I had no plans to stay. I shut the door behind me, locked up my possessions, and exited the hotel without checking on Henry and Genevieve upstairs.

The night before, I had awoken in a panicked sweat from a dream in which I smashed a sledgehammer over a gravestone marked RHODES.

Instead of confronting that fear, I preferred to walk back home and cling to the illusion that everything would unfold as planned.

WITHOUT GERDA'S HELP, I SOMEHOW MANAGED TO BUT- ton myself up in the same eggplant-purple dress I'd worn to Sadie's party, the only gown in my wardrobe suitable for an election-night soiree. Gerda must have scrubbed the mud off the hem Saturday morning, for the fabric betrayed no signs of Percy chasing me down in his buggy.

I descended the staircase toward Father, who was reading

the mail in his best wool suit and a crisp black bow tie. The air was rich with the scent of Macassar hair oil.

He peeked up at me. "You're finally ready. Why are you wearing that lace scarf?"

I left the bottom step. "It's the latest fashion."

"Don't be ridiculous."

"How would you know what young ladies are wearing?"

"I know what does and doesn't look garish." He set down the mail on the hall table. "Please take that off."

I pressed the lace against my neck. "I can't."

"You can't?"

"It's covering a blemish."

"There's no such thing as a neck blemish, Olivia. Now, take that thing off"—he reached for the scarf—"before the ladies at the party see you."

He gave a firm tug, and the lace unspooled.

My neck fell bare.

"The marks are from Percy," I said before he could match words to his open-mouthed stare. "He tried forcing himself upon me the night of Sadie Eiderling's party, but all I could say was 'All is well.'" I yanked the scarf free of Father's hands and wound the lace back around my neck. "I worried you'd ask Mr. Reverie to do something more to me if I told you what had happened."

He just stood there, paralyzed and mute.

"Are you ready?" I asked with a glance at the door.

"Um . . . yes." He blinked and fitted his head with a tall silk hat dating back to the Garfield administration. "I've hired a driver and carriage for the night. We're traveling in high style, which ought to tell you how important I consider this event. Behave as if your life depended on it."

"Of course," I said. "My life indeed depends on it."

FIREWORKS LIT UP THE PORTLAND SKYLINE IN BLASTS OF indigo that rattled my seat in the carriage. Along the side of one of downtown's tallest buildings, an enormous projection of President McKinley's clean-shaven face and balding head glowed across a sandstone wall.

"It doesn't actually feel as if my eyes are playing tricks on me right now," I said to Father, whose toes kept bumping into mine, "but I see President McKinley's giant white face watching over the city. Do you see it, too?"

Father craned his neck to get a peek outside the carriage window. "That's a stereopticon slide. The newspaper said that's how the city would announce who's ahead in the election."

"He looks like the Wonderful Wizard of Oz when he was just a huge head sitting in a chair." I gawked at the passing black-and-white image. "How peculiar."

The whimsical rooftop dormers and chimneys of the eight-story Portland Hotel would be coming up next, within a block, across from the courthouse on Sixth Street. I had walked by its opulent grounds hundreds of times.

The carriage eased down the Yamhill Street slope, but to

my consternation, I did not see all those wonderful chimneys. On a tall, lumpy hill, in the erratic shots of light from the streaks of blue fireworks, stood a castle with towers severe and black.

"No, that's absurd." I turned away from the carriage window and covered my eyes with the lace scarf.

"What's absurd?" asked Father.

"It's not a good sign." I squeezed the lace and spoke more to myself than Father. "It shouldn't look like Dracula's castle—and death. I shouldn't be afraid."

"No, you shouldn't." Father shifted his position on his seat with a squeak of leather. "And you should stop reading that damned horror novel. Perhaps that's one more item I should have Mr. Reverie remove from—"

He cut himself off, and at first I wondered if he was about to revise his stance on the hypnosis. A second later, a sound that must have distracted him reached my ears.

Singing.

Women's voices singing.

I lowered the scarf and shifted toward the window again.

Outside our carriage, females of all ages, sizes, and backgrounds lined the lamp-lit sidewalks in front of our beautiful Portland Hotel with its soaring walls of dark stone and terra-cotta. The women and girls wore yellow ribbons on their coats and their hats, and they belted out a song while raising homemade cloth flags bearing the words VOTES FOR WOMEN!

I slid across the seat and stuck my head into the chimney-scented air to better hear them sing the satirical lyrics of "Oh, Dear, What Can the Matter Be?"

"Put your head back inside the carriage." Father pulled me down to my seat by my shoulder. "If those are the type of women I think they are, you'll get sick to your stomach."

The driver steered the trotting horses into the hotel's circular driveway, a grand roundabout surrounded by shrubberies and ornamental trees, almost as green in the nighttime lighting as during the sunshine splendor of day. The line of singing women and girls stretched clear up to the front doors.

The carriage rocked to a stop, and Father opened the door and clambered out. He turned around to help me down, just as the chorus of females switched to "Keep Woman in Her Sphere," another saucy anthem, sung to the tune of "Auld Lang Syne."

I spotted Frannie and Kate near the hotel's front doors, but I turned my face away and pretended not to notice or hear them, even though my eyes swam with tears of gratitude.

Father offered me his elbow and helped me down to the ground. With my head held high—I swear, I grew four inches—we trod forward to my fate.

A wind snapped at my ears.

The world went black and tipped off balance, and the ladies' voices seemed distorted into muffled wails. The scents of death and decay breathed in my face, and fiery torches guided our way to the hotel's double doors, which stretched open before us like a pair of jaws with jagged teeth.

"I can't do this." I pulled back. "Something's not right. It reminds me too much of death."

"Don't be silly." Father tugged me onward. "Your fears are all in your head."

With a firm pull, he wrenched me inside.

# CHAPTER TWENTY-FOUR

# A REMEDY FOR REVERIES

A banner for the Oregon Association Opposed to the Extension of Suffrage to Women hung above a white semicircular stage, its letters as bold and red as knife wounds. Below the sign a twelve-piece orchestra strummed their bows at a dizzying pace for the brisk Viennese waltz careering around the waxed parquet floor.

The first dancer I saw was none other than Sadie Eiderling, dressed in a long scarlet gown, whirling about in the arms of bespectacled Teddy from her party. Sunken-Eyed John waltzed with a blond girl in black, while his sister, Eugenia, danced with the leering, long-nosed fellow who had called me a tart. They held their upper bodies as stiff as shop-window mannequins, and their faces appeared handsome and young in the bright wattage of the crystal chandeliers.

Whenever they veered into shadow, however, oh, how they changed. Their teeth, their burning eyes, the black-tinged blood on their lips—all their hidden savagery—triggered an ache in the marks on my neck.

Percy, primped like a peacock in a dark suit and tails, strutted our way with his hands folded behind his back. "Dr. Mead, Olivia, how lovely to see you. Pretty scarf, Olivia."

"Father knows about my neck," I said, and Percy turned and skedaddled to the opposite end of the room.

Father kept me pulled against his side and didn't even mention a word about Percy. "I don't see the hypnotist." He gazed about the throng of Portland's wealthiest, who danced and milled about and drank champagne at round tables draped in red, white, and blue. "Let's go pay our regards to the Underhills."

I scanned the room for Henry as well, but he was nowhere to be found amid all the jewels and stiff collars. Waiters in white coats glided about with trays of savory-smelling appetizers and flutes of bubbling gold liquid, but they and Father were the only non-society men in the entire place.

On our way to the Underhills, we passed Percy's bald father, Judge Acklen, whom I recognized from the newspapers. He sipped a dark drink that resembled a vial of blood and appeared to be alone, until a vaporous haze of a woman, perhaps Mrs. Acklen, slipped into view beside him.

Father pressed onward to Mr. Underhill, who was conversing with another young couple I recognized from Sadie's birthday party. They chatted in front of an eight-foot-tall ice sculpture carved like the Statue of Liberty, propped on a round table with a star-spangled cloth. The air around them chilled me more than our mudroom in January.

"Mr. Underhill." Father thrust out his hand, interrupting their chat. "Thank you again for inviting us."

"Oh. Dr. Mead." Mr. Underhill shook Father's hand, and his white mustache wriggled with a smile. "So you arrived."

"Have you spotted our entertainment for the evening yet?" asked Father.

"I think she's right here." Mr. Underhill gestured toward me with his champagne. "This is the girl I was telling you about, Lizzie. Go ahead, say the word to her—but stand back."

The female half of the young couple, a pretty brunette with glossy ringlets, leaned forward with pouty lips and said with a chirp, "Suffrage."

I slapped my mouth and hacked a deep, retching sound.

The girl squealed and clapped her hands, and her broad-shouldered escort gave one of those firm-lipped sorts of nods that males seem to make when they're feeling especially mannish. I swallowed down my humiliation.

"You haven't seen young Mr. Reverie, then?" asked Father.

"No," said Mr. Underhill. "But all of our guests will be

especially interested in his cure after that disgusting display outside the hotel just now."

"I've always told Mother," said chirpy little Lizzie, "that women like that remind me of freakish men with bosoms."

Her escort laughed. "Lizzie!"

"I'm sorry, James, but it's true. Just look at this one." She nodded toward me.

I picked at the tips of my hot gloves and pretended not to have heard the insult. My blood simmered. My chest felt overly exposed.

Sadie and Teddy strolled our way, arm in arm, and under no circumstances was I about to bear the brunt of *her* wicked barbs, too. I pulled free of Father and veered toward the exit.

Ten feet before I reached the doorway, Henry walked into the ballroom while fussing with his tie.

I released a pent-up breath and stopped in my tracks.

Henry halted, too, and something worse than his usual fatigue weighed down his shoulders. He looked deathly ill—his lips cracked, his face drawn, his eyes devoid of all fire.

Father snatched my elbow and jerked me away before I could ask what was wrong.

"Henry looks sick," I said, twisting my head to see his red vest disappearing behind us.

"You cannot interact with him before the demonstration." Father tripped me over my feet to the farthest corner of the ballroom. "People will think the hypnosis is a fake, and that I'm a fake—or a fool."

"I just want to find out what's wrong with him. I don't think that was an illusion."

"He probably just drank too much last night. Showmen tend to do that."

"Dentists, too, from what I've seen."

Father plunked me down in a cream-colored chair near the stage. "Sit here for now," he said over the frenzy of strings. "Mrs. Underhill will likely let us know when she's ready."

I leaned forward to better see through the throng of dancing bodies and spotted Henry wandering behind them as if he didn't know where to go. The waiters with the trays of food didn't even stop to talk to him. The frantic strumming of the orchestra propelled everyone in the room into a faster-than-average speed; people were flitting and swerving all over the place, rushing, rushing, rushing—except for Henry.

"Go check on him." I tugged on Father's coat. "He doesn't even know where you want him to be. He looks even more out of place than we do."

"We do not look out of place."

"You were the one who wanted him here. Go take care of him."

Father grunted and circled around the dance floor to meet up with Henry on the other side. He then gestured with his arms while speaking to Henry and pointed toward Mrs. Underhill, who had joined her husband by the frozen Statue of Liberty. Henry headed over to the ice sculpture as well, raking a hand through his hair.

Father hurried back to my side. "He hasn't been feeling his best, but he assured me that everything will go as planned. He's going to ask Mrs. Underhill if we should start soon."

"Did he say anything about his sister?"

"No, and please, just sit here and stop fretting about everything. All will be well once we start the demonstration." Father tugged his handkerchief out of his pocket and mopped his forehead.

I rubbed the tops of my legs through the purple sheen of my skirt. "Show me Henry's money."

Father blinked as if he hadn't heard me quite right. "I beg your pardon."

"Prove to me you intend to pay him if I go up there and let him hypnotize me again. I won't play nicely until you do."

His jaw stiffened.

"Please," I said.

He rustled an envelope out of his breast pocket, gave me a quick peek at the cash inside, and then tucked the envelope straight back into the folds of his coat. "He had better remove every last shred of your sass tonight, young lady. I'm getting tired of this."

The orchestra's song dwindled to a much-needed end, and the room slowed its pace and settled to a stop. Mrs. Underhill climbed aboard the stage in a royal-blue gown with a long train that swished behind her like a cat's tail. She waved at the conductor to keep the music at bay and walked to center stage.

"Ladies and gentlemen, welcome to our election-night ball, sponsored by the Oregon Association Opposed to the Extension of Suffrage to Women."

I gagged over the word *suffrage*, while everyone else applauded and cheered.

"To the Republicans in the crowd," continued Mrs. Underhill, "a hearty congratulations. It looks as though President William McKinley and his running mate, Theodore Roosevelt, will be helming the country as we sail into this glorious new century."

Fewer than half of the attendees smiled and slapped their gloved hands together, while the anti-imperialist Democrats folded their arms across their chests and sat there with a wilted air of defeat.

"What we can all celebrate together as a group, however"—Mrs. Underhill lifted her index finger and waited for the applause to fade—"is the continued tradition of men alone voting for president while we women devote our attention to more ladylike pursuits."

An astounding abundance of women and girls clapped at this sentiment, including bold Sadie Eiderling, who seemed far too despotic to be opposed to female empowerment. I ground my molars.

"My sincerest apologies," said Mrs. Underhill, folding her hands together in front of her waist, "for the unpleasant display that greeted your arrival at the hotel this evening. More than ever it seems we need a remedy for the growing army of loud, obnoxious women who insist they are the same as men." She shifted her royal-blue bosom our way. "And I have good news for you on that account. Some wise men in our very own community have used their innovative brains to create such a remedy."

Silence befell the mesmerized crowd.

"My dear friends," continued Mrs. Underhill, "you may have noticed a few extra people at this party whom you may not have expected to see tonight. Dr. Walter Mead, a local dentist." She stretched out her hand in Father's direction. "And Monsieur Henri Reverie, the talented young hypnotist from Montreal, Canada." She extended her right arm to Henry, who stood in front of the opposite side of the stage from us. "Together, they have invented a cure for female rebellion, using the astounding power of hypnotism. Young Monsieur Reverie is going to demonstrate this revolutionary antidote for wayward women right here, right now, in front of all of you. Please welcome to the stage Henri Reverie and his subject, young rabble-rouser Olivia Mead."

The audience's applause walloped me in the face like a sack of rocks, and I couldn't even think to stand on my own. Father had to yank me out of the chair to get me to come to my senses and move.

"Go up, go up," he said, spinning me toward a small staircase at the side of the stage. "He's waiting for you."

I tripped over my skirt and petticoat on my way up the steps, for the whole room spun, and all I could see were crystal chandeliers whisking over my head. A warm hand slipped into mine and helped guide me to my feet.

"It's all right, Olivia," said Henry, putting his other hand around my waist. "I'm here. Just keep breathing."

With his assistance, I regained my balance and found myself wandering with him to the middle of the stage. Unlike the last time I joined him in such a way, it was the audience below us that resembled devils, not he. No matter how hard I blinked, I couldn't shake the sight of sharp teeth, anemic skin, and hungry stares in that sea of sky-high pompadours and slicked male hair that glistened with greasy spiced oils. Sadie Eiderling stood in the front row, peering at me with a viper-toothed grin, her hair a huge and untamed nest on the top of her head.

Henry slid his hand out of mine and turned to face the monsters. After a deep inhale, he rolled back his shoulders, lifted his chin, and with the magic of a metamorphosing butterfly, transformed into the performer version of himself.

"Good evening, *mesdames et messieurs.* My name is Henri Reverie, and I have been studying the arts of mesmerism and hypnotism with my uncle ever since I was twelve. I use a combination of techniques from the great masters, including animal magnetism, deep relaxation, and the remarkable power of suggestion. As you heard from our lovely hostess, Madame Underhill, I recently received the fascinating challenge of curing this young woman"—he half turned toward me—"of her dreams to vote for president. *Un remède pour des rêveries*. A remedy for daydreams." He rubbed his right fingers together in the air and seemed to taste the phrase on his tongue. "The cure for dreaming. A beguiling possibility, no?"

Spellbound, the rapt devil faces in the audience watched him walk toward them across the stage. "Over the past five days," he said, "I have administered two separate treatments to this young woman. When I first came to her, just last Thursday, she was participating in scandalous rallies for the vote and scrambling to finish her high school diploma so she could attend a university."

"You actually met her last Wednesday," called the gaunt and long-toothed version of Percy from the crowd, his hands cupped around his mouth, "when you stood on top of her at your Halloween show."

"Yes, *merci*. Thank you for reminding me, Monsieur Acklen. I first saw Miss Mead the very day she attended the rally, and I subdued her in front of the eyes of Portland that very night. Now she cannot even hear certain words related to the vote and higher education without getting sick to her stomach. Shall I demonstrate?"

The audience, at first, seemed taken aback by his proposal. They darted skeptical glances at one another, chuckled, and shook their heads. My eyes stopped seeing them as monsters. Now they were a crowd in white summer dresses and suits, gathered to witness a miracle maker at a county fair.

Sadie, decked out in a straw hat and red gingham, lifted her hand and asked, "Will this demonstration be disgusting?"

"Only if we badger her with the words too long," said Henry. "Go ahead, Mademoiselle Eiderling. Say something to her yourself. Try the word that starts with an *s*—the one those singing women out there adore."

Sadie shrugged. "Song?"

"No"—Henry helped her along—"s-u-f-f . . ."

"Ohhh." Sadie balled her hands into fists and drew a large intake of air through her nose. "Suffrage," she said with the breath of a birthday-candle wish.

I covered my mouth and made yet another gagging racket, and I glared at Henry out of the tops of my eyes. *Do not prolong this part of the demonstration*, I mentally willed him. *Do not.*

"Susan B. Anthony," called Mrs. Underhill from her new position down below the stage, and I coughed into my hand until my throat hurt. "Votes for women," she also added. "Women's rights."

*"Merci."* Henry held up his hands. "Thank you, ladies, for helping me with that particular demonstration. I am proud to say that with the subtlest of commands"—he circled around me with solid thumps of his soles—"I have also instilled in Miss Mead a higher moral standard. This virtuous girl before you now possesses a hatred of higher education, bicycle bloomers, and dalliances with the wrong sorts of boys."

I sank my teeth into my bottom lip to keep from grinning at those last parts. My nerves settled a tad, and the audience shifted back to its regular appearance. Rich folk in ball gowns and evening suits.

Henry stopped right beside me and clasped hold of his lapel. "However, as Madame Underhill so eloquently stated, one of the most pressing problems with these suff—" He cut the word short. "The problem with these young ladies is that they are loud. They certainly want to have a voice, don't they?"

"They certainly do," shouted a red-cheeked gentleman in the midst of the nodding male and female heads.

"Wouldn't it be *magnifique* if we could silence these girls?" asked Henry in a tone that worried me a little with its seriousness. "Simply take away their voices and make them as quiet and gentle as women ought to be?"

Another round of applause echoed across the room.

"Would you like me to prove to you that the silencing of wayward young women is a genuine possibility in this modern era of hypnosis?"

The applause strengthened in volume—its vibrations trembled in the soles of my shoes and the surfaces of my teeth.

"Monsieur Conductor . . ." Henry whisked around to face the orchestra. "Would you kindly have your orchestra play a soothing piece of music for me? A lullaby, if you please."

The conductor and the orchestra flipped through their sheet music, and Henry peeked at me for the swiftest of moments. His gallant stage voice and mannerisms failed to conceal the dark circles beneath his eyes or the fact that his bottom lip was so dry and cracked, it now bled almost as much as when Father had gagged him. I wondered when he last took a sip of water, and I sealed my mouth shut so I wouldn't feel compelled to ask.

The conductor must have raised his baton and signaled to his orchestra to commence, for the strings played a lullaby that filled the room with the delicacy of the fog settling over the roofs and the pines and the big-leaf maples of my street.

"Miss Mead." Henry faced me with his side to the audience. He bumped his fingers against my wrist so that I would position myself the same way.

I hesitated. A spark of fear shot through me. Before I could even think to try the tongue trick, he grabbed my wrist and pulled me toward him.

"Sleep!"

My face smashed against his shoulder blade, and I dropped down, down, down, until the orchestra's lullaby folded over me in black sheets of musical ecstasy. Henry turned me toward the audience and tipped me backward, dragging me with my heels skiing across the stage. My arms flopped below me, and my fingertips skated along the wood.

"Olivia," said Henry with his mouth behind my head. The strings of the orchestra nearly swallowed up his voice, but I heard him say, for my ears alone, "You no longer feel compelled to cover your mouth and make a gagging sound when you hear the words *suffrage, women's rights, suffragist, votes for women, Susan B. Anthony,* or *college.* You can argue with your father as much as you'd like and be as angry as you'd like."

He draped my body in a chair in front of the gentle purr of the violins. My utter lack of control over my limbs sent my legs falling open and my head tipping backward, and I could feel him hurrying to close my knees and reposition my torso.

"Stop." He took his hands off me. "Wait, wait, wait. Stop the music. I'm sorry, but this particular feat seems ridiculously easy. Hypnotizing one girl into losing her voice means nothing to the giant world outside those doors. Hundreds to thousands of suffragists are busily working away right now, spinning their webs, making their next plans to slap another referendum onto your ballots. If we want to rid this state and this country of suffragists, I need to prove to you that I can hypnotize an entire stage full of women into silence."

Henry's hand cupped my forehead.

"Awake," he said while sitting me upright. "Please stand, Miss Mead, to allow room for more chairs."

I let him help me to my feet, even though my legs bent and bobbed at all sorts of odd angles.

Henry readdressed the audience. "Would some of you gentlemen kindly fetch at least five of those singing women from outside this hotel? And then I'll need a few more volunteers to help bring some chairs upon this stage."

The young men and their fathers just stood there and stared as if they had never been asked to carry a stick of furniture in their lives. Before long, the poor waiters were setting down their trays, lugging around chairs, and running out to the street to wrangle women.

I pulled at my lace scarf and pleaded to Frannie and the other girls, *Please be gone! Be gone!* My grand scheme for the evening suddenly struck me as ridiculous and selfish, and I hated myself for convincing Henry to conspire with me.

A curly-haired waiter ran back inside from the lobby. "The women left."

I covered a relieved smile with my hand.

"They left?" asked Mrs. Underhill, and other disappointed murmurings and snorts shook loose from the crowd.

Henry held up his hands. "Do not worry, *mesdames et messieurs.* I am still able to show you how to tame a roomful of tigresses into docile, silent kittens. I simply need some of the beautiful ladies in this audience to temporarily stand in as the rebels."

The women froze.

Henry clasped his hands together in the direction of Sadie's bloodstain of a dress. "Mademoiselle Eiderling, would you care to be one of our volunteers?"

Sadie narrowed her eyes. "No."

"I believe I owe you the chance for an operatic solo," said Henry, "which can certainly be arranged while you're up on this stage. I do not think there would be a sound more breathtaking this election night than your sweet voice filling this room with the national anthem."

Sadie folded her arms over her chest and didn't budge.

Teddy slung his hand over her shoulder. "Do it, Sadie."

Sunken-Eyed John raised a champagne flute and said,

"Yes, do it," and his sister Eugenia clapped and added, "Yes, please, go up there, Sadie. What a laugh that would be"—all of them prodding at Sadie just as she had tried to bully Henry at her party.

"All right." Sadie jutted her chin in the air. "But Eugenia and my mother have to come with me, and my voice had better sound like an angel's when I sing the national anthem."

"*Bien sûr*, an angel," said Henry with a wobble in his footing that got me worrying about his health again. "Certainly, *mademoiselle*. Please come up and sit in one of these chairs."

The partygoers cleared a path for Sadie, Eugenia, and an older woman in a gown dripping in ecru lace, her hair a squat version of Sadie's strawberry-gold pompadour. Mrs. Underhill trooped up on stage with them as well, followed by Lizzie—the squeaky girl who had called me a freakish man with bosoms—and her equally sulky-lipped mother.

I perched myself on the leftmost chair and cleared the nervousness from my throat as the six other ladies joined me in sitting up there, all of us facing the audience in front of the orchestra.

"Thank you for helping us, ladies," said Henry, angled toward both us and the crowd below. "Your cooperation will reward you in the future, for when we silence the suffragists—"

I forgot to gag, but Henry's pause pushed me into action. I choked with passion to compensate.

"—you will no longer need to concern yourselves with organizations such as this one. You will be able to devote your time to charities and other, worthier endeavors instead of hushing up women with pluck."

The mothers on the stage nodded their approval, while their daughters fussed with their skirts and slumped as if bored. I folded my hands in my lap and tried to ignore Father's watchful face out of the corner of my eye.

"Ladies and gentlemen"—Henry pivoted toward the audience and raised his hands—"I present to you America's idyllic future."

He swirled around to us ladies and started work on Lizzie at the opposite end of the line from me.

"Close your eyes." He stroked the girl's head of jostling brown ringlets. "You are drowsy. You can think of nothing but sleep. Melt down, melt down into sleep."

He moved on to Lizzie's mother and embarked upon the same routine. "Close your eyes." He kneaded the woman's supple forehead. "Think of nothing but sleep. You feel very sleepy. You are so tired. Melt down."

He continued down the line of women, repeating the same phrases and massaging everyone's skulls and foreheads. This time I had ample warning to keep myself alert. I wedged my tongue against the roof of my mouth. Henry's silky voice alone was already persuading my chin to drop to my chest, but I forced myself to envision slamming a door in his face.

"You feel very sleepy," he said to Mrs. Eiderling next to me. "You are drowsy. Think of nothing but sleep."

Mrs. Eiderling's head and shoulders slumped forward.

Henry moved over to me and put his hands on the sides of my head. "Close your eyes."

I pressed my tongue to my palate with all my might and shut my lids.

"Think of nothing but sleep." He caressed my temples. "Go to sleep."

I held my breath and strained to block out the potency of his words. *Slam the door. Slam it hard!* My thoughts strained toward suffragist anthems, train rides to New York City, moonlit bicycle rides in garnet-brown bloomers . . .

Henry left my side. My mind remained my own.

"You now feel your right arm drifting into the air," he said. "You cannot help it—the arm is simply moving on its own, rising higher and higher."

I played along and raised my arm, my eyes still closed.

"As you can see, ladies and gentlemen," he said, "some subjects are more susceptible to hypnosis than others. Miss . . . what is your name, *mademoiselle?*"

"Lizzie Yves," said the chirpy girl in a wide-awake voice.

"You still seem awake, Lizzie. Stand up, please—and sleep! Go down, go down, you are so tired you can do nothing but sleep. Very good. You are doing beautifully."

I found myself tapping my foot to get him to hurry along with everything, but I stopped myself as soon as I realized the blunder.

"Now, ladies . . ." His footsteps traveled to the center of the stage. "What I am about to tell you is extremely important, so you must listen carefully. When I say the word *awake,* you will open your eyes, and you will not be able to speak. You will have no voice. No matter what anyone says to you, if you try to talk, all that will exit your mouth is soundless air. You will be silent."

I bowed my head and heard the patter of his shoes leaving the stage, as if he were running away from the mess he was about to create.

"Awake!"

We all opened our eyes. Mrs. Eiderling spread her lips apart beside me, but all that came out was an empty gasp. Next to her, Sadie clutched her right hand around her throat and squirmed in her chair until the legs of the furniture tapped against the stage. Mrs. Underhill and Eugenia flapped their lips open and shut like wide-eyed fish.

"This, ladies and gentlemen," said Henry from down in the middle of the crowd, "is the sound of silent women."

The men in the audience let loose applause that threw us back in our chairs.

"Bravo," shouted Judge Acklen. "Well done!"

Mr. Underhill whistled his approval, and his wife sat up with a fierce-eyed glare.

"Go ahead." Henry grabbed Percy by the arm. "Tell those girls what you really think of women. They can't say a word back to you."

"Oh, I don't know about that." Percy lifted his hands and

retreated out of Henry's grasp. "They can still slap, can't they?"

The gentlemen laughed and patted Percy on the back.

Sadie stood and waved her arms.

"Oh, wait." Henry wiggled a piece of paper and a pen out of his breast pocket. "One of them is trying to communicate."

Sadie snatched the writing utensils from his hands and kneeled on the stage to scribble a note. She then shoved the paper down at Henry's nose.

Henry read the note over and shifted back to the crowd. "Well, this is a historic moment indeed. For the first time ever, an anti-suffragist woman has written the words 'Give us our voices!'"

A few gentlemen laughed, but a sobering silence threw a bucket of ice water over the party. Glimmers of suspicion awakened in the eyes of the Oregon Association crowd. The hairs on the back of my neck bristled.

"Ladies." Henry turned toward us, and he swayed for a moment, as if he had moved too fast. "Gentlemen are not kind when it comes to you speaking your minds. You must be cautious about giving us full custody of your voices. I am afraid we will take unfair advantage, *mes chéries.*"

Sadie stomped her foot on the stage and made the whole room jump.

"All right, sit down, sit down." Henry waved her back to her chair.

He moved to take a step away from the crowd, but he stopped and tipped as though dizzy, and his eyes rolled toward the back of his head. He fell forward but caught himself by bracing his hands against the front edge of the stage.

I bolted upright in my chair. "Henry?"

He stayed still for a moment, panting as though breathing were a struggle, his head hanging between his arms.

"I'm sorry." He managed to lift his face, now as white as ash. "Oh, God . . . maybe the orchestra . . . I'm really sorry . . ." He staggered backward and collapsed on the waxed ballroom floor.

# CHAPTER TWENTY-FIVE

# SILENCE

I'm not sure how I got off that stage—I believe I may have taken a running leap and jumped to the hard parquet below. All I remember is Henry's skin growing cold and gray beneath my hands.

"Are you breathing, Henry?" I shook his shoulders. "Oh, God. Please breathe! Please breathe!"

He turned paler by the second. The only thing I could think to do was jostle him.

"Don't die. Don't die. You can't die. Isn't there a doctor in this room? Why isn't someone helping him?"

I peeked up at the crowd and discovered that the floor

around us had cleared. Everyone stood back in their fine tailored clothing, watching me fumble to save his life.

"Why are you just standing there?" I asked. "This isn't part of the show. Someone needs to get him to a hospital. Put him in one of your carriages. Help him!"

Mr. Underhill grimaced at Henry. "He's a theater person. Some of us would rather not have him in our carriages."

"Oh, Christ, you're idiots." I cradled Henry's head against my chest. "If he dies, then your wives and daughters are going to be stuck without voices forever."

Some of the men and boys actually laughed at that statement—*they laughed!*

Claps of thunder erupted from the stage behind me. I gave a start and peered over my shoulder to discover the silenced mothers and daughters hurling themselves down the staircases at the sides of the stage in their long, shimmering gowns. They barreled toward us and shoved me away from Henry. Sadie and her mother lifted him by his shoulders. Mrs. Underhill and Eugenia grabbed his legs. Lizzie and her mother hoisted him up beneath his back. In less than two seconds, those women had his limp body up in the air and were rushing him across the room.

I jumped to my feet and chased after them through the palm-lined lobby and out to the cold night air. With Henry bouncing in their arms, the ladies reached an enclosed black carriage parked near Sixth.

I lunged to help them open the door and told them, "Be

careful," as they maneuvered Henry's head inside and spread him across a padded seat.

Sadie waved her arms at the driver and mouthed the word *hospital.*

The driver shrugged his broad shoulders. "Speak up. I don't know what you're saying."

"You need to drive this carriage to the hospital," I said for her. "Quickly!"

Sadie dove inside the vehicle with her mother and Henry, and the other ladies ran to the carriage behind them. I tried to follow Sadie into her carriage, but the door slammed shut in my face, and the horses trotted away.

"Olivia!" Father stormed toward me with my coat hanging off his arm. "We're going home. That was a shocking thing you two did in there. I'm appalled beyond words."

"What are you talking about?"

He gripped my arm with a squeeze that made me gasp.

"I'm not stupid, Olivia. You're able to speak when the rest of those women were silenced."

"I just—"

"You conspired with that hypnotist behind my back again and put those ladies in peril. What else have you been doing with him in secret, you lying little hussy?"

"I . . . what does any of that matter right now? Something's terribly wrong with Henry. His sister's waiting for him in the hotel. She's supposed to have surgery in San Francisco this Friday."

"That's Reverie's problem, not mine."

"We only conspired against you because he thought what you were doing to me was horrible. Don't punish his sister for our actions."

Father hardened his jaw but eased his grip.

"Please," I said, "she's done nothing wrong, and she's waiting for her brother. Go with me to fetch her so we can tell her about Henry and take her to him."

He puffed a loud sigh.

"Father?"

"All right, I'll give that poor girl a ride, but I'm not paying her brother one cent of my money. Come along." He wrapped my coat around my shoulders. "Let's go find our driver and be quick about this."

GENEVIEVE'S DOOR ALREADY SAT AJAR.

"Oh, no! What's happened here?" I hurried down the hall and pushed my way inside, expecting kidnappers and murderers and chaos.

Instead, I encountered the strange scene of Genevieve, Frannie, Kate, and Agnes sipping mugs of steaming tea on the Rhodeses' hotel sofa. Genevieve—solid and sturdy—wiped away tears with a handkerchief and smiled.

I blinked to ensure they wouldn't all disappear. "What's happening?"

Father strode into view behind me, and all four pairs of eyes seemed to ask the same question of me.

Frannie stood up from the right-hand arm of the sofa. "We raised money for Genevieve, just in case . . ." She looked between Father and me. "In case there was no other money to be had."

Father and I eyed each other.

"Between school, the bookstore, and this evening," said Kate, nestled beside Genevieve on one of the sofa cushions, "Frannie was able to collect close to seventy-five dollars."

"Seventy-five?" I stumbled toward them.

"Isn't it wonderful?" Genevieve rose with her mug. "I don't even know what to say. I never dreamed of such kindness." She stood on tiptoe and peeked over my shoulder. "Where's Henry?"

"He's . . ." I swallowed and clamped my hands into fists.

Genevieve's tea sloshed over the rim. "What's wrong?"

"Your brother," said Father, "collapsed after he and Olivia played a dirty hypnotist trick upon a group of women. He's on his way to the hospital."

Genevieve flickered out.

"I don't know what's wrong with him," I said, rubbing my temples to bring her back into view, "but he's there, and we'll take you to him."

"Is he all right?" she asked, now a weak sputter of light. "Was he able to speak?"

I shook my head. "You had better come."

The mugs were set aside, the door locked, and our six pairs of feet thundered down the hotel staircase.

Out by the carriage, Frannie folded me up in a hug. "You're still leaving after all of this, aren't you?"

"As I told you," I said into her ear, "train rides are faster and easier these days. Thank you for helping Genevieve."

"You're welcome. Please be extremely careful, Responsible Woman." She gave my lips a quick peck and sent me into the hired carriage with Father and Henry's wavering ghost of a sister.

THE LAMP-LIT HOSPITAL ON DARK AND HILLY CORNELL Street appeared to me as a regular brick-and-stone medical building—not a mausoleum or an undertaker's parlor or anything else more funereal than an actual hospital. All the same, a helpless sense of panic gripped my chest when I jumped out of the carriage below the five-story structure. I felt I'd forgotten something, or I'd lost something, and my mind kept racing back to shaking Henry's heavy shoulders as he lay there on the cold parquet floor. If only I'd moved a little faster to reach him, rustled him a little harder. If only I could have kept him from slipping out of reach.

I put my arm around Genevieve, and we climbed the steps to the hospital's tall doorway beneath an archway of bricks, with Father following us.

Inside the lobby—a cold, wood-paneled room I remembered from my grandmother's battle with pneumonia—the Eiderling, Underhill, and Yves ladies paced across a worn beige rug with their hands on their hips. The floral garden of their perfumes melded into the sticky smells of sweet medicine.

A nurse in a small white cap and an apron-covered dress peeked up from the front desk. "May I help you?"

Genevieve and I walked over to her, still attached to each other.

"You just admitted this girl's brother, Henry Rhodes," I said. "Or . . . Henri Reverie, as these ladies might have called him."

"They didn't call him anything." The nurse craned her neck toward the pacing collection of ladies in ball gowns. "What is wrong with their voices?"

"This is all the result of a hypnotism show gone terribly wrong."

"They're hypnotized?"

"How is Henry?" asked Genevieve. "May we see him?"

The nurse shook her head. "Visiting hours already ended, I'm afraid."

"Is he alive?" I asked.

"I'm sorry, but I don't know how he is. I only filled out his paperwork . . . or what I could of it." She glanced at the mute women again. "You'll need to wait here in the lobby, and the doctors will speak to his sister when they have information to give."

I turned and bumped straight into Father's chest.

"Oh, I didn't know you were there . . ."

"I don't want to stay here with these . . . women," he said

under his breath with a sharp eye on Mrs. Underhill. "They're probably plotting a way to murder me right now. We're going home."

"I can't."

"We took care of Miss Reverie. Now it's time for you to leave." He took me by the hand and jerked me away from Genevieve.

"Wait! I need to fix all the messes I've made."

He hauled me toward the door.

"Father, please"—I pushed his fingers off mine—"stop! I need to take responsibility—"

"Do not test me any further tonight," he said through gritted teeth, leaning toward me, "or I swear, I'll—"

"You'll what? What more can you possibly do?"

"Don't you dare complain again about my choice to help you."

"You hired someone to make me sick and helpless."

"I spared the rod and spoiled the child, is what I did."

"I'm 'A Responsible Woman,'" I said, and the words echoed across the hospital's walls and stopped the silenced ladies from pacing. "I'm the person who wrote that letter to Judge Acklen in Saturday's paper, and I'm more of a suffragist now than when you first hired Henry to control me. You struck a match and lit a fire."

Father's chin quivered. "Well . . ." He fumbled for his handkerchief in his coat pocket. "It's a damned good thing Mr. Reverie—or Rhodes, or whatever the hell his name is—

it's a damned good thing he might already be dead, because I would love more than anything to kill him right now."

"No, *you* did this to me. You made me want to fight. And I bet you did this to Mother, too."

"Women belong—"

I covered my ears. "I don't want to hear any more of your theories about women. I want you to go home and live by yourself, because I'm done living with you and cooking for you and worrying about you drinking away your misery. If Henry is gone, then I'm taking Genevieve to San Francisco. If he's able to take her himself, then I'm traveling to New York. My bags are already packed."

"Olivia—"

"All is well." I closed my eyes and kept my hands over my ears.

Father didn't respond. When I raised my lashes, all I saw was an eight-year-old boy in a long evening coat and an oversized silk hat. He backed toward the hospital's front entrance in shoes too big for his feet, his lips sputtering to find something more to say.

A tear slid down my cheek to my mouth.

"You and your mother deserve each other," said the boy, and he slipped out the door—his most painful extraction yet.

# CHAPTER TWENTY-SIX

# A QUIET VIGIL

Around nine o'clock at night, Mr. Underhill, John, and two waiters from the party lugged in baskets full of leftover food. Mrs. Underhill greeted them with flailing arms and an attack of noiseless mouthed words.

"I don't know what you're saying, Margaret." Mr. Underhill plunked down a bottle of wine on a small lobby table and squinted at his wife's lips. "I know you're upset we all laughed, but it was funny at the moment, dear."

Mrs. Underhill slugged him in the arm.

"Ouch! Margaret!"

Eugenia shot up and yelled without words as well.

"I don't know what either of you are saying." Mr. Underhill scratched his head. "This is all very frustrating. We'll check back here when you're calmer. Come along, John."

The gentlemen grabbed hold of each other and retreated as quickly as they'd arrived.

Sadie tore open one of the baskets and scooped out wrapped breads, cakes, and crab salad.

My stomach refused to register hunger. Beside me on our shared bench, Genevieve held her arms around herself and shivered.

"Do you know how to undo the hypnosis?" I asked her.

She shook her head. "Uncle Lewis only ever wanted me to provide the accompaniment. At most, he'd make me the human plank and show how he could break boulders with a sledgehammer on top of me."

I winced. "Oh. Well . . . then I suppose I've committed my worst transgression yet."

"What's that?"

I leaned forward and sank my head into my hands. "I made a group of women entirely dependent on a man."

OUR QUIET VIGIL FOR HENRY STRETCHED LATE INTO THE night, with no news of his health from any of the doctors. Mrs. Underhill shared some of the food with Genevieve and me, an act that drove another spike of guilt through my heart. These women were my equals, I realized, as we sat there and dined as a group in the lobby. Despite our differences in wealth and political opinions, they were no better than me.

And . . . I was no better than them.

The nurse at the front desk fetched us glasses of water around eleven thirty, but she left her station at midnight, and the hospital slept. The lobby was transformed into an uncomfortable bedroom for seven females in lace and silk gowns, plus a fifteen-year-old girl in a gray traveling dress who should have been on her way to San Francisco.

I kept my arm around Genevieve on our creaking bench and refused to drift off until I heard her soft snores against my shoulder. Her flushed red cheeks radiated the heat of a fever.

Both Reveries were slipping out of my reach.

AT ONE POINT DURING THE NIGHT, I SLEPT ENOUGH TO dream I was typing up an article for a suffrage newspaper in an apartment overlooking the brick buildings of Barnard College. Below my opened window, young women walked the green grounds with books tucked under their arms.

Mother—her curls still red and soft, her white dress fragrant with the tea-rose perfume I remembered from our rocking-chair days—walked over to me with a smile on her lips.

"This came for you, Livie," she said, and she set a postcard on the desk beside my typewriter.

On the front of the card was an illustration of Market

Street in San Francisco, with cable cars trekking down the center of the road between flag-topped skyscrapers.

I flipped the postcard over to read the note.

*All is well, ma chérie.*

I awoke with a start and disturbed Genevieve with my elbow.

"What's happening?" she asked—just a shadow of a girl in the hospital's dim, early-morning light.

"Genevieve," I said in a whisper, "do you remember Henry saying, because of my Halloween birthday, I'm a charmed individual who can read dreams?"

"Mmm. I think so."

"Was he making that up?"

"I don't know." She shrugged against my arm. "Sometimes he just seems like a talented boy with a wild imagination. Other times . . . I don't know . . . Sometimes all his magic feels real."

"Well"—I snuggled back down beside her, this time with my head on her shoulder—"if it is true, then we're going to be all right. Soon."

"Hmm. I like your dreams," she said, and we eased back into sleep a while longer.

DAYLIGHT PUSHED THROUGH THE DRAFTY LOBBY WIN-dows sometime after seven in the morning. Across the room from me, the anti-suffragists wilted across the chairs and the benches, their colors as filmy as the delicate wings of moths. Genevieve rested her head against the armrest beside me and wavered between light and shadow.

The echo of approaching footsteps stirred us all out of our melancholy.

A doctor in a white coat similar to Father's dentistry garb approached a new nurse at the front desk—a petite woman with big dark eyes who reminded me of ladies from Coca-Cola advertisements.

"Miss Reverie," called the nurse, and all eight of us lobby dwellers sat up straight.

Genevieve, now a solid streak of a girl, jumped to her feet and walked over to the front desk. The doctor put his arm around her back, rumpling her long golden hair, and whisked her off to the far reaches of the hospital. I imagined her traveling in the central elevator that transported patients up and down floors without them needing to climb out of beds, and I hoped she was soaring upward, not down to the morgue.

*Oh, Lord.*

*The morgue.*

I stood up, wrapped my arms around my ribs, and paced the worn rug the way the silent anti-suffragists had done the night before. Sadie and the other girls and their mothers watched me with fear in the blacks of their pupils. When I wiped away tears, their eyes watered, and they sniffed along with me.

"I'm sorry," I said, and I spun in the opposite direction with a swift whoosh of purple satin. "You were all just so cruel. Why'd you have to be so awful to me?"

They didn't answer, of course, so I continued pacing.

"No one should ever be silenced. Not you. Not me. Not any other woman or man. Please, open your eyes and see"—I stopped and swept my gaze across every single one of them—"we're all on the same side. We're all being treated as second-class citizens. Why are you just sitting beside your husbands and fathers and accepting this rubbish?"

Their dead-eyed lack of a response troubled me more than if they had shouted vicious retorts. I left the hospital and walked the length of Irving Street for the better part of an hour, crunching through thick piles of leaves and brushing my hand across brittle overhead branches.

When I returned—no wiser or calmer than when I'd left—I found Genevieve standing on the front steps in Henry's black coat, her hands hidden inside the sleeves. A gentle wind tugged on her skirts and loose hair.

"The fool still wasn't eating or drinking," she called down to me. "The doctor said he had an attack of fatigue and anxiety. They're feeding him his third meal since his arrival right now, and he's dopey with laudanum. His chest hurt him too much to breathe."

A smile stretched across my face. "He's alive, then?"

She nodded.

I ran up the steps. "You saw him?"

"He's eating and restoring those ladies' voices as we speak. The men's ward is a circus, but the staff members were getting tired of seeing millionaires' wives and daughters glaring like vultures in the lobby."

"May I see him?"

She shook her head. "Not until he's discharged. They made an exception for the hypnotized women."

I joined her inside, and another long bout of painful waiting ensued, interrupted early on by the society ladies in their red, white, and blue dresses, parading out to the hospital's exit from somewhere in the back. They spoke again—I heard complaints about sore backs and idiotic husbands mainly— but the return of those voices allowed me to better breathe.

Before she reached the front door with the others, Sadie turned her face my way, and I braced myself for bared teeth or a verbal dart that would make me feel even worse than I already did about the silencing.

She offered neither.

But I saw her—the true Sadie, a newer version. The rest of the hospital dulled around her, and she brightened before my eyes, a girl in plaid trousers and a thick red tie, with a bouquet of yellow ribbons pinned to her left shoulder. I swear she even offered me a smile of camaraderie, but perhaps that was my imagination stretching too far.

In any case, Mademoiselle Sadie Eiderling, the beer baron's daughter, left the hospital that morning a burgeoning suffragist and a modern woman.

Of that, I'm certain.

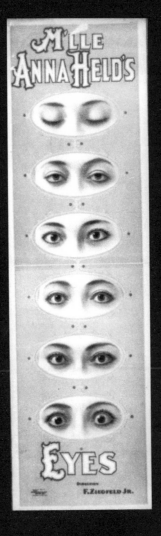

"Perhaps it is better to wake up after all, even to suffer, rather than to remain a dupe to illusions all one's life."

—KATE CHOPIN, *The Awakening*, 1899

# CHAPTER TWENTY-SEVEN

# AWAKE UNTO ME

Near three o'clock in the afternoon, Henry materialized. Not from a cloud of orange smoke on a stage but from the back hallway of the hospital— a far more impressive feat, considering the state of him the night before. His red vest and black necktie dangled over his arm, and he wore just his striped shirtsleeves and trousers and a pair of brown suspenders.

Genevieve and I sprang up from the bench and hurried toward him. I lagged behind a couple of feet so she could embrace him first.

She clamped his middle like a vise. "Are you all right?"

"I am," he told her. "No need to worry anymore."

She lowered her arms, and Henry moved on to me with an embarrassed-looking smile and a warm hug. His lips nuzzled against my hair near the top of my head.

"That wasn't part of the plan, Monsieur Reverie," I said into the soft sheen of his shirt.

"Those women were in a hell of a panic, weren't they?"

"We all were."

"I know." He rubbed my back. "I'm sorry."

"What about the hospital bill, Henry?" asked Genevieve.

"I told them to send it to Anne's house in San Francisco."

"Did Genevieve tell you about Frannie's collection?" I asked.

"Yes, that was far too kind. I'm deeply grateful." He stepped back and regarded my purple gown, his hand in mine. "You never went home last night?"

"I'm never going back home. Father knows."

"New York City, then?"

"Yes." I gave a small nod and a weak smile.

He swallowed as if tasting a bitter pill.

Genevieve cleared her throat. "Our bags are at the hotel. We still have the rooms if you want to change first. There's a nearby streetcar if you're too tired to walk all that way."

Henry dropped his hand away from mine. "Then let's get going. I don't want to think about this departure much longer."

· · · · ·

BRUSHED AND SCRUBBED AND DRESSED IN MY ORDINARY brown skirt and winter coat, I stood in front of Henry and Genevieve on the vast tile floor of Portland's Union Depot, waiting to purchase a railroad ticket that would take me up through Washington and then east. By the time I reached the ticket counter, my hands were sweating. I dropped my slick coins all over the place.

"I'm sorry," I said to the grandfatherly man working the counter, and I caught a nickel before it clanked to the ground. "I'm a little nervous."

"Going on a grand adventure?" he asked.

"That's my hope."

I sorted out the money, and in a matter of seconds I clutched a ticket between my fingers. The Rhodeses purchased their southbound fares and tucked the papers in their coat pockets.

Henry peeked at my ticket over my shoulder. "Your train leaves soon. We had better walk you out to the platform."

I nodded and ventured outside the depot with the two of them by my side.

A black locomotive breathed white steam on the north-bound tracks, while arriving travelers climbed out of the green passenger cars in their winter hats and traveling coats. Porters in blue jackets and caps lugged large leather bags and pointed the lost in the correct directions.

"Henry." I grabbed his arm before we strayed too far from the bright terra-cotta bricks of the main building. "Don't forget, I'm still under hypnosis."

"Ah." He swung around to face me. "I was wondering if you wanted to let go of that one lingering part."

"Of course I do. I don't want to keep seeing the world the way it truly is."

He cocked his head. "Are you sure about that?"

"Help her, Henry." Genevieve pushed at his shoulder. "Don't you dare leave her stuck like that."

"I want my mind to be entirely my own," I added.

"Olivia 'Scorcher' Mead . . ." Henry cracked a smile, and the corners of his eyes crinkled with amusement. "There's no doubt at all that your mind has remained your own this entire time."

"Do it quickly, eh, before she needs to go." Genevieve backed away with her plump black case—the smallest of their bags. "I'll even leave you two alone for a few minutes if you want to be by yourselves."

"You don't have—"

"Do it." Genevieve turned and wandered off to the opposite side of the platform.

Henry lowered their two larger bags to the ground beside him, which prompted me to set my Gladstone next to my feet alongside my skirt. We stood up straight and faced each other.

"Close your eyes—they're exceptionally heavy." He cupped my cheek, and my eyes fell shut, as if lead lined my lashes. "Keep them closed," he said in a voice soft and lush, and he pulled my body toward him. "Your lids are now stuck together. Try opening them."

I couldn't.

"Good. Very good. I am now going to stroke the back of your neck with my free hand, and each caress will send you deeper and deeper into hypnosis." He rubbed his palm down the base of my neck, over the topmost vertebrae. "Do you feel that wonderful sense of relaxation?"

"Yesss," I whispered from somewhere inside a deep, delicious pocket of darkness.

"Now, listen carefully, because what I am about to say is extremely important." His breath warmed my ear. "You will see the world the way it has always been. You will ensure your mind remains your own and never, ever allow a hypnotist or a domineering suitor or your father—or anyone else—to alter your thoughts beyond your control. Do you understand?"

"Yesss. My mind . . . will remain . . . my own."

"You will not allow people like Percy Acklen to make you feel as though you're lesser than they."

"I . . ." I tried to reach my fingers up to Henry's hand on my cheek, but my arm was built of limp rubber.

"Will you promise, Olivia? Don't let people like him make you feel like dirt."

"I promise."

"Your mind will remain your own."

"Yesss."

I heard him swallow. "I am going to wake you up now. Are you ready?"

I nodded on the wobbly hinge of my neck.

"I'll count forward to ten—we'll take it slowly. One . . . two . . . three . . ."

"I want . . . to make sure . . . you're going to be . . . all right, too."

He lowered his hand from my face. *"Pardonnez-moi?"*

My eyes stayed shut, still too thick and dense to unseal, and my tongue remained heavy and cumbersome. "I feel . . . the urge . . . to tell you . . . things. Waking up . . . might change . . . my boldness."

"It won't."

"You're only . . . eighteen. Hospitalized . . . chest pains. Fatigue. Collapsed. Just eighteen. I can't . . . be with you . . . need to be . . . on my own. But . . . I care . . . about you."

"I'm all right."

"No. Not convinced."

He was silent, and for a moment I just stood there with my arms dangling by my sides, relaxing in the mesmerizing hold of peaceful blackness.

"Are you ready to wake up now?" he asked.

"Swear . . . you'll take care . . . of yourself."

"I—"

"Swear. Let me speak . . . with less heaviness."

His thumb traced my jawline. "All right. You're easing upward to a lesser stage of relaxation. Keep rising up . . . up . . . up. Your tongue is no longer heavy. You can talk with clarity."

My tongue loosened and stretched inside my mouth. I licked my drying lips.

"What did you want to say?" he asked with hesitation.

"There's beauty in this world, Henry, and not everyone dies young. There's so much hope. There's so much work, too—ridiculous amounts of work—but above all, hope. I've seen it out there, alongside the darkness. Look at Frannie and what she did. Look at the times we had together."

He didn't answer. His hand trembled against my face.

"Henry?"

"I'll count forward," he said, a quaver in his voice, "slowly, so you can come up gently. One . . . two . . . three . . ."

"Were you listening to me, Henry?"

"Yes."

"Will you put yourself back together?"

"Yes."

"Promise?"

"*Mon Dieu*, Olivia"—he emitted a weak flutter of a laugh— "are you hypnotizing me while under hypnosis?"

"We're partners, remember?"

"Yes, I definitely remember."

"Then let my words persuade you to become the type of person you're not afraid of looking at in the mirror. If you think your life is a farce, Henry, then change it."

"All right. I'll fix myself up."

"Promise?"

"Yes. If it means that much to you, then . . . yes." A self-relaxing breath loosened his voice. "Um . . . where was I?"

"Four," I said. "And I want you to open up your eyes, too, when we get to ten. Five . . ."

"All right." He took another breath. "Six . . ."

"Seven," I said.

"Eight . . ."

"Nine . . ."

He removed his hand from my face. "Ten."

We awoke, and I took a long look around me. Passengers and porters hurried about, and a train's black smokestack hissed with impatience. In front of me, a boy blinked to keep his eyes dry before letting me go.

"They have to remove her whole breast," he said. "It's a fairly new procedure, but it's the only thing that will save her. She'll have a better chance than our mother did."

I cast my eyes down to Genevieve waiting on a bench with her leather bag. "She looks brave." I peeked back up at him. "And so do you. You'll both be strong for each other."

He nodded without breathing.

I reached up and kissed his lips, which faltered beneath mine. We clasped our arms around each other and hugged instead, and Henry whispered in my ear, *"Un jour, lorsque tu es prête, on se reverra encore."*

"What does that mean?" I asked with the left side of my face pressed against his shoulder.

"One day, when you are ready, we will meet again."

No words found their way to my mouth. My eyes welled with tears and turned Genevieve's brown coat and gray skirt, down the way, into blurs.

A blue-capped conductor checked his pocket watch and called out, "All aboard," and a crowd of people clamored forward to the passenger cars.

Genevieve shot off her bench and jogged past them all to reach me.

"Thank you." She grabbed my face and kissed my wet cheek. "Thank you for your help. Please send me Frannie's address so I may write to her."

"Oh, that reminds me"—I pulled a piece of paper out of my coat pocket—"here's my mother's address." I slipped the paper into Henry's hands. "Please promise to send me a postcard when Genevieve has recovered."

Everyone bustled past us as if they couldn't get on board quickly enough. Time shoved against me.

Henry grabbed hold of my hand, and I kissed him again—a proper good-bye kiss, just in case we were about to turn into mere memories for each other. He pulled me against him by my waist, and we stayed together until the conductor shouted his last boarding call.

I broke loose and climbed aboard the train without looking back at either of them.

A young black Pullman porter in a white coat greeted me at the head of the aisle. "May I help you with your luggage, miss?"

"Yes, thank you." I handed him my bag, and for a moment I saw straight through him to the green floral rug running down the aisle.

*No*, I told myself, and I rubbed at my eyes. *No—you see the world the way it has always been.*

I followed the porter, and four seats in we passed a man with engorged lips and his dissolving wife, whose neck bled in a bright red bloom.

"No! Oh, no." I turned to leave.

Two young ladies in wide-brimmed hats maneuvered their bags up the aisle and blocked my exit.

"Oh, dear, are you trying to get off?" asked the woman in front, turning sideways.

"I just . . ." I cupped my hand over my forehead and heard the rustle of paper in the left sleeve of my blouse.

"Personally, I think you're traveling in the right direction," said the second woman, who had a distinctive glow in her cheeks. "This train passes through Idaho, where women voted yesterday. That's where we're headed."

"I don't know where I'm going."

I swiveled back around and grabbed hold of the wooden backs of seats to navigate my way down the aisle behind the porter. The floor swayed and bobbed below my feet, as if in a dream. I reached under my left sleeve and drew out a folded piece of paper that had been stuffed up there like the tickets Henry had snuck into my glove while we were in the restaurant with Percy.

Another message, written in the same hand as that previous note, met my eyes.

*I believe you have always seen the vampires and the fading souls in the world, Olivia. You just never paid close attention to them before. As I've learned through my own ordeals, once you start viewing the world the way it truly is, it is impossible to ignore both its beauty and its ugliness. Look around you.*

*You can't stop seeing it, can you?*

I glanced up and witnessed a girl near my age with a bruise swelling near her eye. A second later, her body puffed into a thin haze of smoke.

A young bearded man with burning coals for irises glared at the black porter walking by him with my bag, and I swore I saw the man tying a rope into a noose.

My eyes strayed back to the message.

*There is some of the unexplainable in me, ma chérie, but there is also a great deal of enchantment in you. Keep telling the world what you see.*

*Help others to see it, too.*

I dropped into an empty seat and slid across the bench to the window. Using my fist, I rubbed a circle against the condensation fogging up the glass.

Down below, Henry and Genevieve roamed the length of

the car with their bags at their sides and craned their necks, as if they were looking for me as well. With a frenzied wave, I caught Henry's eye, and I pressed the letter against the glass. He stopped and gave a small nod.

The train lurched forward, and the Rhodeses stood there on the platform, amid other travelers in black and gray and the faded browns of the autumn leaves. They blended in with the surroundings, and I held my breath in fear of them going one step farther and disappearing.

"Don't fade," I said. "Please don't fade."

Time seemed poised to swallow them up, but before the train chugged past them, a switch flipped. Henry and Genevieve ignited into the blaze of colors from their Halloween performance, Henry in his bold crimson vest and Genevieve in her peacock-blue gown. I pushed my palm harder against the glass to see them more clearly—a beautiful, blinding brilliance.

Another light flared to life in the glass—the reflection of a girl with an ordinary face and unremarkable black hair, but she shone like the brightest stage lights of the Metropolitan.

The train clacked onward, gathering speed. My reflection remained, but the Reveries fell out of my view. I felt them around me, though, in the velvet-padded seats, between the strangers. Henry and Genevieve. Frannie and Kate. Agnes, Gerda, and Mr. and Mrs. Harrison. Even Mother and Father. They were all there, everyone a part of me, by my side, making sure I stayed on that train until I reached my destination.

# ACKNOWLEDGMENTS

I'M EXTREMELY GRATEFUL TO THE FOLLOWING INDIVIDU-
als and organizations.

My husband and two kids, my parents, my sister, and the
rest of my close family and friends, for *always* being support-
ive of my dreams, even when they've seemed impossible.

My agent, Barbara Poelle, for becoming an instant
champion of this book as soon as she read the first chapters.

My editor, Maggie Lehrman, for believing in me a second
time around and for spinning her magic to make my work
shine.

The rest of the team at Abrams: Susan Van Metre, Tamar
Brazis, Laura Mihalick, Jason Wells, Maria T. Middleton
(designer extraordinaire!), Tina Mories in the UK, the
copyeditor, proofreaders, and everyone else who played a
role in making this book as strong as it could possibly be and
putting it into the hands of readers. Such diligent work is
much appreciated.

My early readers, Carrie Raleigh, Kim Murphy, Francesca Miller, Adam Karp, and Meggie, for their enthusiasm and much-needed feedback.

Miriam Forster, Teri Brown, Amber J. Keyser, and Kelly Garrett—my Thursday Morning Coffee and Writing Team—for getting me out of the house!

My fellow members of The Lucky 13s, Corsets, Cutlasses, & Candlesticks, and SCBWI Oregon, whom I can always count on for advice, emotional support, and exuberant cheers of celebration.

The Mark Twain Foundation, for assistance and permission to quote the great Mr. Clemens.

The Oregon Historical Society, the University of Oregon Libraries, the Library of Congress, the National Library of Medicine, and the Women of the West Museum, for their indispensable research archives.

David Burke, Wade Major, Oliver Fabris, and Jamie Lucero for their help with Henri Reverie's French. *Merci!* Any errors in translation are entirely my own.

Last of all, my deepest gratitude extends to every single woman and man who fought to end inequality at the voting polls in the United States and elsewhere. Their sacrifices and struggles to give the silenced a voice should never be forgotten.

May equality spread even farther across the globe in the very near future.

# WHEN AND WHERE U.S. WOMEN
# GAINED FULL SUFFRAGE

**1869** Wyoming territory[1]

**1893** Colorado

**1896** Utah[2] and Idaho

**1910** Washington State[3]

**1911** California

**1912** Oregon,[4] Kansas, and Arizona

**1913** Alaska[5]

**1914** Montana and Nevada

**1917** New York

**1918** Michigan, South Dakota, and Oklahoma

---

[1] Wyoming became a state in 1890, and Wyoming women retained the right to vote.
[2] Women in the territory of Utah were given full suffrage in 1870. In 1887 that right was taken away until Utah became a state in 1896.
[3] The territory of Washington briefly granted women, including African American women, full suffrage in 1883, but in 1887 the Territorial Supreme Court overturned that law.
[4] The men of Oregon voted down suffrage referendums in 1884, 1900, 1906, 1908, and 1910, before approving the sixth measure in 1911.
[5] The territory of Alaska granted women full suffrage forty-six years before it became a state in 1959.

**August 26, 1920** The 19th Amendment to the Constitution is signed into law. Female U.S. citizens age twenty-one and older are granted the right to vote in all states.

**1924** The Indian Citizenship Act gives Native Americans, both male and female, U.S. citizenship, yet Native Americans will not be granted suffrage in every state until 1962.

**1965–2006** The U.S. government passes legislation to protect the voting rights of minorities, Americans with disabilities, and other citizens who had encountered obstacles in exercising their freedom to vote.

**1971** The voting age is dropped to eighteen in all fifty states.

## RECOMMENDED READING

Bly, Nellie. *Ten Days in a Mad-House.* New York: Ian L. Munro, 1887.

Browning, John Edgar (ed.). *Bram Stoker's Dracula: The Critical Feast.* Berkeley, Calif.: Apocryphile Press, 2011.

Crichton, Judy. *America 1900: The Turning Point.* New York: Henry Holt, Inc., 1998.

Edwards, G. Thomas. *Sowing Good Seeds: The Northwest Suffrage Campaigns of Susan B. Anthony.* Portland: Oregon Historical Society, 1990.

John, Finn J. D. *Wicked Portland: The Wild and Lusty Underworld of a Frontier Seaport Town,* Charleston, S.C.: History Press, 2012.

Lansing, Jewel. *Portland: People, Politics, and Power, 1851–2001.* Corvallis: Oregon State University Press, 2005.

McGill, Ormond. *The New Encyclopedia of Stage Hypnotism.* Bethel, Conn.: Crown House Publishing, 1996.

Nation, Carry Amelia. *The Use and Need of the Life of Carry A. Nation.* Topeka, Kans.: F. M. Steves & Sons, 1908. (*Note:* Newspapers in 1900 spelled Mrs. Nation's name "Carrie," which is believed to be the official spelling. However, she opted to use "Carry" for her temperance campaign and autobiography.)

Ross-Nazzal, Jennifer M. *Winning the West for Women: The Life of Suffragist Emma Smith Devoe.* Seattle: University of Washington Press, 2011.

Sherr, Lynn. *Failure Is Impossible: Susan B. Anthony in Her Own Words.* New York: Times Books, 1995.

Streeter, Michael. *Hypnosis: Secrets of the Mind.* Hauppauge, N.Y.: Barron's, 2004.

Twain, Mark. "Happy Memories of the Dental Chair." In *Who Is Mark Twain?*, 77–86. New York: HarperCollins, 2009.

Ward, Jean M., and Elaine A. Maveety (eds.). *"Yours for Liberty": Selections from Abigail Scott Duniway's Suffrage Newspaper.* Corvallis: Oregon State University Press, 2000.

Winter, Alison. *Mesmerized: Powers of Mind in Victorian Britain.* Chicago: University of Chicago Press, 1998.

Wynbrandt, James. *The Excruciating History of Dentistry: Toothsome Tales & Oral Oddities from Babylon to Braces.* New York: St. Martin's Griffin, 2000.

Read on for an excerpt from
Cat Winters's newest novel.

# THE STEEP & THORNY WAY

# CHAPTER 1

# MURDER MOST FOUL

 I DREW A DEEP BREATH AND marched into the woods behind my house with a two-barreled pistol hidden beneath my blue cotton skirt. The pocket-size derringer rode against my outer right thigh, tucked inside a holster that had, according to the boy who'd given it to me, once belonged to a lady bootlegger who'd been arrested with three different guns strapped to her legs. Twigs snapped beneath my shoes. My eyes watered and burned. The air tasted of damp earth and metal.

Several yards ahead, amid a cluster of maples blanketed in scaly green lichen, stood a fir tree blackened by lightning.

If I turned right on the deer trail next to that tree and followed a line of ferns, I'd find myself amid rows of shriveled
grapevines in the shut-down vineyard belonging to my closest
friend, Fleur, her older brother, Laurence, and their war-
widowed mama.

But I didn't turn.

I kept trekking toward the little white shed that hid the
murderer Joe Adder.

Fleur's whispers from church that morning ran through
my head, nearly tipping me off balance during my clamber
across moss-slick rocks in the creek. "Reverend Adder doesn't
even want his boy around anymore," she had told me before
the sermon, her face bent close to mine, fine blond hair
brushing across her cheeks. "He won't let Joe back in the
house with the rest of the kids. Laurence is hiding him in our
old shed. And Joe wants to talk to you. He's got something to
say about the night his car hit your father."

I broke away from the creek and hiked up a short embank-
ment covered in sedges and rushes that tickled my bare shins.
At the top of the bank, about twenty-five feet away, sat a little
white structure built of plaster and wood. Before he left for
the Great War, Fleur's father used to store his fishing gear
and liquor in the place, and he sometimes invited my father
over for a glass of whiskey, even after Oregon went bone-dry
in 1916. Bigleaf maples hugged the rain-beaten shingles with
arms covered in leaves as bright green as under-ripe apples. A
stovepipe poked out from the roof, and I smelled the sharp

scent of leftover ashes—the ghost of a fire Joe must have lit the night before, when the temperature dropped into the fifties.

I came to a stop in front of the shed, my pulse pounding in the side of my throat. My scalp sweltered beneath my knitted blue hat, along with the long brown curls I'd stuffed and pinned inside. I leaned over and drew the hem of my skirt above my right knee, exposing the worn leather of the holster. I took another deep breath and wiggled the little derringer out of its hiding place.

With my legs spread apart, I stood up straight and pointed the pistol at the shed's closed door. "Are you in there, Joe?"

A hawk screeched from high above the trees, and some sort of animal splashed in the pond that lay beyond the shed and the foliage. But I didn't hear one single peep out of Joe Adder.

"Joe?" I asked again, this time in as loud and deep a voice as I could muster. Tree-trunk strong, I sounded. Sticky sweat rolled down my cheeks, and my legs refused to stop rocking back and forth. "Are you in there?"

"Who's there?"

I gripped the pistol with both my hands. The voice I heard was a husky growl that couldn't have belonged to clean-cut, preacher's-boy Joe, from what I remembered of him. It and a splashing sound seemed to come from the pond, not the shed.

"Who's there?" he asked again. I heard another splash.

I lowered the pistol to my side and crept around to the

back of the shed, feeling my tongue dry up from panting. I pushed past a tangle of blackberry bushes, pricking a thumb on a thorn, and came to a stop on the edge of the bank. My feet teetered on the gnarled white root of a birch.

In the pond, submerged up to his navel in the murky green water, stood a tanned and naked Joe Adder, arms akimbo, a lock of dark brown hair hanging over his right eye. His shoulders were broad and sturdy, his biceps surprisingly muscular, as though prison had worked that scrawny little white boy hard.

My mouth fell open, and my stomach gave an odd jump. The last time I'd seen Joe, back in February 1921, seventeen months earlier, he'd been a slick-haired, sixteen-year-old kid in a fancy black suit, blubbering on a courthouse bench between his mama and daddy.

This new version of my father's killer—now just a few months shy of his eighteenth birthday, almost brawny, his hair tousled and wild—peered at me without blinking. Drops of water plunked to the pond's surface from his elbows.

"You don't want to shoot me, Hanalee," he said in that husky voice of his. "I don't recommend prison to anyone but the devils who threw me in there."

I pointed the pistol at his bare chest, my right fingers wrapped around the grip. "If you had run over and killed a white man with your daddy's Model T," I said, "you'd still be behind bars, serving your full two years . . . and more."

"I didn't kill anyone."

"I bet you don't know this"—I shifted my weight from one leg to the other—"but people tell ghost stories about my father wandering the road where you ran him down, and I hate those tales with a powerful passion."

"I'm sorry, but—"

"But those stories don't make me half as sick as you standing there, saying you didn't kill anyone. If you didn't kill him, you no-good liar, then why didn't you defend yourself at your trial?"

Joe sank down into the water and let his chin graze the surface. Long, thick lashes framed his brown eyes, and he seemed to know precisely how to tilt his head and peek up at a girl to use those lashes to his advantage. "They never gave me a chance to speak on the witness stand," he said. "They hurried me into that trial, and then they rushed me off to prison by the first week of February. And I didn't get to say a goddamn word."

I pulled the hammer into a half-cocked position with a click that echoed across the pond. Joe's eyes widened, and he sucked in his breath.

"You lied to your family about delivering food to the poor that Christmas Eve," I said, "and you crashed into my father because you were drunk on booze from some damn party. My new stepfather witnessed him die from injuries caused by *you*, so don't you dare fib to me."

"Don't you dare shoot me before I talk to you about that stepdaddy of yours."

"I don't want to hear what you have to say about Uncle Clyde. I'm not happy he married my mama, but he's a decent man."

"Stop pointing that gun at me and let me talk."

"Give me one good reason why I should listen to you." I aimed the pistol at the skin between Joe's eyebrows. "Give me one good reason why I shouldn't squeeze this trigger and sh—"

"You should listen to me, Hanalee, because you're living with your father's murderer."

A shallow breath fluttered through my lips. All the doubts and fears I'd harbored about Dr. Koning since he married my grieving mama last winter squirmed around in my gut. I stared Joe down, and he stared me down, and the gun quaked in my hand until the metal blurred before my eyes.

"For Christ's sake, Hanalee, stop pointing that gun at me and let me talk to you."

"Clyde Koning did not kill my father."

"Your father was alive when I helped him into my house. He even joked with me—he said he thought he'd been hit by Santa's sleigh as punishment for misbehaving on Christmas Eve."

I shook my head. "My father wouldn't have said any such thing. The only thing he did wrong that night was to walk down the dark highway to try to join us at church. He wasn't feeling well, and—"

"His leg was bleeding and maybe broken," continued Joe,

ignoring me, rattling off words as if he had them memorized from a script. "So I let him lean his weight against me while I helped him inside. My family was running the Christmas Eve service, so I laid your father on my bed and telephoned Dr. Koning."

"I don't—"

"The last thing your father said to me before I opened the door for the doctor was 'The doc's going to be the death of me. I just know it.'"

I stepped off the gnarled root, landing so hard I jarred my neck. "That's a lie."

"And when I asked, 'Do you want me to send Dr. Koning away?' he told me, 'No, just make sure no one ever hurts my Hanalee.'"

My eyes itched and moistened. I blinked and rocked back and forth. "You don't know what you're talking about."

"When Dr. Koning arrived, he shut my bedroom door behind him and left me to wait in the living room." Joe rose back up to a standing position. Water rained off his body and splattered into the pond, and a wave lapped at his stomach, just above his hip bones. "The next time that bedroom door opened, your father was dead. He wasn't hardly even bleeding before that point—he seemed to have only suffered a busted leg and a sore arm from the crash. But suddenly he was dead, as if someone had just shot a poisonous dose of morphine through his veins."

I shook my head. "That's not true."

"People shut me up at my trial. No one, not even my own lawyer, let me speak, as if they'd all gotten paid to keep me quiet, and I suffered for it." His voice cracked. "I can't . . . do you know . . ." He pushed his hair out of his eyes and exposed a C-shaped scar above his right eyebrow. "Do you know how badly I fared as a sixteen-year-old kid in that godforsaken prison, Hanalee?"

My hand sweated against the gun. "I don't feel a shred of pity for you."

"Just one week before the accident, someone—my father wouldn't say who—came by the church and tried to recruit him into the local chapter of the Ku Klux Klan, which I'm certain had something—"

"No!" I marched right into the pond's shallow edge with the pistol still aimed at Joe's head, and I pulled the hammer into the full-cock position. "I know full well there's a Klan church up the highway in Bentley. I know they host baseball games and print anti-Catholic pamphlets, but they never once gave a damn that my black Christian father lived in this measly spit stain of a town."

"I'm not the one you should be shooting, Hanalee." Joe backed away in the water. "I'm not the one who deserves to die."

"I've never even heard about a single Klan-provoked killing in this state, Joe. You can try to scare me all you want, but I know you're just switching your guilt onto other people because you—"

"No, I'm not. Look in your stepfather's bedroom." He stopped backing up. "I bet you'll find a robe and a hood stashed among his clothing somewhere. I bet he married your white mother just to piss on the memory of your father. And I bet the Klan promoted him to a powerful position for killing the last full-blooded Negro in Elston, Ore—"

I squeezed the trigger with an explosion of gunpowder and fired a bullet straight past Joe's ear—not close enough to hit him, but enough to make his face go as white as those hooded robes he talked about. I staggered backward from the kick, and my ears rang with a horrendous screeching that sounded like a crowd of keening mourners wailing inside my head.

Beyond the cloud of dissipating smoke, Joe thrashed his arms about in the water and struggled to stay upright, but I didn't wait to see if he'd recover from the shock. Instead, I tucked that gun back into my holster and hightailed it out of the woods.

Also by
Cat Winters